Parlor Games

ARE YOU THERE, MORIARTY?

AE LISTER

Are You There, Moriarty?
ISBN # 978-1-80250-594-8
©Copyright AE Lister 2024
Cover Art by Kelly Martin ©Copyright February 2024
Interior text design by Claire Siemaszkiewicz
Pride Publishing

Published in 2024 by Pride Publishing, United Kingdom.

Pride Publishing Publishing books by AE Lister

Persuasions
Various Persuasions
Various Distractions
Various Intentions

Northern Horizons
760 Miles
Repentance and Absolution
Return to Telegraph Creek
A Port Essington Christmas

Parlor Games
Are You There, Moriarty?

Collections
Dark and Deadly: Skeletal Equation
We Three Kings: A Spoonful of Sugar
His Harem: Alternative Medicine
Hot Bite: Bloodlines

ARE YOU THERE, MORIARTY?

Dedication

To safe spaces and good times.

A Note on the Title

The Victorian parlor game *Are You There, Moriarty?* is similar to Marco Polo, except instead of playing in a pool, a pair of players lay face down on the floor about arm's length apart. Both participants are blindfolded, and each is equipped with a rolled-up newspaper. The game begins when the first player calls out "Are you there, Moriarty?" When the second player responds, the caller attempts to bop him over the head with his makeshift weapon. The newspaper swordfight proceeds until both parties feel too silly to continue.

— *Mental Floss*, November 16, 2016

No doubt a kinky version of this parlor game could include a flogger or a crop – and a submissive trying to evade the reach of his Dom.

Chapter One

Late

"Fuck, fuck, fuck," I cursed as I gripped the metal handle by the folding doors, mentally chastising the bus for taking so long to brake and let me off. I hated being late. One of my most valued traits was my punctuality. Everyone said so. What would they say now?

The bus finally screeched to a stop, and the doors parted with a swish. I stepped down into a huge pile of slush.

"*Fuck,*" I cursed.

I waded through melting snow on the sidewalk, wondering for the fortieth time this season why I didn't live somewhere—*anywhere*—else. Someplace warm, where they didn't get snow or slush or freezing rain or any of the other things that assailed this godforsaken city between the months of November and April.

Icy water seeped into my leaky boots, and for the umpteenth time this winter, I told myself I needed to get new ones. I was saving up for quality footwear. Sure, I could buy a pair of supposedly waterproof boots at Walmart, and *maybe* they would work until the end of winter…but maybe they wouldn't. I could wait another month until I had the money to buy half-decent boots that might last me three winters.

I liked my job, which was why I was pissed off that I was late. Sebastian would wonder where I was and might not have enough servers to manage the patrons who tended to fill the place on a Friday night.

I trudged down the sidewalk, shivering, although the temperature was mild, passing an imposing and ancient stone church, a boutique hotel and some small apartment buildings. The wind was picking up, and the temperature was falling now that dark had descended. When the front lights and imposing signage of Maverick Molly's came into view, I sighed with relief.

Maverick Molly's would be warm. It would be full of soft lamplight and Victorian ambience, and I couldn't wait to get there. I could already smell the wood fire burning in the massive hearth in the gaming parlor.

I'd been lucky enough to get a job at Molly's, serving snacks and beverages, dressed in a corset and pretty underthings like a Victorian molly boy. It was a goddamned dream job for someone like me, who didn't mind getting dolled up for the particular clientele that Molly's attracted. Plus, it was advantageous to get in on a good thing early on.

Jacob Moriarty, who ran the place, was a visionary. He'd gotten the idea for Maverick Molly's while researching the Victorian sex trade for an article he'd written, and his partner, Sebastian, had done the hiring for the first group of servers.

I knew Sebastian from an acting gig we'd done together. He'd told me I'd be perfect, if I was willing to don some bloomers and a corset and bring food and drinks to kinky men who would rent the Bordello — the spacious and beautifully decorated back room filled with vintage kink furniture and accessories — to engage in X-rated games with their partners or hookups. We were also encouraged to perform in short burlesque skits or sing bawdy songs in front of the clientele in the public room where men gathered at tables to play cards and old-fashioned board games.

Molly's didn't run a sex trade. The servers were there as titillating décor and entertainment…and also as practical employees. We helped to create the ambience of a different time, when being gay was truly a counter-culture, and safe spaces were scattered through the underground for men to meet and enjoy each other. It probably wasn't very romantic, especially when molly houses were raided and the men inside them taken by the police for having the audacity to be true to themselves and each other. But now that homosexuality was considered, by most, to be a part of the great quilt of human sexuality, the costumes and accouterments of the Victorian gay underground provided a change of pace to men used to meeting in modern hotels or bathhouses — or living their domestic married lives together.

It was a kink club, a cabaret and a gaming parlor, and Jacob and Sebastian raked in the cash most evenings. I was proud to be a part of that. But tonight, I was fucking late, and that wasn't like me. I didn't usually jaywalk but, fuck it.

I ignored the red light and dodged across the street, narrowly avoiding a tragic incident and causing one driver to yell out a curse as I ran in front of his car.

"Sorry, sorry. Shit, fuck, sorry," I said, waving a vague apology as I made it to the sidewalk, my heart beating in my chest like a rabbit's as I ran up the steps of the ancient stone building, pushing the heavy wood door open and slipping inside.

A plump young man with dark skin and deep brown eyes in frilly Victorian bloomers and a chemise with a vintage corset over the top, turned to me.

"Where the fuck have you been, then?" Robin asked, reducing the harshness of his words with a saucy sway of his substantial behind.

"Sorry, sorry," I mumbled, taking off my coat. "Family issues."

"Yeah?" Robin took a piece of half-eaten fruit cake off the plate he held in his hand and popped it into his mouth, chewing while giving me a fake look of sympathy. I was used to that, though. It was part of Robin's schtick.

"Yeah. My mom's on a rampage. I need to find a place of my own."

"Bad luck," he said, with mock gravitas.

I cackled at the look on his face as he attempted real sympathy. Robin didn't have a sympathetic bone in his body, but he kept trying.

"Yeah, well, I'm here now," I said.

"Better get changed. Can you check on the new guy? He's been back there for ages, probably stuck in his corset."

"Sure, sure. What's his name?" I asked.

Robin's face relaxed into an expression of genuine delight, and his eyebrows waggled. "Patrick." Then he narrowed his eyes. "Hands off. He's mine."

"What the fuck? What gives you first dibs?" I asked. Kid must be something to get Robin all possessive on his first day.

Robin's smile vanished. "*I* wasn't late, was I?"

He had a point. I watched him carry the now-empty plate to the kitchen, his much-prized, bloomered rear end swaying as he walked. There was a black fascinator pinned into his short curls with a huge silver feather sticking out of it.

"Nice head piece," I said, and it wasn't sardonic. I did like it.

He turned back to me, the smile there again. One thing great about Robin... He never stayed mad.

"Do you like it?" He touched the tip of his finger to the edge of the feather. "Sebastian says it makes me look like a nineteen-twenties flapper."

I nodded as I put my boots in the tray. "It's cute."

He threw me a saucy smile. "Like *me*?"

"Of course."

"Ta-ta, then. We've got a good-looking crowd tonight, by the way." He waggled his eyebrows again.

Robin Webb was British. Customers loved him because of his cheeky attitude, cockney accent and soft, plump curves. Robin was on the chubby side, and it totally worked for him. He could pull off innocent and diabolically perverse in one goddamned sentence. I alternately loved and hated him.

He looked incredible in a corset and stockings. That kind of self-confidence and the ability to feel comfortable wearing women's underthings was an asset for any server at Molly's. It was more important than objective good looks. Working the tables at Maverick Molly's in Victorian lingerie all evening was not an easy way to make a living, but it was more amusing than working at a regular eatery. It still involved being on one's feet for long stretches of time, fielding curious questions from the men who came to enjoy the ambience and pretending to be amused by suggestive jokes that had been heard countless times already.

We were also required to perform. By that I mean that over the course of an evening, two or more of us had to get on the small stage and perform bawdy skits, sing scandalous ditties and otherwise entertain the gents who were drinking, playing cards and engaging in other vintage games like backgammon and chess.

Most of the men who came to Maverick Molly's behaved themselves. Jacob and Sebastian ran a tight operation, and the regulars—men who enjoyed the alternative types of entertainment Molly's offered—knew what they could, and couldn't, get away with. Occasionally, men who dropped in out of curiosity violated one of the set boundaries and were promptly and summarily dealt with. Rules of behavior were posted in several places, and there was rarely any real trouble. It was a safe and entertaining place to work.

I went past the door to the kitchen and through the one that led to the staff changing area.

"Heyo," I said, in case of anyone in a state of undress who needed to cover their bits. But the only person in the room was still wearing his jeans and staring at the pile of vintage-looking undergarments before him with terror.

"You must be Patrick."

He had a shock of red hair that would have made Raggedy Andy jealous and freckles that made him look like an adolescent. But what I could see of his slimly muscled body was all man.

14

"Yeah. Hi."

I dumped my backpack on the hideously patterned settee. When Jacob and Sebastian had been looking for antiques to furnish their club, someone had donated this eyesore, and they'd found a place for it in here, where we needed something practical but customers wouldn't be turned off by the unappealing aesthetic. Maybe they also figured we wouldn't linger on our breaks, but honestly, we didn't care what it looked like when we were exhausted and just wanted to sit down.

"I'm Toby. I was supposed to be here an hour ago, so I need to get moving. But I can help you with all that."

Patrick seemed relieved but still overwhelmed by the task ahead.

"Um. You did realize you were gonna have to put on women's knickers for this job?"

He swallowed. "I...yeah. But it just now hit me."

"Yeah, it's intimidating at first. You'll look amazing, though."

He blew out a breath and attempted a smile. "God, I hope so."

I laughed. "Trust me... The customers'll be passing you their business cards all night. Smile and pocket them but don't say anything. All you have to do is bring them the food and drinks they ask for. Anything else is not your mandate."

"Right. Sure."

"Unless you want to follow up when you're not at work. But it's your choice. Jacob and Sebastian don't want you serving more than they have a license for, if you get my drift."

Patrick seemed to relax. "Yeah, I get it. Thanks."

I grabbed the stuff off my shelf and threw it all onto the settee.

"Right. Strip," I said to Patrick.

Patrick blinked. "Like, everything?"

"You can't put this stuff on over jeans. It doesn't work that way."

Patrick glanced at the door.

"Nobody's going to come in. Everyone's busy as hell out there. That's why we need to get changed and go help out, right?"

"Okay. Yeah."

I had my clothes off in a moment and stood watching Patrick with silent appreciation. He was a good-looking kid with a swimmer's body. He was going to look incredible in the Maverick Molly's get-up. The confidence would come with time. That was the most important thing in this job, but it wasn't always there at the beginning. Patrick definitely had the looks, but he needed an injection of chutzpah to have a chance at this gig.

I sifted through my things and found the black silk garter belt. I held it up and waggled the straps. "You should have something like this in your pile?"

Patrick's gaze locked onto my crotch, so I glanced down to see if my dick was hanging out or something. But everything was tucked away in the neat little pouch of my lace panties. *Oh...*

"Wait! You're wearing panties. Nobody told me I had to wear panties." Patrick's eyes had bugged, and his voice held a shrill timbre.

"You don't have to wear panties. They just work well with the outfit, you know? And I like 'em."

I loved panties. Why men got the short end of the stick on this one, I'd never understand. I, on the other hand, didn't abide by many gender expectations. I'd worn men's bikini underwear since I'd started shopping for my own clothes, which had been earlier than most kids, seeing as my mom wasn't the best parent on the block, to put it mildly. Once I was brave enough, I'd started buying the prettier, lacier panties that were now available for people with penises.

"Your panties are" — Patrick swallowed — "really cute."

"Why, thank you, Patrick," I said, posing with one hand on my hip and grinning with contentment. "You have some in your pile. So do I. But these are my own," I said, waggling my behind.

"Oh." He smiled, and he went from cute to breathtaking in an instant. Yeah, he'd do.

I fanned my face. "My, my, you do have a lovely smile, Patrick. I think you'll do just fine."

I went over to where Patrick was standing and gestured to the pile of garments in front of him. "May I?"

He nodded.

I rifled through his 'uniform' and quickly found a pair of black lace men's panties.

"Here." I held them up. "Start with these."

Patrick looked down at himself in his snug blue boxer briefs, then eyed me in my lacy red panties, and took the black ones from me. "Okay."

I turned around politely while he changed his underwear and grabbed the garter belt from my pile before I turned around.

"Oh, hell. Yeah, those work," I said, fixating on Patrick's, *ahem...package*, now tucked tidily in the front pouch of his lacy panties.

"They're so soft!" Patrick said, stroking the fabric as a giggle bubbled from his lips.

"Trust me... It'll be hard to go back to boxer briefs after this."

"What now?"

I helped Patrick get sorted out with the garter belt and stockings, which did take some getting used to. Then I showed him the frilly bloomers with a cheeky smile. "The guys love these...almost as much as they like the corsets."

I pulled mine on over my stockings and fastened the buttons on the gusset. Wide pink ribbon weaved through the leg openings above the frilly fabric on mine, baby blue on Patrick's. The bloomers and chemises were exact replicas of what would have been worn—by women, mostly—at the time, and that Sebastian had requisitioned from a local seamstress.

"Next—the chemise," I said.

We pulled on the blousy cotton garments with their elbow-length sleeves that fanned out in soft frills at our elbows.

Patrick caught a glimpse of himself in the full-length mirror.

"Holy shit," he said, checking himself out in several angles.

"I know, right? What a trip."

I'd been a server at Molly's for almost two years now, and it was all a part of my job. It was cool to see it from Patrick's point of view—as something new, exciting and different.

"Now, shoes. The shoes are easier to lace up before you put on the corset. Trust me."

We put on the light brown, kid leather ankle boots and laced them up.

"Do they fit okay?" They would have taken Patrick's measurements and shoe size when they'd given him the job offer.

"Yeah. I look so fucking weird."

"You look real cute. Just wait until you've got the corset on...and the choker. The choker pulls it all together."

"Do all the servers wear the same thing?" Patrick asked, as I lifted the boned corset from my diminishing pile.

"This is the basic outfit, what we're getting into. But sometimes you can find stuff at thrift shops and places like that. Robin has a gorgeous magenta kimono with gold dragons on it that he wears sometimes. If you want to, you can wear makeup and earrings — or other jewelry. Whatever floats your boat, really, as long as it goes with the overall vibe."

"Which is?"

"Nineteenth-century male hooker?"

"Right." Patrick laughed.

"Well, molly boy, actually. Hence the name."

"Molly what?" Patrick said, screwing up his face. "I just thought it was named after someone called Molly."

"Nah, you see, Patrick," I said, wrapping the short corset around my middle and making sure my chemise was straight. I fastened the tiny clasps up the front. "In those days, the hustlers who worked at the whorehouses that catered to gay men wore the same outfits the girls wore at the other places. And they were called molly boys."

"Huh."

"It was a fascinating period in history, really. I wouldn't want to have lived back then, but the stories of the men who defied convention and got up to mischief regardless are very inspiring. Imagine if you had to risk imprisonment or hanging every time you met a man for sex? Those guys were legends."

"Wow. How do you know all that?"

"Well, Jacob gave me a rundown. And I'm a compulsive researcher. I've read some really good books about Victorian sex rebels," I said. "You need help?"

Patrick was trying to put his corset on upside down. "Yes, please. How the fuck did they do this every day?"

"I don't fucking know," I said, taking the corset from Patrick and turning it the right way around. "You get used to it, though. And once it's all on, it's not too bad. Don't lace the corset too tight or you'll have problems. You want it to be snug but not constrain," I said, pulling the laces tight enough to hold him securely. "The design is handy, because you only need to lace it once. Then you just use the little clasps in the front – unless you lose or gain a lot of weight or something."

I tied the strings in a double bow and went around in front of him to fluff the chemise over his nipples. "You want to let it gape a bit so they can see them, but make it titillating, not blatant. Trust me," I said, winking. "I've got this down to an art form."

Patrick's gaze swept along my body from the top of my head to my feet in the brown shoes. "You sure do."

I might have preened a bit as I put on my velvet choker and glimpsed my reflection. But there wasn't time to dawdle.

"All right. You look amazing, by the way. Let's go."

"Do I need to do something to my hair?" Patrick asked.

"Nah, it looks fine. I usually dab some gel on mine, but I don't have time right now," I said, taking the lead as we headed out into the hall and through the double doors of the gaming parlor.

Chapter Two

Maverick Molly's

The grand and spacious room was decorated the way a Victorian parlor would have been, with a lush carpet, antique lamps and five large, round tables for the customers to play a game or sit and drink with each other. There was a bar to the left where I could see Jacob pouring a drink and a huge fireplace on the right wall beside the door to the kitchen. Ahead of us, across the room, a half-circle platform jutted from the wall, with a settee off to one side and a movable screen on the other, and a window at the corner that was covered with red velvet drapes. At multiple times over the course of an evening shift, we would get up and perform impromptu skits, tell bawdy jokes or sing scandalous songs for the men, to much applause and the lifting of glasses.

"There you are," Robin said, giving us a look over and practically salivating at the sight of Patrick in his outfit. "Can you train him? I'm up to my tits in needy men tonight."

"Sure," I said.

I led the way to a group of men playing at cards by the massive fireplace.

"Good evening, gents. What's the game tonight?" I asked.

"Toby!" The black-haired man greeted me. "I was hoping you'd be here."

"And why is that, Mr. Youngblood?" I asked, before turning to whisper to Patrick. "Never use their first names, even if they use yours."

"Oh, you know how it is," Mr. Youngblood said, blushing as he cleared his throat.

"He likes the way your ass looks in the bloomers," another man at the table said as he put a card face down in front of him. "But who doesn't?"

The other men gave their agreement, and I grinned.

"Well, shucks. You know I love to show it off."

I turned and displayed it, pleased to have all gazes directed to that prime real estate.

Mr. Youngblood made a noise in his throat. "Fuck. This hands-off policy Moriarty has going on is fucking torture. I just want to…want to—"

"Now, now," I said, with amusement, "what would your husband say?"

The man sitting beside Mr. Youngblood threw back his head below the antique lamp that hung from the high ceiling, and cackled with glee. His name was Mr. Youngblood, too.

"Look… I can't blame Michael. I can barely control *myself*," he admitted.

I gave them a slow and seductive smile, wondering how nice it would be to be sandwiched between them in their luxurious bed in the Glebe. "Now, now, that's enough of that. I need to concentrate on doing my job."

"What, to look pretty and fuckable? You're doing just fine on that front," said the other Mr. Youngblood. *Lawrence*. We knew everyone's first names, of course. We just weren't allowed to use them.

I turned and pressed my hand into Patrick's lower back, urging him forward. He almost tripped but gave the Youngbloods a shy smile.

"*Curtsey*," I whispered, keeping the smile on my face.

Patrick's gaze flew to mine in alarm, but then he turned back to the Youngbloods and attempted a very amateur curtsey. At least he knew what a curtsey was.

"This is our new server, Patrick. He's learning the ropes tonight." I knew they'd take that and run with it.

"Hello, Patrick," Lawrence said.

"We've got a real nice set of ropes back at our place," Michael Youngblood said, his gaze roaming over Patrick like he wanted to see him bound, gagged and strung upside down in his living room.

"Michael, you'll scare the poor thing. He looks terrified," Lawrence admonished, putting down his cards. "Toby, can we get some peanuts, please? It's been ages since we had supper."

"Of course, Mr. Youngblood. Look after Patrick while I'm gone, will you?"

"Yes, yes. We'll be on our best behavior."

Patrick looked as if he wanted to punch me, but I merely smiled and winked. "Back soon."

It was best to leave the new staff on their own right away, if you asked me. I had no doubt the Youngbloods and the other two men at the table—a Mr. Solomon and a Dr. Agabwe—would help Patrick feel more comfortable. They were longstanding members of

Maverick Molly's and, although they would joke about inappropriate things, they'd behave themselves.

Jacob was on the bar tonight, and he eyed me suspiciously as I lifted the trap and joined him, grabbing a stoneware bowl from under the counter. He was an imposing black man, with an impish face that belied his stern disposition. Sebastian was the more easygoing of the two.

"A little late tonight, are we?" he asked. It wasn't said in a mean way at all, just in a curious and surprised one. I couldn't blame him. Like I'd said, punctuality was something I was known for.

"Held up at home," I muttered. There was no way I was going into detail. I was already embarrassed, and talking about my mom and her stupid habits would only make me more so. "Sorry."

Jacob passed me the peanuts. "No worries. I guess you can be late once in a while."

"I fucking hate being late. It won't happen again…if I can help it," I said, pouring the roasted nuts into the bowl.

Jacob glanced into the other room. "How's Patrick doing?"

I shrugged. "He had a little trouble with his knickers, but I sorted him out."

Jacob laughed. "Yeah, they take some getting used to. He seemed competent in his interview."

I grinned. "Sure. But even if these guys have worked in restaurants before, Molly's can be an education."

"Oh, I know," Jacob said, leaning on the bar and resting his chin in his hand as he gazed at Patrick trying to make conversation with the Youngbloods. "He's cute."

"Very. But that's a job requirement."

Jacob gave me a stern look. "Not officially."

"Yeah, yeah."

He laughed. "Fine. Just don't go saying that anywhere else. I don't want to get on the wrong side of the Better Business Bureau."

I rolled my eyes. "They wouldn't touch Molly's with a ten-foot pole. This place is a municipal gold mine. The taxes alone!"

"Yeah, we do all right," Jacob said with a nod.

Technically, the serving staff were hired as 'models and entertainers', and Maverick Molly's was listed as a gay club, so that Jacob and Sebastian could get away with only hiring male-presenting people.

And Maverick Molly's did more than all right. As far as I knew, Jacob Moriarty and his boyfriend, Sebastian Declan, were raking in the dough. The gay subculture in this city was more substantial than you'd think when you compared it to the major metropolitan centers like Vancouver and Toronto. I'd wager on a higher percentage of the overall population in the queer community here in conservative old Ottawa, with a larger-than-average kink component.

Was it the same in all government towns? Who knew? I could tell you that a good proportion of our clientele came from offices on Albert and Slater, and in Old Hull, now called Gatineau. We didn't ask questions, and I was pretty sure no state secrets were being shared at Maverick Molly's. But folks who had to be serious and responsible during the day might be drawn to places like Molly's so they could live their truth and let loose during the cover of the night.

And they had money to burn.

The staff at Maverick Molly's was hand-picked from the local colleges and universities — young adults who were on a path to a bright future and who needed a way to make money that wasn't swinging from a stripper pole or working retail. Not that there was anything wrong with either of those jobs, but most of us jumped at the chance to do something unique and fun, with a historical component as well. And, sure, we did burlesque skits and sang bawdy songs for entertainment, but that was only a fraction of our duties. Most of the time, we were encouraged to lounge around the gaming parlor looking cute and bringing drinks to men who thought we were adorable and sexy. It was a good gig.

Jacob and Sebastian paid us well, and even had a group benefits plan in place for regular employees, which was a step up from most service jobs in the city. In return, we showed up on time — mostly — and went above and beyond what was required, helping to make Maverick Molly's one of the most prestigious gay clubs around.

It was the best place I'd ever worked. Still, by eight-thirty, I desperately needed a cigarette.

I sidled up to Robin, tucking my hair behind my ear. It felt weird not having eyeliner and lipstick on. Molly's was one of the few places where I could indulge my taste for gender bending without concern, but I'd been late then I'd been busy training Patrick, so there'd been no time to get properly made up. I promised myself that after I had a ciggy, I'd duck into the change room and pretty myself up.

"I'm going for a smoke."

"When are you gonna quit that damn habit, Toby?" Robin said with a withering look. "It's so gross."

I shrugged, not concerned with his distaste. "When are you gonna stop eating donuts?"

Robin gasped and put a hand to his choker.

"Can you keep an eye on Patrick?" I asked. "He's doing okay so far, but some of these men can be a bit much."

Robin grinned with salacious pleasure. "Oh, I know."

"Yeah, you and I know how to handle them. He's still learning," I muttered, heading for the entry.

"Fine. I'll watch him. But don't be too long. I've got my hands full."

"You always do."

Robin stuck his tongue out at me and mimed giving a blow job, making me laugh as I exited the parlor and went to get my jacket.

He didn't actually hand out blow jobs at Molly's — that was explicitly against staff rules. At least, I didn't *think* he did. But I knew he liked to give them, so who knows how many men he had agreed to meet up with after hours? I was sure he got requests, like we all did, disguised as jokes but meant in earnest, at least some of the time. You learned to laugh and play along. If the guy got super rude or overly suggestive, all it took was a word to Jacob or Sebastian, and they would be dealt with.

Our regulars — men who enjoyed the vibe at Molly's and had made it their go-to hangout — were careful not to upset the 'entertainment'. Because they knew we could have them banished with a word, and they liked it here.

I grabbed my coat but only draped it over my shoulders as I stepped outside, careful to hold the railing as I went down the steps in case some ice hadn't succumbed to the vast amounts of salt we dumped on them. The soft leather shoes we wore were cute, but they didn't have the best treads.

Some dude in a motorcycle jacket walked by and threw me a look, probably wondering why there was a Victorian male tart on the streets of Ottawa. Not everyone knew about Maverick Molly's, although it was a popular spot in the gay BDSM scene.

I winked at him. "Just having a smoke between blow jobs."

The guy cursed under his breath and continued walking.

Ottawa was a weird place. It was conservative on the surface and in the rural areas right through. But in the urban core, things were different. Ottawa contained a vast community of kinksters who owned bars and other businesses and held events all over the city. You didn't have to look too hard to find them.

I stood in the shoveled-out space at the bottom of the stairs and dug out my pack of cigarettes, listening to the wine of sirens in the distance. I was lucky that Jacob and Sebastian understood my need to take a break and didn't begrudge me indulging in front of their club. In a way, it was good advertising to have one of their seductively dressed 'entertainers' in front of the place, sucking on a paper pipe. Most of the men who came here had more questionable habits than an occasional cigarette.

I didn't smoke that much. I'd cut down to half a pack a day, and I was proud of that. It was part of my plan for this year, along with moving out of my mom's place and not getting any marks below a B at school. I wasn't quite ready to quit smoking completely, and trying to do so while I was still living with...her...was a losing proposal. Right now, I needed it, or else I'd have to go on some kind of antidepressant, and I just felt like smoking was more fun and less complicated. I wasn't even sure I'd make it to thirty, so worrying about lung cancer way down the line wasn't a deterrent.

I found my lighter in my coat pocket and lit up, then tucked everything away and stood there, gazing at the mix of stone houses, and steel buildings that contained offices and coffee shops and delis. Most of the traffic in this area came around during the day — at this time of night there weren't a lot of folks about. And although that might seem like a bad thing for a business, a place like Maverick Molly's thrived, since men could enter and exit without a crowd of people seeing them do so.

Sure, being queer wasn't illegal anymore, but being queer and kinky could still be seen in a less-than-desirable light by conservative politicians or business leaders with an ax to grind.

When I wasn't drawing the lung-killing smoke into my lungs, I took deep breaths of the cold air and closed my eyes, wondering when life would become more interesting than a constant round of schoolwork, work-work and trying to deal with Mom's mood swings and passive aggressive manipulations.

A car door slammed shut, then a squeal of tires sounded in the darkness and I heard footsteps approaching. I opened my eyes.

A man in a dark gray coat walked in my direction. There was no sign of the car — perhaps he'd gotten a lift from a friend or used an Uber. He was tall, with a casual way of walking and a confident demeanor. I had no idea if he was planning on coming to Molly's, but I couldn't take my eyes off him.

I placed the cigarette between my lips and inhaled, my gaze running over the gentleman as he ambled toward me. Our eyes met, and he smiled.

"Taking a break?" he said, his voice a caramel macchiato to my ears — smooth and strong and decadent, with a kick.

I smiled around my cigarette and nodded.

"Aren't you cold?" he asked, his forehead creased with concern.

I shrugged. *How sweet of him.*

He stopped at the bottom of the steps and glanced up at the elegant main door, then back at me.

"Going in?" I said, my eyebrows raised.

He stared at me, and I couldn't quite glean what he thought. I liked his face. He had a neatly trimmed goatee and a head of black curls that seemed like they'd be hard to tame — and an eyebrow piercing, which was hot. He looked older than me, but not ancient.

"Yeah. I think so."

"You think so?" I laughed. "Oh, you're going in."

"Well, I didn't plan to be waylaid by a saucy little tart having a smoke." He grinned. "I might stay out here for a bit."

Well, well, well. I'd been called worse things.

I took the cigarette out of my mouth. "You want one?"

His eyes widened. "Nope. But I'll watch you smoke it."

I grunted. *Suit yourself,* I thought.

We stood there in the frigid darkness. He gazed across the street as if he were trying to think of something to say. I decided to help him out. Sometimes I liked to let people wallow in their own awkwardness, but there was something about this man that made me want to smooth things out for him. It was probably witchcraft. He'd put some kind of spell on me, but I was helpless to fight it.

"You been here before?"

"To Molly's?" he said. "Yeah."

"Huh. I haven't seen you." I took in his strong features and eyebrow piercing again, his mop of black hair. No, I'd have remembered him.

"Normally I'm...with someone. And we just...you know, go straight to the back."

Ah. So he didn't hang out with the rabble, just took his squeeze straight to the Bordello. I wondered what exactly they got up to there. Was this man a top or a bottom? Did he order his partner around or did he submit for another, even more commanding, presence?

"Where's your someone tonight?" I asked.

He shrugged. "Well, I... I decided to spend some time in the gaming parlor for a change. Drown my sorrows." He smiled.

Not so sorrowful, then.

I raised my eyebrows and summoned a sympathetic expression, even though I felt anything but upset about it. "Oh no. Did your someone break up with you?"

He laughed and shook his head. "No, no. I have a lot of different someones. New one every week, usually. Only I couldn't find anyone, ah, convenient, tonight. It...doesn't happen often."

I looked him over. "I'm sure it doesn't." I could tell that this man had his pick of casual partners, which was a bit of a bummer, to be honest. I wondered why he was still talking to me out here in the cold.

He cleared his throat, and his gaze drifted from my feet in the brown leather shoes, up over the white bloomers with their frills and the corset with the chemise puffing above it. It wasn't gaping suggestively—I'd pulled the edges closed while I was outside — but my coat was open, so he could see what I looked like.

Ah. He likes the outfit. Maybe he liked the way it looked on me. Or he was only bored and wasting time.

"Would you be interested...?" He raised his eyebrows and licked his lips.

"Oh, I'm interested," I said, my gaze locking onto his. "But it's against the rules." I flicked the ash from my cigarette and smiled in apology. "I'm kind of on duty."

"Oh." He seemed genuinely disappointed. "Can I at least have a puff on your cigarette?"

Some folks sounded incredibly entitled and rude when they asked that. This man, though, channeled his desire for something so pedestrian as a shared puff into something else entirely, and I was helpless to resist.

I smiled, even though I felt out of my depth. He was annoyingly charming. I think I disliked him a little because he was pushing all of my buttons — the good ones — and had already declared himself a profligate man-whore, which I didn't hold against him at all, but it wasn't something I was looking for. Or...was it?

Watching him, as he stood there in the cold and dark, all fine and gorgeous and...interesting, I thought maybe it was. If all I could have of this man was a night of passion and careless intimacy, maybe that was okay.

But it couldn't be tonight.

Chapter Three

Games

I passed it over.

He took the cigarette from me with his slender fingers and placed the part that would have had my lipstick on it if I'd not been late to work — *dammit* — to his own. He held my gaze as he drew the smoke into his lungs, the tip glowing red, and let it out in soft puffs.

My dick got hard in my panties.

"I'm wearing panties," I blurted. I don't really know why. It just came out.

He choked on what was left of the smoke and waved a hand to disperse the hazy clouds between us.

"Pardon?"

Okay, genius, now what?

"I thought you might want to know…what I had on…underneath all this." I gestured at my fancy clothes.

He stared at me, his eyes narrowing, cheeks pinking up and breaths coming quicker once he stopped coughing.

"Thank you," he said, with a seriousness that seemed out of place.

"For what?" Now it was my turn to laugh. It sounded like the bark of a startled chihuahua, because, you know, I was all class.

The man grinned. "For telling me that."

We stood there watching each other. Then he turned and went up the steps and into the club.

"Fuck. *Jesus*," I said, my breath leaving my body as my poor cock protested his departure. I glared at my groin. "Settle down, you traitor. No nookie tonight. I just met the bastard."

Five minutes later—and only because I was technically working and thought maybe they'd noticed I'd been gone a while—I stubbed out what was left of the cigarette in the receptacle Sebastian had installed and went back inside.

"That was a long smoke break," Robin said as he swished by me in a swirl of bloomers, his dragon kimono puffing out like a sail.

"Fuck off."

"I won't tell on you. Did you see the guy that came in?" he asked in hushed but excited tones as I hung up my coat.

"Yeah."

"Hot, right?"

I was not going to admit to Robin that I thought Mr. Goatee Eyebrow Piercing was hot.

I shrugged. "Meh."

Robin blinked. "Hmm. Because he's talking to Patrick right now, and they seem to be getting along very well."

I jerked my head around, but I couldn't see into the parlor from where I was currently standing. I glanced at Robin, who gave me a devilish smile.

"*Meh*, huh? Something tells me you think he's as hot as I do—and as Patrick does."

"Fine. He's hot. So?" I said, tugging at the bottom of my corset to set it to rights and nudging the edges of the chemise apart so some of my chest was visible. "I want to go put on my face."

Robin sighed. "Holy shit, Toby. Are you going to work at all or just fucking take breaks all night?"

I flipped him the bird as I hastened into the staff changing room.

I grabbed my makeup bag out of my backpack and went into the tiny staff restroom. Shit, I looked okay, I guess. My cheeks were flushed from the cold and from my sudden arousal as well. My dick had settled down, finally.

I squirted gel into my palm and rubbed my hands together, then fixed my short shag into an orchestrated mess that looked like I'd just gotten out of bed. Then I washed my hands and applied dark brown liner around my eyes and a touch of matte burgundy to my lips. The darker tones worked well with my complexion.

That was much better. Now I could compete with Robin and Patrick for Mr. Goatee Eyebrow Piercing's attention.

Oh fuck.

I'd only just met the guy, and I was going out of my way to attract him. No, no, he had nothing to do with it. I'd already felt weird without my makeup. I was supposed to look tempting. It was part of the job, goddammit.

I nodded firmly to my reflection, made sure everything else was in place, widened the gap in my chemise — *oh look, a nipple* — and headed out to the floor.

Mr. Goatee Eyebrow Piercing was still talking to Patrick and Patrick was — Patrick was blushing like a virgin and avoiding the guy's eyes, as if his gorgeousness was just too much. It was pathetic, and I needed to put a stop to it. He would only embarrass himself.

I marched over there, giving the Mr. Youngbloods a smile as I passed, and swooped in to save Patrick from himself.

"They need you in the back."

Patrick gazed at me, wide-eyed and confused. "Oh, sorry. I'll go now?"

I nodded briskly. "Yes, that would be best. I'll look after Mr.... Oh, I don't know your name..."

I met the stunning man's amused gaze and raised my eyebrows, putting a hand on one hip as Patrick scurried from the room.

Mr. Goatee Eyebrow Piercing smiled as he looked me over. "It's Alastair Kenney."

Ooh. That sounded British and upper class. I had no idea if it was, but I liked it.

I held out my hand. "Mr. Kenney, would you like to join a game?"

"You've put on makeup," he said, gaze fixed on my lips.

"Yes, I was late to my shift, so hadn't put it on yet when we met...outside. Do you like it?" I pursed my lips.

"I do. Although I don't think it's necessary. Your lips are... Well, I mean, they were very nice...when I saw them outside...around your cigarette." He seemed flustered all of a sudden. "But the lipstick," he said, gesturing with a finger at his own lips as I widened my eyes, hoping to look like a baby deer. "That looks good, too." He cleared his throat and averted his gaze.

Well, well, well.

I couldn't help smiling. "Thank you. That's gracious of you."

He looked at me again, this time taking in my scandalous outfit, now that my coat wasn't in the way. "I do like how the makeup enhances the whole" — he waved at me — "effect."

He seemed breathless and not at all upset about Patrick leaving, thank God.

I mean…what?

"About that game. Did you want to join one of these tables? I can inquire if there's a place for you."

This was my job. I'd been hired to make men feel welcomed, accommodated and entertained.

"No, that's all right. I'd rather stand and observe." He slid his gaze over me again, then met mine.

My cheeks heated and my traitorous dick started to swell. I parted my lips. "Oh, sure. I mean, certainly. That's fine." I scrambled for something to say. "Drink?"

He nodded. "That would be great."

Thank God. It would give me something to do besides wallow in my unexpected fascination.

"What's your poison?" I asked.

"Hmm. What do you recommend?"

Oh, we were flirting. We were definitely flirting, which wasn't so unusual here at Maverick Molly's. What *was* unusual was the way it was affecting *me*. Mr. Alastair Kenney made me feel like an actual nineteenth-century molly boy in the sights of a rakish gentleman with clandestine desires.

"Have you tried the Sazerac?" I asked, channeling all my powers of sophistication.

He smiled wider, and I noticed a dimple in one cheek.

Damn him.

He laughed and scratched at his chin. "I don't know what that is."

"Oh, it's very nice," I said, running my fingers along the buttons on the front of my corset as his gaze tracked them. "It's a whiskey base with sugar, bitters and a splash of absinthe." I drew my fingers to my neck, touching the velvet choker. "You'll love it," I said, fluttering my lashes.

"All right. I'll have one of those, please. Thank you."

I turned to go.

"You never told me *your* name."

I turned back to Mr. Kenney. "It's Toby."

He nodded. "Thank you, Toby. I'll be right here."

"And I'll be right back."

I turned and walked to the bar, my heart beating a merry dance as my inner dialogue went *fuck, fuck, fuck.*

I went up to Jacob at the bar and ordered a Sazerac for Mr. Kenney. Patrick came back, looking confused.

Huh.

"They didn't ask for me. They didn't know what you were talking about."

"Oh, shit, I thought they needed you. My mistake," I said, with my best approach at a sympathetic expression. "I'm sorry."

He sighed and fingered the hem of his bloomers. "It's fine. I was feeling kind of overwhelmed, anyway."

"Yeah, I remember my first shift. You're doing great, though."

"Really?" he asked.

"Sure," I said. "Only don't get too close to that guy." I nodded at Mr. Kenney.

"Why?" Patrick asked, blinking in confusion.

"Oh, I just…heard he gets handsy when he's been drinking."

Lies, all lies. I didn't know Mr. Kenney at all. I'd never seen him before tonight. But I went all in.

"…which is against the rules, but sometimes the newer staff don't know how to handle it."

"Oh, right," Patrick said, regarding Mr. Kenney with wariness.

"I'll look after him. You entertain the Youngbloods. They're pretty wholesome."

"Okay." He glanced back at Mr. Kenney. "He's fucking hot though, right? I'm not imagining it?"

I frowned. *Back off, Patrick.*

"Yeah, I don't know. He had a bit of BO when I got close," I said with an offhand air, like I wasn't completely slandering the guy. Then I doubled down. "And his breath stinks."

Patrick's expression soured. "Gross. I'll go check on the Youngbloods."

"Yes, that's a good idea," I said, playing with the neck of my chemise.

Wow, I had sunk to a new low.

When Jacob handed me the Sazerac for Mr. Kenney, I contemplated downing the entire thing myself, except I never drank alcohol. But all of a sudden, I could see the appeal.

I sauntered back to Mr. Kenney, swaying my hips and pretending that I wasn't a lying, cutthroat, selfish person.

"Here you are," I said, smiling sweetly as I handed him the amber beverage in the cut-glass whiskey tumbler.

Jacob and Sebastian had argued about whether to shell out for crystal glassware, but in the end had opted for the more economical cut-glass option, primarily since they could be bunged in the dishwasher for cleanup. The selected glassware was fancy enough that they rivaled crystal glasses for elegance and class anyway, in my humble opinion, not that I'd had the opportunity to drink out of crystal very often…or ever. But the glasses they'd chosen were lovely and had a good weight in the palm.

Mr. Kenney wrapped his fingers around the tumbler with as much grace as the object held within them. I found myself transfixed, wondering where else those fingers might prove a delicate and teasing fit.

Goddammit.

Mr. Kenney tilted his head to examine the drink.

"Mmm. Looks delicious."

"It's very tasty. Watch out for the absinthe, though."

He frowned. "Really?"

I laughed. "Nah. It's only a splash." I examined him. Perhaps he wasn't as worldly as he seemed. "Have you had absinthe before?"

"No. Never." He examined the amber liquid in the glass. "Is it as deadly as the rumors?"

"Deadly? No. It's…potent. But you won't see the green fairy, even if you drink a glass of it."

"Huh." He examined me as he took a sip. "Mm. That's tasty. Thanks."

I nodded and gave him a quick curtsy, because I knew I looked cute as fuck, and it seemed my mission to seduce this man. I wasn't even sure I wanted him if he was as fickle as he'd proclaimed, but I couldn't help myself from trying to get him.

"You're welcome. Now I must go attend to my other customers," I said, even though it was the last thing I wanted to do.

He looked disappointed, which made me inordinately happy.

"Please do flag me down if you need a refill…or really, anything at all." I glanced to where Patrick was serving drinks to the Youngbloods. "And see that fellow?"

Mr. Kenney smiled, his gaze sweeping over young Patrick. "Oh yes. I was speaking with him earlier."

I narrowed my eyes for a second, until Mr. Kenney returned his attention to me, at which point I attempted to look concerned and conscientious.

"He's very new and a tad uncomfortable with all the attention, so maybe just don't bother him for now? I'm sure he'll adjust, but I don't want him to feel overwhelmed on his first shift," I said, swallowing my guilt and silently apologizing to our new server. "And if you need anything, I'm very happy to oblige."

We gazed at each other, and I could tell he'd seen through my attempt at dissuasion, because he eyed me sternly for a long moment, during which I felt my cock go completely hard. But then he smiled, and it lit up his face and melted my resolve. And I really didn't think he wanted to talk to Patrick.

"Of course. I'll let you know." He lifted his drink in a salute, and I forced myself to leave him, which proved an excruciating exercise.

Once I was away, though, I wondered if I'd finally lost my fucking mind. What the hell was I doing? Had I been bewitched? I spent the rest of my shift shuffling drinks back and forth from the bar to the patrons, giving Patrick the easy jobs and making sure to keep Mr. Kenney in view and content at all times. I knew he was watching me, and on the few occasions when he wasn't doing that, I watched him.

I figured the evening could go one of two ways. Either Mr. Kenney would see my burlesque bit with Robin, find it hilarious and ever-so-slightly embarrassing and leave without another word, or worse, scoop up Patrick on his way out somehow...*or*, he'd see my burlesque bit with Robin and fall completely in lust with me and proposition me, at which point I would tell him that, although I was attracted to him, I didn't make a habit of going home with strangers who had already confessed to being on the lookout for an amuse-bouche — *but* with the taste of victory on my tongue.

At eleven o'clock, Sebastian Declan — Jacob Moriarty's husband and co-owner of Maverick Molly's — stepped up onto the stage and tapped a glass with a metal spoon. He was a bit shorter and a lot whiter than Jacob, and in charge of the entertainment aspects of the place. The ringing noise did the job of attracting everyone's attention. The regulars leaned back in their chairs and clapped, hooting in some cases. They knew what came next.

"May I please have your attention on the stage!" Sebastian asked in a booming bass, flourishing his hand at the curved platform. Both he and Jacob dressed the part of Victorian dandies while at work, with suspendered pants, fancy waistcoats and crisp white shirts. They were in their mid-forties, and sometimes I wondered what it would be like having a sugar daddy or two who happened to own a gay club, but they were pretty big on appropriate workplace behavior and had never made a move on me. They were good-looking guys and very professional, and I might have had the occasional fantasy about being taken to bed after a long shift, but that would never happen.

He stepped down and sat at the apartment-sized piano to the left of the stage as Robin flounced up. Robin gathered his kimono close and held the edges together to hide his racier undergarments. Now he threw it open, drew it off and tossed it to the floor.

The men whistled and clapped. One of the Mr. Youngbloods shouted his name.

Robin took a pose, with one leg forward and his toe in the little shoe pointed, before smiling like a maiden, resting his chin on his folded hands, and starting to sing his favorite little ditty. The crisp white of his Victorian undergarments and the gold embroidery of his corset set off his dark complexion most beguilingly.

"*I'm a young girl and have just come over, over from the country where they do things big,*" He emphasized the word *big* and glanced down at his crotch, to much laughter. "*And amongst the boys,*" he said as he gazed at the men surrounding their tables, "*I've got a lover,*"

Hoots.

"*And since I've got a lover, why I don't care a fig.*" Robin smiled. "*The boy I love is up in the gallery,*" he said, gazing wistfully at a made-up person in an imaginary gallery. "*The boy I love is looking now at me. There he is, can't you see*" — he pointed — "*waving his handkerchief, as merry as a Robin*" — he grinned and looked directly at the audience — "*that sings on a tree.*"

"Have I got a tree for you, my pretty Robin," someone called out.

Robin pretended to look shocked, shook his head slightly then resumed. '*The boy that I love, they call him a cobbler, but he's not a cobbler, allow me to state. For Johnny is a tradesman and he works in the Boro' where they*" — he put a hand to his lips and emphasized the next words so they sounded like a reference to something else — "*sole and heel them, while you wait.*"

The crowd hooted and clapped again. Everyone loved Robin — probably not as much as Robin loved Robin, but there you go. He was a born performer.

"*Now, if I were a duchess*" — Robin flashed his eyes and stood taller, pretending to walk in heels and clasping the edge of his robe like it was a skirt — "*and had a lot of money, I'd give it,*" he said as he grabbed imaginary hips and thrust madly, to much applause, *"to the boy who's going to marry me. But I haven't got a penny, so we'll live on"* — he mimed sucking a cock — *"love and kisses, and be just as happy as the birds on the tree."*

He repeated the chorus and when he sang *"As merry as a robin that sings on a tree!"* someone yelled out "I can make you sing pretty, Robin. You can sit on my perch!"

Robin cackled. "I know how many have perched on your twig, sir, and I shall politely decline."

This caused more laughter and some curses.

"Now behave yourselves, gentlemen," he said, beckoning me to the stage as he descended. "You be nice to Toby. He's a delicate flower."

Chapter Four

Seduction

I rolled my eyes as the crowd laughed, since they knew that was far from the truth.

Robin flounced off the stage as I marched up onto it in his place and clapped my hands together.

"Right then, what do you gents want this evening? A striptease?"

There was applause and a cacophony of hoots all around.

I frowned and put a finger to my chin. "Hmm, can't do that," I said, looking at Sebastian, who shook his head. I gazed back at the audience. "A poem?"

"Not unless it's got the words cunt or cock in it!" someone yelled.

"Hmm, let me see…" I said, tapping the finger on my chin and pretending to think. "What about a song?"

"Yes, a song, Toby!"

"Give us a song!"

"Do the bow-wow song, Toby!" Mr. Youngblood begged. His husband tilted his head back and howled, then howled like a dog, as everyone laughed.

"Oh, you like that one?" I asked, as they clapped and whistled.

I found Alastair in the crowd. He was watching the men in the parlor going gaga for me, and I puffed up a bit. I walked over and grabbed the straight chair that we used as a prop and set it in the center of the stage facing backward. Then I straddled it with my hands on my knees, perched on the toes of my leather shoes and gazed out at my adoring audience.

"Here!" Robin said, and I looked over. He pulled a stuffed gray elephant from the prop basket and threw it to me. I caught it in my hand and quipped to the audience, "You'll have to pretend this is a kitty cat, all right?"

"What's the elephant prop for, I'd like to know," someone muttered.

"Is there a song about a giant-sized—?"

"Never mind," I said promptly, cuddling the stuffed elephant to my chest, where it nudged my chemise apart to bare a nipple.

"Oh, fuck me," someone commented, so I knew I was on the right track.

This particular ditty required me to assume the character of a young child. What that said about the men who demanded it, well, I mean, I know what it said about them. The gay Daddy/boy thing was something I enjoyed messing around with, although I tended more to the feminine in my performance.

Sebastian started playing the jaunty music hall tune.

"*I love my little cat, I do, with long black silky hair*," I purred in a most childlike way, batting my lashes and smiling with as much innocence as I could muster. "*It comes each day with me to school and sits upon the chair. When teacher says 'Why do you bring that little pet of yours?', I tell her that I bring my cat along with me because…"*

I held up the stuffed elephant and looked at it, then dropped it to the floor, folded my arms on the back of the chair, and rested my chin on them as I sang with a pout. *"Daddy wouldn't buy me a bow-wow, bow-wow. Daddy wouldn't buy me a bow-wow, bow-wow."* I made a big show of sighing. *"I've got a little cat, and I guess I'm fond of that,"* I said, nudging the stuffy with the toe of my boot. Then I gazed at my audience with a young girl's misery. *"But I'd rather have a bow-wow, wow-wow, wow-wow."*

There was much clapping as I launched into the second verse, this time leaning back on my hands and swinging my feet forward to plant my heels apart on the rug.

"We used to have two tiny dogs, such pretty little dears. But Daddy sold 'em 'cause they used to bite each other's ears. I cried all day. At eight each night Papa sent me to bed. When Ma came home and wiped my eyes, I cried again and said."

I leaned forward again with my chin on my arms and gazed directly at Alastair this time, pretending to be a sad little boy. *"Daddy wouldn't buy me a bow-wow, bow-wow, Daddy wouldn't buy me a bow-wow, bow-wow."* I blinked my eyes at him, slowly, like a cat. *"I have a little cat, and I guess I'm fond of that, but I'd rather have a bow-wow, wow-wow, wow-wow."*

The current flowing between us was white hot. Alastair parted his lips, and I sat up slowly, getting off the chair to much applause. I picked the stuffed elephant off the floor and launched it into the audience, where Dr. Agabwe plucked it out of the air as I descended from the stage.

I met Mr. Kenney's gaze again but then looked away. I had to play it cool, to prove I wasn't completely desperate for what he could offer me, even though I was.

As I brushed by him, he stopped me with a hand on my arm. I looked at it in shock, and he immediately dropped it, then glanced at Jacob, who hadn't seen.

"Sorry. Only, that was...quite a performance," he said, meeting my gaze sheepishly.

His cheeks were flushed, and I could tell he had a boner.

"Yes, well it's all a part of the job," I said, smiling with pleasure.

"You're very good at what you do, Toby. I'm impressed."

"Thank you. Would you like another drink?" I asked, gesturing to his empty glass. "You enjoyed that one."

"Yes, I did," he said in a subdued voice, as if he wasn't just referring to his drink. "That would be great. Thank you."

By the time eleven rolled around, the crowd in the parlor had thinned. It was Wednesday, and most of these people had jobs to get to in the morning. The Youngbloods were enjoying themselves in the Bordello.

Sebastian and Jacob had shown it to me back when I'd been hired, but other than peeking in that one time, I'd given it a wide berth. I had no issues with kink or with kinky folks, and I had had my share of kinky fantasies, but in terms of using actual implements or furniture, I was a neophyte. I hadn't even been spanked properly. It all seemed a little out of my depth.

I sprawled on the green velvet settee in the corner under the window, with one leg hooked over the broad arm. My foot in its sweet leather shoe dangled as I stared at the ceiling and dozed, listening to the crackling of the low fire and the murmured hum of dwindling conversation. My other foot was braced against the floor, so I didn't fall off my narrow perch.

I worked hard, and Jacob didn't begrudge me the occasional downtime. In fact, lying in such a scintillating position tied right into the atmosphere we were attempting to recreate. Even if Patrick, Robin and I weren't actual *trollops* — the verdict was still out on Robin — we were encouraged to convey the air of pretty young things on display.

A ragged sigh above me caused me to open my eyes. There was Alastair Kenney, holding his third Sazerac, a rosy glow to his skin and a satisfying warmth to his gaze. I hadn't heard his footsteps. He'd taken off his suit jacket and rolled up his sleeves to reveal shapely forearms dusted with dark hair.

His smile held notes of melancholy and hope. "Hello, Toby."

I laced my fingers together over my corset, and gazed up at him, blinking my eyes with exaggerated innocence.

"Mr. Kenney," I purred, "what can I do for you?"

He ran his gaze over me and lingered on the puffy white bloomers with the lace at the edge and the pink ribbon running through, then paused on my calf in its midnight black stocking and finally fixed on my soft leather shoe.

"Your shoe is undone," he said, gesturing with a finger.

I glanced at the lace in question. It wasn't completely untied, but it had loosened and looked on the verge of coming loose. I met his gaze, about to say it was fine and that I'd fix it in a minute. But his smile widened, lost its sadness and took my breath away.

"May I?" he asked, with a gentleness I'd not expected.

I glanced at the bar. Jacob wasn't there, probably sorting things in the kitchen for closing. *Technically*, it wasn't allowed. But there was nobody close enough to care, and I certainly didn't mind. And he *had* asked for my consent.

"You're not really supposed to touch me," I said, blinking up at him with exaggerated naiveté. "But yes, you may."

I smiled, then, to let him know I appreciated the kind gesture.

Mr. Kenney glanced behind him to see if anyone was looking. He angled his body so that it blocked me and my shoe from Patrick and Robin, who were talking animatedly about something by the fire, Patrick nodding and giggling as Robin gestured wildly.

He tugged the end of the lace to pull it fully free, his fingers trembling ever-so-slightly. I don't know why that was so hot, but it felt like he'd untied the back of my corset instead of my shoelace.

He stood there, gazing at my shoe, breaths audible as he licked his lips. He didn't look up from the laces as he whispered, "I want to do much more than this, Toby."

Then he glanced up, and his eyes burned black into mine.

My cock had already started getting hard while he'd looked me over so self-indulgently. Now I wanted him to pull my shoe off and kiss the arch of my foot, as if I were a fancy prostitute and he was trying to convince me to lower my fee.

"Well, Mr. Kenney, I'm afraid you can't possibly go that far," I said, bracing my hands against the cushion of the settee as Alastair stroked the tips of his fingers along the arch of my shoe, his gaze following.

"When do you get off, Toby?" he said, his words quick.

I watched as he tied the black laces into a delicate bow, his fingers deft and sure now.

"Uh…" I gulped as the double entendre landed in the horny part of my brain, which was all of it, at the moment. "M-my shift is over at midnight."

Mr. Kenney smiled, that dimple reappearing as he kept his gaze attentively on the laces he tied into a double knot.

"Do you need to help close the place?" he asked, glancing up.

God, why are his eyes so beautiful? Why does he have this power over me? Why do the deep tones of his voice feel like feathers gliding along my skin?

"Not tonight," I breathed, my gaze fixed on those long, agile fingers.

"Lucky me," he said, patting my securely tied shoe and straightening. "There."

Somehow, I reined in my desire and reasserted some control.

"You have no idea how lucky you are, Mr. Kenney," I murmured, taking my hands and running them up the front of my corset so I could tug the edges of my chemise farther apart.

"Jesus," he cursed. "Shit. Maybe a hotel? I can—?"

I held up my hand. *Whoa, whoa, whoa.*

"I can't talk about this here," I said. "I'll meet you outside at twelve fifteen, because I need to change. Wait for me at the bottom of the steps, and we can figure things out from there. All right?"

He couldn't stop staring at my exposed nipples.

"All right," he said, finally, and I curled the edges of my lips into a satisfied smile.

"You know I can't wear this outfit once I'm off my shift, right?"

He sighed. "Such a damn shame. You look so good in it."

At least the lace panties were my own. They would be a nice surprise for him.

I waved my fingers. "Off you go then. I'll see you in a bit."

He laughed and wandered away, collecting his jacket from the back of a chair as I tried and failed to ignore how good those suit pants hung on his narrow hips. I put a hand to my forehead, trying to get my heart to slow down. *Holy shit.* What the hell was *that* about?

I only had a few more things to do before my shift ended. When the clock struck twelve, I hastened into the changing room and got out of my tarty things, reverting back to my jeans and black T-shirt with a twinge of regret. Normally I was glad to get out of my costume, because the corset started to pinch after a while. But tonight, all I could think about was how naughty and illicit I'd felt watching Mr. Alastair Kenney untie the lace of my leather shoe, and how much fun it would be to get dolled up again in the privacy of a hotel room or, even maybe his place, and have him undress me.

I stared at the pieces of my uniform, wondering if Jacob would mind if I borrowed it for one night…Would he even notice?

Fuck it.

I was a valued employee. I'd never done anything against the rules – so far – and I'd bring the outfit back tomorrow. They'd never even know it was gone. I glanced around guiltily then stuffed the different pieces into my backpack, including the corset and shoes. Patrick and Robin had to close tonight, so they were still out on the floor and didn't witness my transgression. Mr. Alastair Kenney was going to get the whole Maverick Molly's experience tonight, let me tell you. But I'd have to get him to swear that he'd not seen me in anything but my twenty-first-century clothes, or I'd hear it from Jacob and Sebastian.

I suddenly remembered that one of the things I'd sworn off of this year was hasty casual hookups. But honestly, I was doing so well on the cutting down on cigarettes thing, and I was totally committed to moving out of my mom's place, so I figured I could toss one of my New Year's resolutions into the gutter where it belonged.

I'd had such a crap day until Mr. Alastair Kenney had walked up to me and asked for a puff on my cigarette. I was going to have fun tonight – sex with no strings, with a hot-as-fuck virtual stranger who seemed as into me as I was into him. Maybe a casual hookup was exactly what I needed.

Robin came into the change room, and I swept by him with a raised hand.

"See ya."

"Are you on tomorrow?" he asked.

"Yep. I'll be here," I promised.

"On time?"

"Yes! For fuck's sake." I was a bit terse because I didn't want him to notice how stuffed full my bag was, and I needed to meet Alastair before he got fed up and left without me.

"Bye, bitch," he sneered, somehow sounding amused and pissed at the same time.

"Whatever."

And I was out of there. No one paid me any mind as I strode down the hall, put on my boots, grabbed my coat and headed outside.

Alastair—I could think of him as something other than Mr. Kenney now—stood at the bottom of the steps, exactly where I'd told him to wait for me.

"Hey," he said, with a smile. "All done?"

I skipped down the steps. "All done."

"So, where do you want to go, Toby?"

I shrugged. "I don't care, except we can't go to my place."

"Roommates?" he asked.

I huffed a laugh. *If only.* "No. My mom."

"Oh. Oh! How old are you?"

"Oh, for fuck's sake, relax. It's just"—I waved my hand in the air—"rent's expensive."

"I'm so sorry. I didn't mean anything." It was the first time I'd seen him flustered. It looked kinda good on him. "Obviously, you're working in a bar, so you must be at least nineteen…"

I gave him a look. "I'm twenty. Would you calm down?"

"Oh, wow. That's…that's young." He said it as if it meant he was concerned, but his gaze swept over me like I was a smorgasbord that had just upped its appeal.

I narrowed my eyes at him. "But legal. Maybe you're too old."

"Ouch." He put a hand to his heart.

"Want me to call nine-one-one? Are you having a coronary?"

Alastair stared at me, shocked, then burst into laughter.

"I'll be thirty-six in two months."

I pretended to be shocked. "Shit. That's old."

"Thanks. That's instilling a lot of confidence. Are you even attracted to me?"

"Am I even – *Oh my God.* Pretty sure we've got a mutual thing going on." I eyed him. "Isn't that what this is about?"

"Okay. Good. Because I really want to fuck you."

He'd been keeping up with me as we trudged down the sidewalk, but I stopped abruptly and we almost collided.

"Hold on there, Romeo. I don't know if we're gonna get that far." I looked him up and down. "I mean, maybe? Let's just see where this goes."

"That's fine. Of course," he said.

We started walking again.

"Do you want to get a hotel room?" he asked. "I'll pay…"

"Sure, I guess. But a nice one."

"What about the Chateau?"

I stopped again and this time, Alastair did bump me, but he quickly backed off as I practically went ballistic.

"The Chateau Laurier? Are you fucking kidding me?"

Alastair frowned. "No, I… It's a nice hotel."

I stared at him, trying to figure out if he was for real. "You don't have to spend that much on me."

The Chateau Laurier was the most renowned hotel in Ottawa. Not the most modern, or even the most expensive, maybe, but it was a classy spot. It was where all the important visitors to our city stayed — MPs, dignitaries, royalty.

"Wait. Are you some kind of prince or, shit, a member of Parliament?"

"God no. I work in tech. But I am friends with the manager. She can get me a room there at a good rate."

"But we'll only need it for a handful of hours…" I said, throwing out my arms.

He took out his phone, tapping it with his finger. "It's fine, Toby. Let me do this. The rooms are spacious, and the place is swanky. It's a beautiful hotel." He tapped some more. "I'm getting an Uber."

Of course, it was a gorgeous hotel. Fuck, yeah, I knew *that* — or, I'd heard that. But I'd never stayed there or even gone inside the imposing stone building that served as a backdrop for millions of tourist photos.

"God, now I'm feeling pressure…" I said, putting a hand to my forehead.

"What? No, come on. We don't have to do anything if you don't want to. I'm happy to just hang out. I swear. It's totally up to you."

I eyed him up and down, going over my options. I could insist we go somewhere less expensive, but now that he'd mentioned the Chateau, I kind of wanted to go there. I could say goodnight and give up on this adventure entirely, go home to where my mom was probably in a drunken stupor and wank off in my bed to fantasies of fucking Alastair. Or I could smile and say "Sure, that sounds great."

I smiled. "Sure, that sounds great."

"Fantastic! Car's on its way." He tapped his finger on the screen of his phone and waited, holding my gaze.

"Fairmont Chateau Laurier, Delphine speaking." The voice on speaker sounded slightly bored but unfailing in its professionalism.

"Delphi! How's the hotel business?"

"Alastair Kenney. Jesus. You can't possibly be calling for a room this late. For *tonight*?"

"You've never failed me before, Delphi. There must be something I can have."

Wow. Way to be confronted with Alastair's man-whore status in a very crucial moment. But I suppose if it got me a room at the Chateau and a night of unrestrained passion, I could deal with it.

"Fine," Delphine muttered. There was a pause. "There's a king with a city view. Will that do?"

"Which floor?"

Wow. Picky much?

"It's on the sixth floor. Is that good enough?" Now she sounded annoyed. I was kind of on her side.

"Sure, sure. Can you send up a bottle of champagne and two glasses, please."

Hold-up. I raised my finger. "I don't drink."

Alastair blinked, staring at me in confusion. But he recovered. "Hold on. Never mind. What about some chocolates?"

He raised his eyebrows at me, and I gave him a thumbs-up. Okay, now I was definitely on board.

"Of course, Alastair. Would you like a bouquet of flowers?" The question was dripping with sarcasm, but Alastair raised his eyebrows at me.

I gave him an incredulous, disappointed look, and he frowned.

"No, that's it. We'll be there in about ten minutes."

"It'll be ready for you. Enjoy."

"Thanks, Delphi. You're the best," Alastair said, but she'd already ended the call.

He tapped the screen with his thumb and lowered his phone.

"You don't drink?" he said.

"I'm not sure why that's so surprising."

"Well...the Sazerac... You sounded so sure. I assumed you'd had one."

"Well, I work there, so I know all the good cocktails without having to sample any. Sorry to disappoint you?"

"Fuck, Toby. I'm not disappointed. I have all respect for people who don't drink, as long as they don't stop me from doing it."

"No worries there. You obviously enjoyed the Sazerac, since you had three."

"You kept count?" He smiled.

"Maybe. It was fun seeing you get tipsier as the evening went on."

Alastair ran his fingers through his hair and pulled his coat tighter, looking shy and adorable, *the slick bastard.*

"Kiss me," I said. I don't know why that came out. It was supposed to be in my head. But we were standing on the sidewalk waiting for the Uber, and I guess I panicked.

But it worked out, because Alastair tugged on my coat sleeve and pulled me close, finding my lips with his as if he'd only been waiting for permission. And I got the whole butterflies in my stomach thing and the jolt of lightning as our mouths connected — and the kiss got deeper and more urgent before either of us could stop it.

A car horn honked.

"Shit," Alastair muttered and pulled away, turning his head. "That's our Uber."

I stared at him, wondering what he'd done with my brain.

"Toby?"

"Yeah?"

"Let's go."

Chapter Five

High Society

The Fairmont Chateau Laurier hotel sat upon the bank of the Ottawa river, bordered on the west by the Parliament Buildings and on the east by Sussex Street. The area had an old-world feel — as close to it as it could seeing as Canada didn't have Europe's legacy of rising and falling civilizations. There was a rumor that the Parliament Buildings had been built over an indigenous burial site, and this could be true. This land had been occupied when the settlers from Europe came over and 'discovered' it.

Our Uber driver was a middle-aged man who didn't seem to care that we were two men heading to the fanciest hotel in Ottawa at 12:20 a.m. He let us off at the entrance and pulled away as Alastair ushered me inside. I tried not to be impressed but, really, who wouldn't have been? It was a huge space, for one thing, with a warm glow of light that illuminated the gleaming and luxurious finishes. An arrangement of leather sofas and chairs defined the comfortable lobby.

Alastair made his way to the reception desk as I hung back, gazing up at the second-floor balconies that looked down on the lobby. There was no one around, so I was free to display my astonishment at the grandeur of the old hotel, until Alastair came back with our room cards.

"Shall we?" he said, handing one to me.

I looked at it, expecting it to be in gold or something like that, but it seemed like any other hotel room card. I was honestly a little disappointed.

The number six-fifteen was written on the holder in blue pen.

"It's on the city side."

"Huh?" I asked. "As opposed to the country?"

He laughed. "No, as opposed to having a view of the Parliament Buildings or the courtyard."

"Oh. Wow, look at you. You have stayed here a few times."

He shrugged. "Well, my friend…"

"I know. Her name is Delphine."

Alastair blushed. "Yes. Well, Delphine can usually get me a good deal."

"That's why we're here."

"Yes," he said. He stared at me curiously. "Are you okay?"

I ran a hand through my hair, feeling less brave than I had at Molly's and wondering if this was a good idea or not. Probably it wasn't, but I was trying to figure out how much I cared.

"Yeah, I just feel…a bit lost."

Alastair reached out and took my hand — the one that wasn't holding the room card. He looked around but we were completely alone.

"I'm glad you're here with me."

I contemplated the sincerity of his expression, then nodded. "I'm glad I'm here with you, too."

He led me to the elevators. When we got there, he released my hand.

"Is this too much? I'm sorry. I just really like this place, and I knew I could get us in." He seemed eager to put me at ease, which I appreciated. "I should've just found somewhere—"

"It's fine," I said, as the elevator dinged, and the doors opened. "I'm not used to being treated so well."

He frowned. "Now that's a shame."

We stepped in, and Alastair pressed the button to close the doors. They made a soft swish as they did. We had privacy together for the first time.

In seconds the sexual tension was so thick I was swimming in it.

Alastair gazed at me with heavy-lidded eyes, and I was overtaken by the desire I'd been fighting since that first kiss on the sidewalk.

"Fuck," I breathed, surging forward and grabbing the lapels of his coat.

"Toby," he whispered, just before I attached my lips to his face.

He opened his mouth and let me plunder it with my out-of-control arousal. Whatever we had between us, it flared up like a five-alarm fire. He was hard. I was hard. And the elevator was whisking us up to a luxurious room on the sixth floor.

Ding.

We wrenched apart, breathing hard, as the elevator door swished open.

An elderly woman in a fur coat stood there. She blinked at us as we stepped into the hallway. I hadn't expected to see anyone at this hour, let alone an old lady.

"Hello," I said. "What a lovely evening." I took Alastair's hand and laced our fingers together.

Alastair puffed a laugh, his eyes dancing in a wonderful way, as the old lady looked us over.

"Looks like it will be," she said with a smirk. I put my hand over my mouth as she stepped into the elevator and pressed the button. The doors closed.

Alastair and I gaped at each other, then burst out laughing.

"Shh, shh," I said, "there are people sleeping!"

"Do you suppose she was on her way to an…assignation?" Alastair giggled.

"Oh fuck off. She was at least eighty."

He pointed an accusatory finger at me.

"That's ageism. I hope I'm still fucking people when I'm eighty," Alastair said.

"Something tells me you will be," I quipped, pulling him along. "Come on. By the time we get to our room, you might be that old."

"Cute. You know, you're bossy when you're horny."

"You have no idea."

I found room six-fifteen and slid my key card through the slot, pushed down on the handle and pulled him into the room behind me.

"Okay. I need you to sit down in that chair," I said, pointing to the armchair by the window. "And wait for me."

"Toby, do you like the room? Is it everything you dreamed of?" Alastair asked, sweeping his arm around us at the king-sized bed and the polished wood furniture. There was even a box of Godiva chocolates and a bottle of non-alcoholic wine on the table.

"Yeah, yeah, it's really nice. Honestly, all we need is a bed."

He blinked. "Huh." He put his key card on the table by the bed. "Wham bam thank you ma'am."

He wasn't actually offended by that remark, was he? I was relieved by the soft smile he gave me as he took off his suit jacket.

"Oh, you'll be thanking me in about ten minutes," I said, throwing my coat on the bench by the closet.

"Ten minutes!"

"No, no, no, I mean, for the first part...the very first part. I have a surprise."

"Oh. Okay. Well, get on with it, then."

"That's very romantic," I bemoaned as I ducked into the bathroom with my backpack. "Oh shit, it's pretty fucking nice in here. Swanky." My voice echoed off the tiles.

Alastair laughed, and it sounded surprisingly genuine.

"Are you sitting in the chair?" I asked through the bathroom door.

"Yes. I'm being a very good boy."

Good.

I liked good boys—especially good boys who were actually just-shy-of-thirty-six-year-old men who were tall and hot and kissed you like they did in the movies.

I stumbled out of my jeans and T-shirt. My cock looked obscene trapped in the black lace panties, and I mentally told it to settle down and that we had a little time before the big event. How much time, I wasn't sure, since it was heading on to one a.m., and we'd almost combusted in the elevator.

Anyway. I took the opportunity to give my bits a bit of a wash, in preparation for...whatever was going to happen between us.

"You going to be much longer?" Alastair's voice startled me. The good boy had got out of the chair and must be standing right in front of the door. "You're not having second thoughts, are you? I mean, just tell me because we don't have to—"

I opened the bathroom door and poked my head out.

"I'm not having second thoughts. Are you?"

Alastair looked relieved...and also hot as fuck.

"No. Definitely not. I'm having trouble waiting."

I gave him an ironic smile. "And having trouble sitting in the chair."

He rolled his eyes. "Well, yes. Sorry."

"Go. Sit. I'll be out soon."

"Fine."

I got into the garter and stockings, then sat on the closed toilet to do up my shoes. Then I put on the chemise and corset, making sure it was straight and that the chemise gaped in a pretty way. I touched up my eyeliner and rouged my lips. I messed up my hair a bit, giving myself an air kiss in the mirror. I almost forgot the velvet choker but remembered at the last minute.

Fuck, I looked totally luscious. He was going to die. Not literally...but of lust or something.

"Are you sitting in the chair?" I asked through the door.

"Oh my God. Yes. Are you coming out?"

"Wouldn't be the first time. Close your eyes."

"Fuck. Fine."

"Are they closed?"

"Yes!"

I made my way across the carpeted room, over to where he sat in the armchair like a kid at detention, his ass halfway across the seat, legs splayed, foot tapping with impatience. His broad hand was over his eyes. I hoped he wasn't peeking.

"Are you peeking?"

"Absolutely not." But he sounded very, very turned on, and I had my doubts.

I leaned over and put an elbow on the desk beside the armchair, cradling my chin, and angled my bloomered ass toward him.

"Okay. You can look."

He looked.

"Oh holy fuck." He sounded breathless and impressed…exactly what I'd been hoping for.

His gaze drifted over me as he sat up and leaned forward, his eyes widening.

"Toby."

"Yes, Alastair?"

"I thought you said—"

"Eh," I shrugged. "I took a risk for you."

Alastair could barely smile he was so turned on, but he tried. "Oh, I'm so glad."

"I knew you would be."

"Don't fucking move."

I froze, instantly obedient to the authority in his voice. If I was bossy, then Alastair was commanding. I didn't dare move. I didn't want to.

"What are you gonna do?" I asked, my voice rough.

"Shhh. Quiet."

Oh, fuck me. I think I whimpered, but everything was a horny blur.

He pressed against me as he leaned over my body, circling his arms over mine on the desk, his lips on my chin as he kissed me with a gentleness that belied his easy authority.

His erection nudged me from under the fabric of his pants. He rocked his hips as he licked the shell of my ear, and I almost died.

"Oh fuck," I said.

He groaned and pressed into me with more force. Then, suddenly, he was gone. I felt bereft. I went to stand, but his hand pressed against my lower back, keeping me there. It was so goddamn assertive and hot that I was about to explode.

"Stay still."

"Okay."

"I just want to see," he said, his words practical but the tone almost reverent.

"Okay," I whispered.

He took his hand away, but I stayed where I was, lowering my chest to the desk and stretching my arms out in front.

He slid his fingers under the elastic waistband of the bloomers and dragged it past my ass, until it was mid-thigh.

"Oh, my fucking God," he murmured. I felt the warmth of his breath on my bare skin, then he kissed my buttock, making me gasp as the soft hairs of his goatee tickled it.

"I know, right?" I gulped, wondering how long I could go without embarrassing myself by coming like a teenager.

"This is part of the uniform?"

"Yeah."

"Jesus. Those guys go all out. I figured it would just be modern stuff. Not...not fucking lace and garters."

"You like?" I asked, wiggling my ass.

"Oh my God. Toby." He kissed my other buttock and fingered the strap of my garter. "I want to jerk myself off all over you."

"No! I have to take this stuff back tomorrow!"

He groaned and stroked his hand along my hip and up in between my thighs.

I gasped.

"You're killing me," he said, but I heard the smile in his voice.

"I really hope that's not true."

"No," he laughed, but it sounded like a hiccup. "Anyway, I've got a better idea."

"Cool," I said, trembling like a fucking schoolgirl. I wished he'd get on with it. "I don't want you to fuck me, though," I said. "Anyway, not yet. Maybe later."

"I promise I won't unless you change your mind."

"Thank you."

"It's only common courtesy," he said.

"Not as common as you think."

"Touché. May I take your panties down?" he asked.

"Why, yes, you may."

Alastair's fingers trembled as he hooked them under the edge of the elastic and edged the panties down my ass, slow as treacle.

"Wait. They're snagging on my"—I puffed a laugh—"boner."

"Oh shit, sorry."

I slipped a hand down to pull the edge of the panties over my cock, then got back into position as Alastair tugged them down.

"Wow. You have a gorgeous ass."

I wiggled it for him. "Thanks."

"No, really. It's fucking beautiful."

Nobody had ever called me beautiful before. I tried not to let it go to my head — and failed.

I pressed my forehead against my arm. "Well, Alastair — or should I call you Mr. Kenney? — if it's so damn beautiful, can you please do something to it before I perish into a puddle of goo on this desk?"

"Okay, okay. Wait! *Would* you call me Mr. Kenney?"

"Of course, Mr. Kenney. Whatever you say, Mr. Kenney." Oh, that was super-hot.

"Fucking hell. Yes. Yes, that's good."

I couldn't help a shaky laugh. "Is it?"

"It's perfect. *You're* perfect."

Beautiful? Perfect? This man could sweet-talk me off the edge of a cliff — something that should have made me wary but only reminded me how much I'd been playing it safe lately.

He used his thumbs to spread me, and I was glad I'd washed there with soap and water when I'd changed.

"Oh God, oh God, oh God," I panted.

He swiped his tongue over my hole as I cried out for Jesus. He kept going, making me squirm and pant and beg, his goatee soft on my sensitive skin and his tongue even more so.

I saw stars and couldn't control my breathing. My heart pounded, and my cock dripped. I was a mess.

"I might... I might come..." I warned him, but he only gripped me harder and went at me with more force. "Oooooh, fuck. Oh fuck. Oh *fuck*."

My arm shot out of its own volition and a pencil holder skidded off the desk.

"*Shit*."

"Never mind," Alastair said, pulling back to speak. "Come if you want. I don't care."

I don't know why those careless words made it harder to fight it, but I knew I was losing the battle.

"*Fuck fuck fuck*," I keened.

The tip of his finger breached me.

I whimpered and pushed back against him. He sank his finger in deep and fluttered his tongue on my perineum.

"Oh fuck! Fuck! *Fuck!*" I yelled as I came in violent spasms, my body riding a wave of chaotic ecstasy as Alastair—Mr. Kenney—teased me with his fingertip.

He waited until I'd turned into a wet noodle before saying primly, "Well, that was unexpected."

I blinked and tried to breathe. *What? What!*

"I told you I was gonna come!" I shouted, except it sounded like a dying gasp.

"I thought it was only dirty talk," Alastair confessed.

"You thought... You thought..." I couldn't scramble enough brain cells together to finish the sentence.

"I can't believe you came hands free," he said with amazement. "I thought that only happened in porn."

I couldn't believe he was still talking. I was floating, drifting on clouds of bliss and afterglow.

"Shhh. Shhh," I said.

"What?"

"Quiet, please. I'm enjoying the aftereffects of your very skillful rim job. Don't blow it."

We realized what I'd said at the same time and started laughing.

"Can I get up now?" I asked.

"Let me help you."

He pulled me to standing. I swayed, dizzy from the reorientation as my body came down from my orgasm.

He bent to pull my panties up, but I stopped him with a raised eyebrow.

"I mean, really, what's the point? Might as well take them off," I said.

He smiled. My gaze landed on the outline of his massive erection under the dress pants.

"Ooh, you poor thing," I murmured.

He saw where I was looking and blushed. "Yeah, well, that was pretty fucking hot, Toby." He glanced at the carpet under the desk, and so did I. A decent-sized bubble of milky splooge sat primly on the paisley carpet.

"I'm going to clean that up," Alastair said.

"That was your fault. I said I was gonna come."

He laughed. "Don't worry about it. It was definitely worth the mess."

Alastair cleaned up my spunk with a bit of tissue then used a wet towel to wipe the spot, as I watched with fascination and amusement.

"You are such a gentleman. No wonder you're so popular."

He laughed and threw the towel into the bathroom. "Here... Come sit on the bed, and I'll get these things off for you."

Such a gentleman. And such a goddamn whore when he had me naked in front of him. The perfect combination, really. *No, no, don't think that way. This is only one night. It's perfect for* one *night.*

I walked over to the bed with my panties and stockings around my thighs, my cock tapping out, waving before me like a drunken sailor. I sat on the edge of the mattress and watched, wide-eyed, as Mr. Kenney went to his knees and lifted my booted foot into his lap. He smiled up at me, fire in his gaze.

"These are the sweetest shoes. Honestly. I think they're my favorite part of the whole" — he gestured at me — "outfit."

"A foot fetish, Mr. Kenney? You do surprise me."

He laughed. "I like boots, I guess…and leather. And these are…so cute." He undid the laces and eased the shoe off my stockinged foot.

"I hope my feet don't smell," I said.

He smiled, and lifted the boot to his nose, closing his eyes as he inhaled.

"Oh my *God*. Why is that so hot?" I squirmed, as desire ignited my core and made me half hard again.

He put down the boot and picked up my stockinged foot, lifting it to his face and sliding his nose along the arch. I leaned back on my elbows and watched with an incredulous smile. Whatever this was, I liked it. Nobody'd ever done anything like this before, and I was here for it.

He turned and kissed the bottom of my foot as I wiggled my toes. Then he lowered it to the floor and took off my other boot the exact same way.

"Wow. You are…dedicated."

"I like to take my time. Enjoy things," he murmured. "Enjoy *you*."

I glanced at the clock. "It's almost two. We don't have a lot of time."

"Are you working tomorrow?" Alastair asked.

"Yeah. But not till three. You?"

He didn't answer right away. He was pulling my panties and stockings down. I wondered if he'd sniff those, too.

He did.

Then he bunched them up and placed them to the side.

"I think I might call in sick," he said.

I blinked. "Wow. That's…very privileged of you."

"Yes, I suppose it is." He shrugged. "I've been working there a long time. I have some leave saved up."

"Convenient."

"Very. That is, unless you have somewhere you need to be before your shift starts."

We gazed at each other. This was supposed to have been a quick, let's-get-each-other-off-as-fast-as-possible, results-focused encounter. And, I mean, I had fulfilled my part of that deal. But he didn't seem to be in a rush. And if I was gonna get another nut out of it, well, I was fine with that.

"No."

"No?"

"No, I don't have anywhere to be before my shift."

In fact, if I could avoid going home for a day, that would be fantastic. But he didn't need to know about that.

Alastair smiled and gave a slow, satisfied, nod.

"Good."

He stood and put a knee on the bed, looming over me, making me lean back until I hit the mattress with a giggle.

"Because I want to take my time."

Chapter Six

Debauched

"Fine," I said. I couldn't tear my eyes away from his exquisite forearms — veiny and super masculine.

"Fine," he echoed. "*You* are fine, Toby. *So fucking fine* I just want to eat you the fuck up."

"You already did that," I pointed out.

"No, no. That was nothing but an amuse-bouche, my fine friend."

I snorted. "Could have fooled me. But yeah, it was very, very amusing on my end."

I wasn't sure we were friends. I wasn't sure we were anything but two bodies colliding in the night — *er, early morning*. But maybe I was fooling myself, because this already felt like something I'd never experienced before. I didn't want to get in too deep with someone who was only supposed to be a one-night stand, but it was hard to put up a wall when you didn't want to.

So, I didn't — or not much of one, anyway. Mr. Kenney — Alastair — had oozed sincerity since we'd chatted on the steps of Maverick Molly's, when he'd confessed to a plethora of hookups and not apologized for any of it.

I supposed I was one of those hookups, now. Well, I would commit to it a hundred percent. And if we only had a few hours together, then they might as well be good ones. I could pick up the shattered pieces of my soul later.

He kneeled over me, straddling my hips but not putting his weight on me, examining the silk buttons on the front of the corset. "I love this. Never thought a corset would look so good on a man."

"Yeah," I breathed, "It feels good, too. I like the way it…holds me together? I don't know."

He smiled again. That dimple was gonna be the end of me.

"I like the way it holds you together, too."

He cupped my waist and bent to kiss me.

Kissing on the sidewalk had been hot. In the elevator, even more so. But locking lips with Mr. Alastair Kenney as he loomed over me on the king-sized bed in a room at the Chateau Laurier, after he'd already made me come and half-undressed me so seductively, was fucking epic.

I opened beneath him like a star-struck virgin, thrilling to his masterful tongue and wandering hands. They roamed all over the corset, squeezing, tracing, stroking it…and me underneath.

The kiss started off deep and devastating and only got hotter from there. I thought I was going to suffocate but, *meh*, breathing was overrated. This kiss was everything. If I hadn't yielded completely to him before, I definitely did now. *Take it, it's yours*, my body was saying.

My brain lagged a bit behind, not wanting to go too far in the name of — I don't know what. Modesty? Fuck, no. Comfort? Hell, I was feeling pretty comfortable with Mr. Alastair Kenney. Maybe more of a don't-give-everything-up-on-the-first date vibe.

But then, this was supposed to be a one-off. The question was, did I want all of it? Or did I only want an entertaining, surface tour?

It was hard to decide when I couldn't keep my thoughts straight.

And I was a bit confused that he wasn't suggesting I suck him off — which I was totally willing and eager to do, thank you very much — or give him a hand job — *yes, please* — but seemed content to kiss and fondle me, even though I'd already made a mess of the carpet in a room at the fanciest hotel in Ottawa.

I broke from the kiss. Alastair continued along my jawline as I forced myself to speak.

"Don't you want me to…?"

"This is fine. I want to kiss you, touch you."

"Okay," I sighed.

I wasn't used to this kind of treatment. Maybe it was a testament to the power of a scintillating costume. Would he be so dedicated to worshipping my body if I wasn't dressed up like a Victorian molly boy? I had no idea, and I didn't care. The outfit had been my idea, and it was paying off.

He traced the edge of the velvet choker then found the tiny buttons on the front of the corset.

"Can I take this off?" he asked, voice low and rough.

"God, yes. Please."

Wow, look at me being all polite. What the fuck was up with this? It was unlike any hookup I'd ever had, but I was definitely enjoying it.

He continued to kiss my neck then pulled the cotton of the chemise aside to get at my shoulder as he popped the tiny buttons along the front of my corset. I'd only ever been the one to take the thing off before, and I had to say, having a paramour remove your clothing as skillfully as if they dealt with historic garments on a daily basis was…exhilarating.

"Wait a second," I said breathlessly, because something had occurred to me. "Do you sleep with women?"

Alastair stopped what he was doing and pulled back to meet my gaze. "Well, I'm bisexual. So, yes. I have." He smiled. "Is that a problem for you?"

I let out a breath. Was it? Not exactly.

"No, I just—" I said, licking my lips and wondering what kinds of women Alastair brought to the Chateau Laurier. "I thought you were gay. I assumed…because of Molly's…"

"I don't think it's a good idea to assume anything these days," he said. "Shall I continue?"

I gazed at him and appreciated him being so honest. I kind of wanted to talk about it more, because something about the fact that he slept with women as well as men made me like him even more, even though that didn't make sense. I'd never slept with a woman, so why did it matter that he had? Maybe because I could imagine that I was one of those women and that fulfilled a need I was aware of but had never articulated.

And for some reason, I couldn't leave it alone.

"Do you… Do you prefer women?"

Alastair blinked at me. He slowly shook his head as he gazed at me with real affection. "Not at all. In fact," he said, gaze going back to the corset that wrapped me,

"I'm starting to think that gorgeous men in feminine clothes are really what turns my crank."

I couldn't help a shy and surprised smile from forming as Alastair returned to the work of removing my corset. What was he doing to me?

As the pressure of the boned garment lessened and disappeared altogether, the absence of the corset's structure and compression made me feel more vulnerable and naked, even though the thin chemise still covered me. I lifted onto my elbows as Mr. Kenney tugged the splayed material from under me and tossed it to the pile of things collecting on the floor by the bed.

He gazed at me with dark, aroused eyes and an expression of wonder.

"What?" I asked, my voice a damsel's whisper.

He shook his head. "You just look very delicate and...so, so pretty, Toby. Is it okay that I find you very feminine?"

"No, I don't mind," I said, because it was true. "I'm probably non-binary...or at least gender fluid. I just don't make a big deal out of it, you know?"

After I said it, I wondered if coming out was wise in this situation, when we were only going to be spending a few hours awake together then heading our separate ways. But he had said I was feminine and admitted to sleeping with women. I wanted to be just as forthcoming. And anyway, it was too late, because I'd done it.

He gave me a sober look.

"Thank you for telling me," he said.

Well. I hadn't expected that.

"You're...you're welcome?"

He laughed. "Toby, I don't think you realize how fucking adorable you are to me."

"Like...like a puppy?"

He rolled his eyes. "Obviously not like a puppy. Don't be ridiculous." Then he side-eyed me. "Although, I could see you in a leather hood with a rubber tale coming out of your ass."

I almost choked on my tongue as my arousal went up to Code Red.

"Fuck..." I said, my eyes wide, as a wicked and entirely unrepentant smile formed on Alastair's handsome face.

He sighed. "But right now, you look completely angelic in this blousy thing... I don't know what it's called."

He pinched a bit of the sheer cotton in his fingers.

"It's a chemise." I eyed him carefully. "You know, I'm trying to figure out if you have some kind of ulterior motive, beyond getting me into a hotel room and under your thumb, which is already happening, so you can stop with all the pretty words, you know. I'm kind of a sure thing at this point."

Alastair drew back, looking horrified, which honestly pained my heart, and I wanted to take everything back.

"Oh my God. I'm sorry. I don't mean to... Do I sound like I'm manipulating you?" he asked, holding himself up on his hands and gazing down at me with a comforting amount of regret.

"No, no. I don't know. I mean, I don't know you all that well, and..."

He raised his eyebrows as I stroked the fingers of both hands along his very attractive forearms to assure him I was still into it...him...everything that was happening.

"Alastair, I'm having a fantastic time. I'm just waiting for...for something bad to happen," I confessed.

"Is this a good time to tell you that I'm working for the Russians?"

The line was delivered in such a deadpan way that I almost believed him.

"What?" I said, my blood going cold.

He laughed. "Toby, I'm not."

"Well, duh. I think?" I narrowed my eyes and let my hands fall, palms up, to the mattress. "How the hell would I know?"

"Oh, Toby, Toby, Toby," Alastair murmured, lifting his hand to stroke my cheek. "How can you be so adorable?"

I gave him a weak smile, because I didn't fucking know. "Years of practice?"

He smoothed the cotton fabric of the chemise, and the heel of his hand bumped my now-full erection. I grunted in response and blinked up at him benignly.

"Hmm. I see you've rallied, despite your misgivings."

"I don't have misgivings. And, yeah, I rallied. I'm not a one-trick pony, you know."

He rubbed his palm over my cock where it stood beneath the delicate cotton of my shift.

"Oh...fuck," I moaned, closing my eyes. Then opening them. "Wait."

"Huh?"

"Don't you want a blow job...or something? I feel bad that I'm on my second helping and you haven't even had your first."

"Oh, Toby. I feel like I'm still savoring the appetizer, to be honest. Or are you getting tired?"

"No! Not at all. But, uh, I'd be willing," I said, batting my eyelashes and running my tongue over my bottom lip so he could see what I had to work with.

He smiled, considering. Deciding if he wanted that, or if he wanted to keep doing what he was doing. I had no objections either way.

"Okay," he said, after a long moment.

"Yeah?"

"I think so. Stick out your tongue again."

I laughed and stuck my tongue out as far as it would go, the obedient boy toy to Alastair's demands.

"Well, okay. Something tells me you know how to use that."

"Are you saying I'm a slut?"

"Of course not." He gave me a look, and I felt suitably chastened. "I'm saying you're probably talented — and I'd like to find out."

He gave me room so I could sit up, the gauzy chemise covering all my randy bits as I scooched toward him. He looked so hot kneeling there with his arms crossed, waiting for me. I went onto my hands and knees and reached for him.

"Oh God," he moaned as I slid two fingers into a belt loop and tugged him forward. He unfolded his arms to steady himself as I worked at unbuckling his belt.

"What do you have inside your pants, Mr. Kenney? I'm dying to find out," I said, running a hand over the bulge in front and gasping at the size and solidity beneath.

"I can't wait to show you," he breathed, one hand going to my head and the other pulling his belt out of the loops with practiced ease. He threw it to the floor and watched me unbutton and unzip him, his mouth open and his breaths coming in short puffs.

His cock strained against the cotton of his black boxer briefs where a dark spot was spreading. At the sight of it, a jolt of arousal shot down my spine and into my balls.

"I can smell you," I said, in a breathy, sex-kitten voice that I sincerely hoped he appreciated.

His cock jerked. "I can smell *us*."

We stared at each other as I tugged at the waistband of his briefs and pulled them down over his healthy erection. His cock bounced free—a lovely, average-sized specimen—smooth and juicy. It was just the right size—big enough to make me catch my breath in anticipation rather than terror. Just the right amount of girth on it and about five inches long. *Perfect.*

"Are you measuring my cock, Toby?"

"Um. No," I lied.

He didn't fall for it. "Well? Do you think it will fit?"

"Sure it'll— Wait a minute. I said I didn't want you to fuck me, remember?"

He grinned and snorted a laugh. "Gotcha."

"Very funny." I examined his penis, tilting my head. "It's a little on the small side, if I'm being honest." *It wasn't.*

He winked. "No, it's not. And size *does* matter, at least a little. Any guy who says different is lying."

"You think? Alastair, that's a very outdated concept, I hate to tell you."

He wasn't listening, I didn't think. Because his hand had wrapped around his cock and his gorgeous eyes had gone half-lidded.

I stared at Alastair's cock as he let go of it and dropped his hands to his sides, waiting. I wrapped my fingers around the base and leaned forward. Then I licked the bubble of moisture off the top with the flat of my tongue in one long, lazy stroke.

Alastair—*Mr. Kenney*—made the most delicious sound of surprise and pleasure. Fluid oozed from my own dick as I engulfed his cock, humming and flicking my tongue back and forth.

"Fuuuuck," Alastair cursed, his fingers tightening in my hair. "Oh fuck. Toby."

"Mmm?" I said, continuing my attentions.

"That's so good." He swallowed. "*So* good."

"Mmm."

He tasted fantastic—so clean, as if he'd washed his bits at some point, too. Was it possible he'd cleaned himself at the club? It did smell like the soap we used, to be honest. I pulled off with a slurp, giving him a look.

"Did you wash your cock at the club?"

"Ohhh, God, why did you stop?" he groaned, wrapping his hand around himself and gazing at me in confusion.

"Because I want to know if you washed your bits at the club. You taste…clean."

His smile faltered. "I—God, Toby—I wanted to be clean, for you."

Not a lot of the guys I'd hooked up with in clubs or bars had been thoughtful enough to do something like that. I appreciated it.

I nodded, blinking, trying to wrap my head around it.

"Well…thanks?"

"You're…welcome?"

"C'mere." I grabbed his pants and pulled him forward again. This time I went at him in earnest, determined to make him come. I wanted to take him apart, make him scream my name.

"Toby!" he shouted, as I worked him hard and relentlessly.

Achievement unlocked.

I swallowed and sucked…and sucked and swallowed. Alastair groaned and gasped and gaped down at me as I slipped my hands into his pants and grabbed his ass, keeping him deep as I sucked the jizz out of him.

He stuttered curses and my name again as he shot down my throat. I mentally sent out apologies to all the folks trying to sleep in the rooms near ours, and hoped we didn't get kicked out because of me…because of him…because of how we were together.

I clutched him close, trying not to choke and breathing through my nose. Finally, I let go. He staggered back and tripped over his pants, grunting and cursing as he hit the floor.

"Oh fuck," I said, scrambling off the bed. "Are you okay?"

He was shaking and making a weird choking noise, and it didn't take too long to realize he was laughing. I sat back on my heels as he rolled on the floor in the throes of hilarity.

"Wow. I've heard of post-orgasmic rage but not post-orgasmic hysteria. I guess this is better?"

"Sorry… I'm sorry." He gasped for breath as he lay on the floor, on his back, staring up at the chandelier with his pants around his ankles and a broad smile on his face.

"I know this is a fancy hotel and all, but you should probably get off the carpet." I gestured toward the desk. "God knows what people have done in here."

"Right, right." He kicked off his shoes—he still had his shoes on?—pushed his pants and boxer briefs off and stood. Then he unbuttoned his shirt and dropped it onto the pile. "Take off your chemise, Toby." His lips curved in a sweet smile as he gazed at me. "I really want to see what you look like underneath."

"You do?"

"Duh," he said, pretending to be me, I guessed. He laughed at my visible delight. "I'm having a really good time, by the way."

I couldn't help my broad smile. "Good," I said. "Me, too, for the record."

I took the hem of the white chemise between my fingers and drew it up to my waist. Then I waggled my erection at him. "And so is this guy."

He groaned. "It's so damn cute! Toby, you're adorable."

I gazed down at my swollen dick, then back at Alastair. "Really? You couldn't go with 'intimidating', 'huge' or 'fucking monstrous'?" Of course, it was none of those things, but, you know...

"Your penis is lovely and pretty and sweet, just like you."

I blinked as warmth suffused me.

"Who the fuck are you? How are you so nice and I only just met you—and you're the best goddamn hookup I've ever had. Then again, I'm only twenty."

He sat on the bed and put one foot up, cradling his knee between his entwined fingers. "Well, I'm quite a bit older than you," he said, "and this hookup is"—his gaze landed on me and it seemed like he was going for something very complimentary but then he went with—"right up there."

He cleared his throat and blushed. His words were a bit of a disappointment, but I tried not to let it show.

"Right up there," I said. "Hmm. Okay. I'll take it."

He nodded, avoiding my gaze. "If it makes you feel better, this is the first time I haven't gotten kinky with someone and had so much fun."

Oh. That was…interesting.

"Huh. Is that so?"

His gaze flashed to mine, and he smiled again. "Yeah."

"How kinky do you usually get with your hookups?" I asked.

He tilted his head and gave me a confused look. "Well, I…usually take them into the back room at Molly's."

Oh, right. How had I forgotten that pertinent fact?

"Oh yeah. True," I said. "So, pretty kinky."

He shrugged. "Yeah."

This was a one-night stand—a gloriously decadent hookup with a man who liked his sex a-la-carte, kinky and with many different partners. It would behoove me to remember that.

"It's the best hookup I've had in a long time," he said quietly.

I nodded, dropping the edge of my shift so it covered my erection.

"Toby, come here," he said, in the same hushed tones, his eyes on mine.

I looked at him as I scratched the back of my neck and wondered if it was time to leave. I was clearly getting caught up in something that was supposed to be a lark. But that meant going back home to my dark little room and a house that smelled like booze, and I couldn't fucking bear it.

Maybe letting myself feel more for Alastair than I probably should wouldn't be so bad. I was tough. I'd survive. I'd ride the wave until we parted then I'd be sad, then I'd be fine. It was all good.

I joined him on the bed.

He caught me up in his arms and pulled me into a kiss, like I was the most precious thing in the world. And I have to say, it was addicting, this kind of attention. I let him seduce me and lay me out, and when his hand slipped under my chemise and wrapped around my cock, I didn't stop him. And when he lay back on the bed and jerked me off while we kissed and whispered sweet things to each other, I pretended we had all the time in the world. And when I came with a shuddering cry in his arms, I promised to remember it with no fucking regrets.

Chapter Seven

The Light of Day

We went to sleep. It was easy for me because I'd come twice, I was tired from work and the excitement of a casual dalliance was fading with the remnants of my last orgasm. I drifted into unconsciousness in the king bed next to Alastair with the ease of someone looking for a way out. The luxurious comfort of an expensive mattress and top-of-the-line bed linens helped.

When I woke up to silence and the absence of another person in the bed, I wasn't that surprised, although it took a moment to even remember where I was. There was a strip of light coming in where the curtains met, enough for me to get my bearings, and the clock said it was nine-forty-two. I flipped onto my back and stared at the ceiling in the dark, recalling our magical tryst and feeling an ache in my chest. I knew it wouldn't happen again, and that I'd probably see him with other men at Molly's. I'd joke about what a man-whore he was, while I sobbed inwardly.

No. Come on. I wasn't *that* much of a romantic. I'd be fine.

It had been fun, and there had been more than simply a physical connection between us, which, yeah, made it extra special and had been a surprising twist. But it was still a one-night stand, and thirty-five year-old Alastair Kenney would be fucking a different twink next week. *Maybe even this week.* And I had to wrap my head around that.

It was fine, and I needed a fucking cigarette. I slipped out of bed and had a good stretch, then ambled to the curtains and pulled them partly open. I squinted before taking in the morning view.

The room looked out onto Sussex Street and the buildings there, which I hadn't had the opportunity to appreciate last night. The curtains had been closed for us when we'd arrived, and we'd been rather distracted. It would have been beautiful at night with all the lights. I leaned against the window frame and appreciated the view until the urge to smoke hit me again. I gave my limp dick a glare.

"This is all your fault."

I found my jeans, digging the pack out of the back pocket. I probably wasn't supposed to smoke in the room. Fuck it. I could just light up for a second and take a few drags. I hadn't had one since ten-thirty last night, and I was dying. I guess Alastair was a good distraction from that habit because I hadn't craved one until now.

I took a cigarette out and put the pack on the side table, then got back under the covers. I'd never smoked in such a swanky room, and I got a little excited about it for a second. I put the smoke between my lips and lifted my lighter.

The door opened and Alastair came in, carrying a paper bag and a tray with two cardboard cups.

"Good morning," he said, then saw what I was doing and frowned. "What are you doing? You're not allowed to smoke in the room."

I rolled my eyes, lowered the lighter and let the unlit cigarette fall from my lips.

"Goddammit. It's the morality squad."

Alastair gave me a look that made me annoyed and hard at the same time. "Toby, come on. The smoke detector will go off. I don't know about you, but I don't really want to have to explain this to the concierge."

"Fine." I put the lighter and cigarette beside the pack.

Alastair set down the tray and the bag on the table.

"How did you sleep?"

"Fine," I said, a bit dazed — and really craving that smoke. I scratched at my neck and realized I still had the velvet choker on. Oh well. At least I looked cute.

I was glad he was back, don't get me wrong. But I couldn't wrap my head around it.

Why was he acting like we were more than just a one-night hookup? Or did he bring all his conquests breakfast in bed in the fanciest hotel in the city? *Hmm.* Maybe he did. I knew very little about Alastair Kenney, and the little I did know should make me wary.

He's just making sure you're happy so he can feel good about letting you go.

It was a nice thing to do, a decent, human thing. You didn't meet many decent people these days. Or at least, that had been my experience. I had been waiting for him to do something predictable, like stop being nice after he came, or like taking off without a word. But he kept surprising me, and I wasn't used to that.

"I got you a coffee. Do you like coffee?"

"I like coffee," I said, pulling the sheet up to cover myself, feeling suddenly shy and exposed in the daylight. He, of course, looked radiant. I wasn't so sure about myself.

"Here." He brought the cup over. "I got a double-double. I wasn't sure—"

"That's great," I said, taking it from him. "Thanks."

He grabbed the paper bag and tossed it onto the duvet beside me. "And four chocolate chip cookies to share."

"Hmm. Interesting breakfast choice," I said.

He shrugged. "Not as messy as donuts or muffins."

"Well, you're lucky. I will eat cookies at any time of the day or night."

We sat on the bed, Alastair in his wrinkled dress pants and shirtsleeves, me still naked except for the choker, and under the covers, eating cookies and sipping coffee. If I'd looked around a bit I would have noticed his suit jacket still in the closet. But I'd have probably thought he'd forgotten it, just like he might have forgotten me.

Alastair grabbed the remote off his side table and turned on the TV. He flipped through channels until he found the local news.

"Is this okay?" he asked.

And I couldn't take it anymore.

"Jesus, Alastair. Do you have to be so fucking nice?" I said, unsnapping the choker and crushing it in my hand.

He blinked at me like a startled fawn, holding the remote, in complete shock, as if I'd just called him an asshole for being nice to me.

"What?"

"I'm sorry. That came out…wrong. I'm just not used to"—I gestured at my coffee and the cookies and him—"this."

"You mean, to people being nice?"

"Not after they get what they want."

He stared at me with such concern that I had to look away.

I put down the coffee and wiped the cookie crumbs from my chin. "God, I'm sorry. I had a great time, you're super-hot and a really, really nice man. I don't deserve this."

"Toby, I brought you coffee and cookies. You're acting like—"

"Like you didn't treat me to the best fucking sex I've ever had, in the fanciest fucking hotel in this goddamn stupid city?"

"That wasn't what I was— That was the best sex you've ever had?" he asked, sounding surprised.

"Well, I'm only twenty. And yeah. And don't you dare say that wasn't sex because we didn't get to the fucking part." I thought about it. "No, actually do say that, because then I can tell myself you're an asshole, and not a super nice guy and a fucking amazing hookup."

"I'm not going to say that."

"Fuck you." I dropped the choker to the bed and folded my arms across my chest and pouted. I gazed longingly at the cigarette on the table.

Alastair sighed. "What is the problem here? Are you actually mad because I'm being too *nice*?"

"Yes. I'm trying not to…get too attached."

"Why?"

I gaped at him. *"Why?"*

He smiled, and I wanted to punch him. Seriously, just lay him out flat for being such a goddamn nice asshole that I didn't deserve.

Instead, I explained. I might have upped the volume a bit.

"Because you told me last night that you only do casual sex, and here we are after doing casual sex and I feel like you might actually like me, but maybe you're this nice to all your hookups, and I'm just reading something into it that isn't there, and I really don't want to be made a fool of."

He didn't say anything for a very long time while I inwardly died of embarrassment and cursed my loose tongue. He didn't need to know all that. I could've just held it together for another hour and left with my dignity intact.

"Huh. I didn't actually say that."

I blinked. "You told me you came to Molly's with different guys all the time, to use the Bordello." I narrowed my eyes. "And now that I think of it, maybe you meant girls, too."

"I've never brought a girl—a woman—to Molly's. I don't do kink with women." He ran a hand through his hair. "So just different men, to make use of the kink furniture and the, uh, unique, you know, implements."

"You don't have to spell it out."

"That's a very specific kind of thing, is what I mean."

"It's a sex thing."

"Sometimes. More often it's just a kink thing. And it's easy to be anonymous and casual about it."

"I don't get it," I said. At least, I didn't want to get it. I didn't think it would make me feel better.

He turned off the TV and put the remote down.

"You know, I don't have vanilla hookups with men very often."

"Is that what this was?"

He laughed. "Yes." He inclined his head. "Your outfit made it kinkier than I'd expected, but not as kinky as I usually get."

I snorted. "Yeah, nothing compared to the stuff you do in the Bordello." I had an image of Alastair wielding a flogger and handing me a gimp mask. I didn't hate it.

"It wasn't nothing," he said. "Jeez, Toby, I *like* you. I thought that was obvious."

We gazed at each other for a long moment. I pulled back on the pout a bit, and eventually spoke. "I like you, too. But I thought this was just gonna be a one-off, which is totally fine, by the way. I can do casual sex. I've done it before."

Alastair laughed. "I'm sure you can. And, yeah, I thought it was gonna be a one-off."

I felt a flare of hope and hated myself for it. Why did I have to be so fucking soft?

"So maybe it's not?" I said, my voice small and hesitant. I couldn't look at him. I played with the bedcovers.

"Maybe it's not," he said.

I blushed, feeling more hope and trying not to get carried away. I grabbed a cookie. "Okay. I can handle that," I said, taking a huge bite and chewing thoughtfully.

"I want to see you again. Maybe we should go on a date."

I almost choked on the cookie. "You're asking me out?"

He laughed harder. "Why is that so surprising? I literally had my tongue up your ass, and you're shocked that I'm asking you out?"

He had a point.

"I just…I can't wrap my head around it."

"Well, we don't have to go on a date, but I'd like to see you again. Maybe next week?"

"I mean, I wouldn't say no to a date."

"Great!" He seemed genuinely pleased.

"Thanks for breakfast," I said, gazing around me at our sweet accommodations. "And the swank hotel room."

"You're welcome. I'm glad you enjoyed it."

I tilted my head. "It was...fun."

"It was. And that outfit. Christ, I might come on the spot next time I see you dressed in it at the club, now that I know what you wear underneath."

I grinned. "That would be pretty embarrassing for you."

"Yes, it would."

We touched our cardboard cups together and sipped hot coffee while we ate the rest of the cookies and discussed the finer points of Ottawa dining.

* * * *

I made my shift on time.

I had the pieces of my 'uniform' all folded up neatly in my backpack. I'd made sure there were no signs of any, uh, bodily fluids on them before I'd put them in there. I was almost disappointed not to find anything, but it made things easier.

I had claimed to have errands to run — a lie — and we had parted before lunch with no good-bye kiss or sentimentality. As much as Alastair had talked about seeing me again, I had my doubts.

I finally got to smoke a cigarette, doing my best Audrey Hepburn impression while posing enticingly in front of the ritzy hotel, after Alastair left. I watched him stride down toward Rideau Street in his fancy winter coat and leather gloves, no hat over his wayward curls, and wondered if I'd ever see him again.

When I had finally checked my phone, there'd been some anticipated texts from my mom.

Hey, could you pick up some cigarettes for me? I'll pay you back,

Hey, where are you?

Did you come home last night?

Call me, Tobias

I only sent one text in reply:

B home tonight

It was more than she deserved.

I had to start looking for a place, but I didn't have enough saved for a deposit. I was getting there, but it was taking too long.

Oh, she'd conveniently forget to pay me back for the cigarettes. But if I didn't get them for her, she'd call me a lazy SOB and an ungrateful child — and that was easier to avoid. Yeah, she had me wrapped around her evil little finger, but I was a wimp, okay? At least, when it came to her.

She was my mom, for fuck's sake, and I knew that not all of this was her fault. It couldn't have been easy being a single parent. She'd busted her ass for me for a long time now, wrecking her health and causing her to lean on the booze as an escape from the mindless drudgery of it all. But still, she'd spiraled so far at this point that I just wanted to escape.

I didn't need the guilt of feeling like I was still dependent on her. I don't know why I continued to feel that way. I bought groceries and cigarettes. I tried not to give her cash, no matter how often she asked or how desperate she seemed, because she'd use it to buy booze and drugs. No way was I contributing to *that* part of the train wreck.

Of course, since I wasn't late to work, it meant I was stuck using the changing area with other servers, specifically with Cory and Devin.

Cory was all right, but Devin was a bit of a prick. And when he saw me taking my molly boy gear out of my backpack, he had to call me out.

"Oy, Toby. You got another gig as a molly boy somewhere?"

Cory glanced over. He was halfway into his stockings. He smiled and shrugged, because he didn't give a flying fuck what I was doing with my corset and stockings stuffed in my backpack.

"Nah, I just like to wear it at home on my off days," I said, and flipped him the bird.

"No, seriously. Why is it in your bag?"

"Why don't you mind your own fucking business, Devin?" Cory said, attaching his stocking to the garters. He turned to me. "You don't have to explain yourself, Toby. I, for one, don't give a flying fuck."

I gave him a thumbs-up.

"Anyway," I said, "I just wanted to give them a wash in my own detergent. The soap Sebastian uses irritates my delicate, baby-soft skin."

Cory laughed and got into his leather shoes, putting one on the edge of his chair to do up the laces. He was wearing his chemise already, and the white cotton drifted in cloudlike puffs over his upper half. His blond hair fell to his shoulders in soft ringlets. If anyone at Molly's could be considered a stunner, it was Cory. Most of the men went gaga at the sight of him.

But Cory, wonder of wonders, was straight. He didn't mind wearing the costume, though, and was enough of a performer to pull off the whole 'I'm a gay molly boy from the eighteen hundreds' bit. His girlfriend was as gorgeous as he was and thought it was hilarious that her boyfriend slung drinks at a gay kink club in a corset and stockings. They were cool people, and I was glad to know them.

Devin, on the other hand, was gay, like me and Robin, but I think resented that he had to wear the retro underwear and prance around for the pleasure of his customers. I'm not sure why he'd taken the job, except that the pay was good for the hours we put in, the club was respected and Jacob and Sebastian were awesome bosses. And, you know, the fact that he whined all the time was kind of a turn-on, in a strange way, to the men who frequented the place. I didn't understand the appeal of brats, honestly, but Devin seemed to have it down to a science.

"Yeah, right. You're probably getting all dressed up for your boyfriend so he can rub off against your knickers, right? Right?"

I blushed, because that was...perceptive.

"Fuck off, Devin. I don't have a boyfriend."

"Oh right. Just that weird girl—what's her name? Esmay?"

"Esther. And she's not fucking weird."

She was a little weird, but that was why we were friends. I needed to see her and tell her about Mr. Alastair Kenney and the Chateau Laurier. She'd get a kick out of that and wouldn't hesitate to get real with me about Alastair and what she thought of him.

I had a report due next week that I'd written approximately half of, so I needed to get on that. Maybe a night of passion with Alastair had been a bad idea to begin with, because I couldn't stop thinking about how sweet he had been and how good the sex had been— and I really needed to focus on my studies.

Work was okay, except the whole time I was remembering the private show I gave Alastair in the privacy of a swanky hotel room at the Chateau, and coming hands free over the desk while he rimmed me.

Fuck. I had hoped for a night of cheap thrills and no attachment. I hadn't expected to be so affected by our night together. I hadn't exactly prepared for that. Part of me hoped Alastair would show up at Molly's again tonight, alone, looking for me because he couldn't possibly stay away. I knew it was unreasonable and silly, but I was still disappointed when it didn't happen.

I was on closing duties tonight. By the time Jacob and Sebastian and I had cashed out and cleaned up, I was exhausted and barely able to function. I guessed a night of passion and barely five hours sleep was catching up to me.

"You okay, Toby?" Sebastian asked as we finished up.

"Yeah. Just tired."

"You want a drive home?" he asked, gazing at me with concern.

He'd driven me a few times before — once when I'd gotten two nosebleeds over the course of my shift and again when I'd developed a fever one time.

"Could you? That would save me falling asleep on the bus…"

"Of course. Don't worry about it."

"Thanks…really."

He dropped me off in front of the ratty bungalow in Vanier without a comment, checking his rear-view mirror obsessively in case of hooligans. There were worse places to live and less appealing bungalows. It wouldn't have been so bad if I hadn't once gone to a staff party at Sebastian's and Jacob's gorgeous house in the Glebe. Compared to that place, this was skid row.

My soul left my body as soon as I'd gotten out of his car, and we'd waved good-bye. I took a deep breath and went up the walk.

Her car was in the driveway and the door was unlocked, so she was here. I'd told her to keep it locked, because I always had my key with me, but she was careless about that and many other things. Too much on her mind, she said, to deal with trivialities. But I made sure to lock it behind me after I went inside.

Most of the lights were off, and I didn't hear the TV, so she must have gone to bed. I tiptoed past the kitchen, through the living room and up the stairs, slipped into my bedroom and closed the door. I breathed a sigh of relief as I used the moonlight to guide me to my desk lamp. I switched it on as quietly as possible and pulled my curtains closed, setting my backpack by the door.

I was glad I'd gone to the trouble of making my bed and tidying up before I'd left the other day, so that now, all I had to do was strip off my jeans and T-shirt and climb under the covers. I'd showered at the hotel, so I swiped some antiperspirant under my arms. I didn't want to risk waking up my mom by running the water at this early hour.

I opened my window a crack and lit up a cigarette, remembering how stern Alastair had been when he'd caught me at the hotel. Fuck, that was hot. As I smoked, I thought about the way Alastair's hands had felt on my body, the way he'd eaten me out like he'd been waiting to do it, and how he'd looked at the moment of orgasm. If I hadn't been so tired I'd have jerked off to the memories, but I didn't have the energy.

I must have fallen asleep pretty soon after I lay down because the next thing I knew, someone was banging on my door, and there was light leaking into my room around the edges of my curtains.

"Tobias! Why did you lock your door? I need those cigarettes before I go to work! Jesus, why didn't you give them to me when you got home? You could have left them downstairs!"

Chapter Eight

Rude Awakening

I dragged myself out of bed and hobbled over to my door, unlocking it and opening it a crack. Mom stood there, right in front of my door, with a murderous look on her haggard face.

"It's six a.m. I got back at one. Can't you just let me sleep?"

"Where are my cigarettes? I told you to get me cigarettes."

Fuck.

"I forgot. Sorry."

I wasn't sorry, except that now I'd have to deal with her rage.

"Jesus, Tobias. Get your head screwed on. Why are you like this?"

I stared at her, emotionless, trying not to buy into her bullshit.

"Do you need money?" I asked, because that was always a good deflection. "I can give you some, and you can buy your own cigarettes."

She narrowed her eyes. "Who do you think you are? Who do you think has paid for everything in this house since your fuck-up of a father took off? I just asked you to do something for me, that's all. Jesus."

"I said I was sorry."

Her eyes narrowed. "Where were you last night?"

I pressed my teeth together. It was none of her damn business, and I didn't have to explain. I was twenty years old, for fuck's sake.

"Nowhere. It doesn't matter."

"Nowhere? What the hell, Tobias?"

"My name's Toby. Please call me Toby."

"I named you Tobias, not Toby. That's a name for a fucking dog."

I barked a fake laugh. "Thanks."

"I don't know why you can't tell me where you were. I'm your mom, you know."

"Oh, I know."

She stared at me, maybe noticing that I was dead on my feet. "Are you okay?"

"Yeah, I'm fine. I'm sorry I didn't get your cigarettes."

She waved a hand in front of her. "Forget it. I'll get some today. Can you let me in? I need to talk to you about something, Tobias."

I debated saying no but decided it wasn't worth the trouble. I opened my door all the way. She came in and sat on the edge of my bed. She was actually dressed nice, in a pencil skirt and a blue blouse that had seen better days.

I stood there with my hand on the door, wondering how long she would annoy me before she left for work. I wanted to go back to bed. I was exhausted from my two shifts and my sex romp with Mr. Kenney.

"So," she said, bracing her hands on her knees and stretching her arms, "where were you the night before last?"

Oh, come on!

"I was...*out*. You know..."

"With Esther?"

I shrugged. I didn't want to lie, even though that would be the easiest thing to do.

"Tobias, I don't think you should run around having casual sex with strangers."

I blinked. *How the fuck?*

"I wasn't running around. And I'm not a kid, for fuck's sake."

She crossed her arms over her chest. God, she was skinny. It seemed like every year she got skinnier. I knew it was the drugs and probably an eating disorder. Her hair was dyed brown from a box and looked fake.

"Well, you weren't here. Where did you sleep?"

And I couldn't fucking resist. It was just too tempting.

"At the Chateau Laurier, actually," I said, with a smug look.

She stared at me and almost laughed, but then she noticed how serious I was.

"Don't lie to me."

"I'm not. Do you want to see my room key?"

"What the fuck were you doing there?"

"Having casual sex with a stranger." *A beautiful stranger, actually.* And he wasn't a stranger anymore. I had his phone number. *Alastair Kenney, 343-895-4717.* Yeah, I'd memorized it. Sue me.

Her lips thinned, and she scowled. "You know, you can be really rude sometimes. I thought I raised you better than that."

I rolled my eyes.

"Now tell me where you were, or I'm going to have to give you a curfew."

Oh yeah. That was not happening. I mean, she could give me one. She could say anything she wanted. But she couldn't run my life. I did not say any of that out loud.

"I told you where I was."

She stood, and I instinctively took a step back. I wasn't afraid of her, just cautious. She'd been physical only a couple of times, but I was always prepared.

She put her hands on her hips. "You expect me to believe that some strange man took you to the Chateau Laurier to fuck you?"

Wow. What a time for her to exceed even *my* expectations as to what a shitty person she could be. I wondered if she was on something, but I didn't dare ask.

"I don't care what you believe. That's where I was." I kept my voice level. The last thing I wanted to do was escalate this.

She examined me for a long moment, probably trying to figure out if I was lying. I felt like I had at six years old, holding a granola bar behind my back. She used to get mad at me for eating 'extra' food because we didn't have much. So I'd sneak a granola bar or a cookie, like any other kid, and when she'd ask me about it, I'd lie. I didn't think that made me a bad person—and she'd always known I was lying back then. I'd gotten better at deceiving her over the years, but I tried not to lie anymore. I was an adult now, and I didn't have to explain myself to her.

"Huh. No telling *what* some men will do for a little ass." Her gaze traveled over me, and she scowled as if I was a pile of reeking shit.

"What did you want to talk about?" I asked, gazing at the floor now and trying to keep from losing it. I was so angry and so tired and so fed up. I wanted desperately to be where I had been early yesterday morning—in a beautiful room at the Chateau Laurier, dressed in my work outfit, waiting while a gorgeous stranger undressed me. I felt like Cinderella, except that Alastair wasn't looking for me with a shoe I'd lost.

Dammit. That was a missed opportunity.

"Just wanted to make sure you were being smart. But I guess I got my answer." She walked past me and out of the door, but she turned back and said, "At least you can't get knocked up. But don't come crying to me when you get sick."

I almost said I wasn't gonna get sick, not from what she was referring to, anyway. But there was no point. And she was leaving, and there was no way I wanted her to come back and keep provoking me. So, I bit my tongue and stayed silent.

When she'd gone I stood there, listening to her moving around.

"Tobias!" she yelled from the kitchen. "Do me a fucking favor for once and toss the dishes in the dishwasher before you head to work."

It wasn't a question, so I didn't answer.

I waited until I heard the front door slam shut and the rumble of her beat-up Toyota making a racket as she went to her aesthetician's assistant job that she'd managed to keep longer than a few months.

Once I knew she was gone, I went back into my room, leaving the door open, and sat down on the edge of my bed, closing my eyes and taking deep, cleansing breaths. Then I picked up my phone from the bedside table.

I'd muted it when I'd gone to bed, and there was a text message from Alastair Kenney, as if he'd known I'd been thinking about him and needed a kind word and someone being decent to me.

Hi, Toby.
I hope you're doing well. Did you get caught up on the sleep you missed? You're probably still sleeping. Hope so. I hope you have a good day.

The frustration, disappointment and sheer exhaustion of dealing with my mom, on top of my lack of sleep, evaporated in an instant. Also, it was cute that he used full sentences, with punctuation and everything, like he was fifty instead of thirty-five.

I answered.

thanks
i just woke up
it was good to see your message.

I waited a few minutes, but he didn't text back, and I figured he must be at work already or busy getting ready to leave.

I called Esther, because I knew I could count on her to freak out about my adventure with Alastair in the right way.

She picked up after a couple of rings.

"Toby Dunn, how are you fucking doing?"

I ran my fingers through my hair and huffed a laugh. "I've been better."

"Oh no. What did she do now?"

"Ah, nothing, except basically accused me of being a sex worker. No offense to sex workers, but I'm not one, and I know what she thinks of them."

"What? You? You haven't had sex in months." She laughed like that was the biggest joke. She finally stopped laughing, but when I didn't say anything, she prompted me. "Toby? You haven't had sex in months. Right?"

And suddenly I was smiling. "Only if you don't count last night."

She gasped. "Whaaaat? With *who*? Oh my God. Tell me, tell me, tell me!"

"Wait! Aren't you at work?" I asked.

"Yeah, so? I'm on a break." There was rustling and the scrape of a chair on the floor.

"That's convenient."

"Tell me!" she demanded.

"I need to ask you a huge favor, though," I cautioned.

"You tell me who you had sex with, and I'll do anything you want."

"Really?" I sounded skeptical.

"Wait! What do you want?"

"Esther, I really, really, *really* need to stay at your place for the next few days. *Please*?"

"Aw, Toby," she said in a soft voice, all teasing gone. "Of course, you can sleep here."

There was silence as a lump formed in my throat.

"Anytime," she continued. "You know that."

I laughed, but it was only so I wouldn't sob. I didn't think she bought it.

"Thank you." It was a whisper.

"Do you work tonight?" she asked.

"No."

"Then come over for supper and a movie. We'll order pizza and drink too much Coke and have a burping contest. Okay?"

"Okay." God, how did she know just what to say?

"And you can tell me all about your recent sexcapade."

I laughed, and this time it was sincere.

"Sure."

"I gotta go, but promise you're safe?"

"Yeah. She's gone to work."

"She didn't touch you?"

"Not this time."

"That bitch," Esther growled. "Get over to my place before she comes back. Someone'll let you in. Do you wanna look at ads for rooms? I bet you could find one for, like, a few hundred bucks a month. Better to put up with some random stranger in your house than your mom."

"Yeah. I don't want to live here anymore."

"Oh, honey. I don't want you to live there anymore, either."

* * * *

The dirty dishes that my mom wanted me to throw in the sink were all over the fucking counter. For a person who hardly ate anything, she sure messed up a lot of tableware. She wasn't good at cleaning, or cooking—or anything, really—which was why she'd always had shit jobs while I was growing up. I think this was the longest time she'd stayed at one place, and the job gave her a reasonable amount of money, except that she spent so much of it on sketchy stuff. I'd paid my own way through university, except for a few bursaries that a teacher had advised me to apply for. I was determined to graduate and at least have a post-secondary education, something my mom had never valued.

Maybe I could do one last thing for my mom because she had somehow refrained from murdering me for twenty years and kept a roof over my head. I loaded what dishes would fit into the dishwasher and ran it, then washed what was left in the sink. I cleaned the shitty Formica countertops and linoleum floors and the stove, working out my anger and frustration with physical labor and spiteful housework. It was as if I were giving her a big "fuck you" with a dishrag and dish soap.

See how good I am at respectable living? Better than you, you fucking bitch.

I packed my backpack and a duffle bag with the things I'd need for a few days at Esther's and went to catch the bus. While I was waiting at the stop, a text came through from Alastair.

Toby! Are you working tonight?

nope
this is my night off

Really.

yeah
going to hang out with a friend

Oh.

Three dots came and went. I wondered if he'd been planning to ask me out for *tonight*.

Maybe I'll see you at Molly's sometime soon?

not working til sat
see you then?

See you then. Have a good time with your friend.

ttyl

I was a little disappointed that Alastair hadn't asked me out for later in the week, instead of a vague suggestion that we'd see each other during my next shift. But looking forward to a relaxing evening of pizza and soda and Esther was enough to get past it.

* * * *

"Toby, baby! Come in!" Esther said when her roommate opened the door to me at four-thirty.

"Hi, Deshawn," I said.

Deshawn grinned, and we slapped hands. "Nice to see you, Toby." He turned to Esther. "See ya later."

"Will you be back in time for pizza?"

"Nah, I'll be late," he told her. He turned back to me. "I'll try to come in quietly."

I blinked back emotion. Deshawn was such a nice guy. "Thanks, man."

He smiled with his whole face. "No worries. I know how it can be."

Esther rose from the sofa and came toward me. She was wearing a flowy skirt in rainbow colors and a black tank top. Her long hair was up in a messy bun and the silver stud in her nostril glimmered against her brown skin.

"Baby, are you okay?"

"I'm fine. It's fine," I said, trying to convince myself, but I didn't feel it. I couldn't go back there—I was *so* done—but I couldn't sleep on Esther's couch forever.

Esther frowned, putting her hand to my cheek and gazing into my eyes. "It's really not. But you're here now."

"I didn't know what else to do. I couldn't stay there."

"Toby, I told you that you could stay over whenever. I know what she's like."

"Yeah. But you've got roommates. I don't wanna disrupt everyone."

Esther rolled her eyes. They were a much deeper brown than her complexion and held so much wisdom and heart. "You know Lev isn't around much. And Deshawn comes and goes. Both of them know what you're putting up with at home. They don't give a shit if you have to sleep on our couch for a couple of weeks."

"Yeah. I just feel like I should have things figured out by now."

Esther laughed, taking my duffle bag and putting it on the sofa. "Get comfy, and don't worry about it."

I smiled, feeling safe again. I trusted Esther because I'd known her for so long. I didn't know why I'd trusted Alastair, but he'd made me feel safe and well looked after, too.

"It's hard. I don't want to be a mooch. I should have my shit together."

Esther frowned. "Don't be a self-hating dick. You're only playing into her hands when you do that."

I squared up. "That's true. Thanks."

"I've got your back. You know that."

Suddenly overcome with gratitude, I threw my arms around her, needing to show her just how much I appreciated her friendship.

"Oh, honey, honey," she whispered, enveloping me in her soft, plump arms. "It's okay."

We were around the same height, since I was on the short side for a guy, and she was on the tall side for a girl. I tucked my head into her neck and breathed deep, inhaling her familiar and comforting smell.

"Thanks."

"Always, Toby."

We stayed like that for a bit. She waited until I pulled away, then she frowned and examined me with concern.

"Is everything okay otherwise?"

I blinked. "Yeah."

"Here, come and sit," she said, leading me out of the living room. "Lev is in their room playing Red Dead, so they won't be out for a while."

"Sure." I was glad to have some time alone with Esther, even though I liked Lev and they tended to stay out of my business.

"Are you hungry? We can order the pizza now."

"Yeah, okay." I dug my wallet out of my pocket. "Here… I've got a couple of twenties."

"I told you I'd cover it."

I gave her a look. "I can pay for my share."

"Of course, you can, but I don't want you to. Keep your money. This is my treat," she said. "And I'm not your mom, so you don't have to worry about being beholden." She rolled her eyes.

I laughed. God, it was good to see her.

She picked up her phone. "What do you want? Pepperoni? Vegetarian? Hawaiian?"

"Can we get a medium Hawaiian and a medium Vegetarian?"

"Oh, you wild, wild man. Of course!"

"And a bottle of soda. Coke, if possible?"

She held up a hand. "Don't worry, I've got you covered. I'll even get brownies."

My eyes went wide. "They have *brownies*?"

"The *best.*"

* * * *

Esther's apartment was a mishmash of furniture and décor, but there were mini-lights strung along the windows and the lingering scent of patchouli incense. I'd managed to have a quick smoke on the balcony, so I was chill now and feeling a lot better.

Esther waited until we'd had some bites of pizza before asking about my hookup.

"Sooooo," she said, hooking a thread of cheese that had stretched from the pizza to her lips with her finger and breaking it. "I am dying to know about this recent sexcapade! *If* you are willing to divulge. You don't have to tell me, obviously. I promise not to hate you if you don't."

I laughed. I felt so much better now that I had a belly full of grease and ham and pineapple. And the Coke had perked me up, so that I didn't feel so tired.

"You got me brownies. I'll fucking tell you anything."

"Yass!" She looked seriously pumped. She put aside her plate and settled in, staring at me with an intensity that would have scared me if I didn't know her so well.

"All right. So…I was working at the club, and I needed a cigarette."

Her nose wrinkled. She really didn't appreciate my habit.

"I've cut down."

"To zero?"

"Not yet."

She rolled her eyes. "Fine, I don't care. Keep talking."

"I was taking a break out front, having a cigarette…"

"In your cute molly boy outfit?"

"Duh. I'm not gonna change to go outside for ten minutes."

"Okay. And?" Her eyes were comically wide. I didn't know what she was expecting.

"And so this guy comes along."

"Oh yeah!" She fist-bumped the air over her head.

"And, uh, I guess he liked what he saw. He watched me all night. He even tied my laces when they came undone."

Her eyes popped wider. "On your *corset*?"

"On my shoe. Jesus."

Esther's eyebrows squiggled, and she put a hand to her heart. "Aw!"

"I know, right? Only it wasn't actually adorable. It was super, super-hot."

"Oh really?"

"Yes, really."

She put a hand in front of her mouth, trying to stop her giggles. "He tied your shoe, and that was hot?"

"Fuck off. It was. I can't explain it. I know it sounds ridiculous." I shook my head. "Anyway, he asked if I was into going to a hotel or back to his place or my place—" I made a face. "And I said I'd go to a hotel with him."

"You dog!"

"And we ended up at the Chateau." I shrugged as if I ended up at the Chateau Laurier every weekend.

She blinked. "The Chateau Laurier? Are you fucking kidding me?"

"Nope." I popped the 'p' to emphasize it.

"You got fucked at the Chateau Laurier!" Esther shouted. I gestured for her to keep it down, but she waved her hand toward Lev's room.

"Lev's got their headphones on. It's fine."

The door opened, and Lev stepped out, sans headphones.

"Sorry… I had to see who got boned at the Chateau Laurier. Oh, hi, Toby. Wouldn't have expected it was you."

"Thanks a lot," I said, hiding my face. "I didn't get *boned*."

"Oh," they both said.

"Bummer," Lev added.

"No, no, no. We had fun. We had sex…just not… Never mind."

"Good times," Lev said, moving into the kitchen. "Oooh, pizza!"

"Help yourself," Esther said.

Lev had been living with Esther for over a year now, and I liked them. They had committed to the non-binary label and were unapologetic about anything relating to the genuine expression of their gender. They'd taken their name from the kick-ass trans character in *The Last of Us*, which I thought was amazing.

Esther looked at me, eager for me to continue. I debated whether or not I cared if Lev was here to listen and decided I didn't.

"Well, he was great. I was great. Everything was great."

"Great!" Lev said.

"Come on!" Esther moaned. "I want details!"

"Oh for fuck's sake. He was good with his tongue. That's all I'm saying."

"Oh yeah. Boom chicca wow-wow," Esther sang, grinding like a porn star, making me laugh.

"You liked him?" Lev said.

"Yeah. It was…kinda more than I bargained for," I admitted.

"What do you mean?" Esther asked.

"He was such a gentleman—and I know that's old-fashioned but it's really quite charming—and kind, and hot as hell…and witty. We had a connection. I've never…" I frowned. "I've never been treated so well by someone I'd just met, during a one-night stand."

Esther stared at me. "Maybe it wasn't a one-night stand."

"Esther, he brings guys to Molly's all the time, to use the Bordello."

"Oh." Esther said, evincing disappointment. "Wait! That's the kink room, right?" She slapped a hand over her mouth as her eyes popped wide again.

"Yes. Where naughty boys go to be punished— apparently, by Mr. Alastair Kenney."

"Ooh, is that his name? How distinguished! He sounds like a Dom," Esther commented.

"Well, I know he's a gentleman, first and foremost. And now I'm curious about the kink thing," I admitted.

"But you're not kinky!"

I glared at her. "How the fuck do you know? Maybe I am."

Esther started laughing. I felt rather insulted.

"He could be kinky. Sometimes people are late bloomers," Lev said with a mouthful of pizza.

I blinked. "But…I'm only twenty."

Esther laughed harder, and Lev shook their head. "Oh, you sweet summer child."

"Wait! Lev, are you — ?"

They held up their hand in the stop position. "I'll never tell." But then they winked. So I took that as a yes.

I tapped my chin. "Huh."

"It's good that he treated you well," Lev said, holding a folded piece of pizza in one hand.

"Yeah." I laughed. "Except, if he hadn't treated me quite so well, I wouldn't be in this situation."

"What situation?" Esther asked.

"Of…feeling too much…for him. I was hoping to compartmentalize it. I'm trying."

"Casual sex can be complicated," Lev said. "Ask me how I know."

"Do you regret it?" Esther asked me.

"No. Absolutely not. Not at all."

Chapter Nine

A Temporary Refuge

I stayed at Esther's after that. Deshawn and Lev understood, and they didn't seem to mind, as long as it wasn't going to be a permanent thing. It was crowded, but kind of fun, too. Definitely better than being at my mom's.

She texted me, apologizing for waking me up and asking where I was and when I'd be back. She didn't mean it. She'd wake me up early again tomorrow if she needed something.

Anyway, I didn't reply. I'd have to go back for my other clothes and shit soon, but I wasn't looking forward to it.

Instead of thinking about that, I spent my time remembering everything that had happened in that hotel room on the sixth floor. If that was all I ever got, then I would seal it in my memory bank with countless wanking sessions that happened in the early morning hours when everyone else was asleep and I was alone on the sofa. I was pretty good at being quiet, having lived with my mom for so long.

Saturday came around, and I couldn't help getting a bit excited. I hoped to see Alastair again and half-imagined him inviting me to the Chateau for another round. I had no idea how realistic that was.

I'm embarrassed to say that my heart leapt when he came through the doors of the gaming parlor at around ten-thirty, and promptly sank when I saw the gorgeous man that came in with him.

I had leaned over one of the Mr. Youngbloods, being deliberately flirtatious because that's what I was paid for, flashing a nipple as I gave advice on his hand of cards. I looked up, and there was Alastair. But it became obvious in a moment that he had dragged a very pretty boy along to get kinky with. My smile turned into a frown, and I returned my focus to Mr. Youngblood's cards and ramped up the flirting, hoping that Alastair would notice.

Would he even look for me? Maybe he'd only been pretending and didn't care one way or another if he ever saw me again. The thought made me bitter.

"Oh, well, *that* is a very good hand, Mr. Youngblood," I said. Then I glanced sheepishly at the other players and covered my mouth. "Oh, damn! You probably didn't want me to say that."

"You rascal," he muttered, but then caught an eyeful of my nipple and shrugged. "Never mind. I'm a shit player, anyway."

I laughed and glanced up. Alastair Kenney stood by the window, his young companion looking impatient and annoyingly sexy. Alastair stared at me with...something that I couldn't identify in his eyes. Anger?

I bristled. What the fuck did he have to be mad about?

I was doing my job. He was the one showing up with a kinky boy toy when he'd professed to wanting to ask me out.

My heart beat faster as he started over. My dick got hard, too. The look in his eyes was…something. I didn't know what, but I liked it — or, at least, my body did. My brain was still throwing a hissy fit.

Alastair stopped beside me.

"Hi, Toby," he said, in clipped tones, glancing at Mr. Youngblood with barely concealed contempt.

I waited for a second to make sure that Alastair saw the nipple I was flashing Mr. Youngblood, before I straightened up and put my hands on my hips.

"Mr. Kenney, how nice to see you again." I said, lifting my chin as Mr. Youngblood tossed some chips into the pot.

Mr. Kenney looked between me and Mr. Youngblood, who was focused on his game.

"Can I help you with anything?" I asked.

Alastair opened his mouth, then closed it. I smiled. First point to me. Then his expression relaxed, and he said, "Yes, actually. I need the key to the Bordello, if it's available."

Involuntarily, my gaze shifted to the young Adonis waiting in the doorway. "I can certainly check for you. Do you need it right away?" I glanced back at the boy toy. "Or for another night?" I blinked innocently. "We usually take bookings in advance."

I saw his lip twitch. But he gave me a grave look.

"We need it *now* – or as soon as we can get it."

I straightened, lifting my chin. "I'll find out," I said, with a thin smile. I turned from the games table and walked to the bar, where Jacob was staring at me with an odd expression.

"You okay, Toby?" he asked.

"Sure. Is the Bordello available? Mr. Kenney and his…" I almost said boy toy, but corrected myself, "*guest*…would like to use it." I glanced at them, then turned back to Jacob and rolled my eyes. "Right now, apparently. I told them it might be booked."

Jacob stared at me for a few more seconds. Maybe he could tell that I was close to losing the smile I was only maintaining with superhuman concentration.

"No, it's free." He reached under the bar. "Here."

I took it, holding it out as if it offended me. The small metal key was attached to a large antique, rusted Victorian key that I used to think was cool but now only looked upon with disdain.

I took a deep breath, knowing that now I had to give Alastair the key to the room where he would be taking the pouty twink he had in tow and doing all sorts of perverted things to entertain him.

I did it, somehow without dissolving into a puddle of regret and disappointment and inadequacy on the floor.

"There you are, Mr. Kenney," I said, my voice a strange mix of pitches. I was trying. I really was. "Enjoy yourselves."

"Thanks," Alastair said, taking the key from me and eyeing me curiously. He looked like he was about to say something, but I couldn't keep my composure anymore. I turned tail and went back to Mr. Youngblood, who had just won the hand, despite my faux pas.

"There he is! My good luck charm," Mr. Youngblood said, nodding toward me and giving me a most affectionate smile, that I clung to like a lifeline.

"Wait'll you see what happens when you rub me," I purred, giving him a deliberately salacious look.

Man, I was out of control.

"My goodness," he said, blushing and clearing his throat while his husband, the other Mr. Youngblood, gaped at him over his glasses.

"Settle down, now, you two. You don't want Jacob coming over here."

But it was too late. Jacob was on his way, and he didn't look happy.

"Toby, can I speak to you, please?"

"Of course," I said, a niggling worry in my head that Jacob had noticed something weird between me and Alastair. The serving staff weren't prohibited from having relations with clients, but it had to be outside of work hours, and it might not be something Jacob wanted to deal with, especially if it affected the job.

He led me into the hall where I caught a glimpse of Alastair and his boy toy rounding the corner on their way to the Bordello.

When I glanced at Jacob, he crossed his arms and looked at me with narrowed eyes.

"Toby, what's going on here?"

"Where?" I could play dumb like the best of them.

Jacob gestured toward the back room. "I'm getting some very strange vibes from you and Mr. Kenney. What's going on?"

I gazed at my feet in the brown leather shoes and had a vivid image of Alastair tying the laces for me.

I sighed. "We had a little...encounter."

Jacob seemed startled. "In the *club*?"

"No! Of course not. I know the rules."

"Okay. Good." He glanced around, then met my gaze again. "Well, I don't have a right to police you when you're not on shift, but you are on shift right now, and it seemed like the fact that Mr. Kenney came in with a very attractive man on his arm made you...somewhat agitated."

"*Phhht*. No," I said. "I'm fine."

He raised his eyebrows.

"Mr. Kenney can fuck whoever he wants. I don't care."

Jacob peered at the corner again. "I doubt he's taking him in there to fuck him."

I glared at Jacob. "It's a fucking kink room. What else is he going to do in there?"

Jacob sighed. "You know kink doesn't always involve fucking, right?"

It doesn't?

"Sure. Of course." Kink didn't involve fucking? What the hell was the point of it, then?

Wow, I sounded like a boomer in my own head. I knew there was more to sex than fucking. Of course, I knew that. But I had always equated kink with penetration, for some reason. Color me surprised.

"Then you don't know what they're going to do in there. And it's not any of your business. Right?"

I glared at him, pissed off at my own ignorance and the fact that Jacob was calling me out.

"Right," I admitted.

"Good."

"Fine."

His expression softened. "Look... I'm not *mad*. I'm a little surprised, that's all. You've never done anything like this before."

I cocked my head. "How do you know?"

"Okay, fair. I don't. Have you?"

I shrugged. "Not with anyone from the club."

"Okay. Just be careful."

"Why? Is Mr. Kenney dangerous?"

"No, I don't think so." Jacob gauged my reaction. "But he's in here with a different twink every week."

"Yeah, he told me that."

"Oh." Jacob seemed surprised. "Okay, then. It's only —"

"What?"

"Well, when he came in tonight, you were acting like a jilted lover."

Was I that transparent? *Goddammit.*

"Well, I'm not. Mr. Kenney can fuck, or spank, or paddle whoever he wants. It's none of my business. Are we done here?"

He nodded. I'm not sure if he believed me, but he wasn't calling me out on it.

"Yes. And, uh, pull back on flirting with Mr. Youngblood, will you? He had a heart bypass last year."

"Oh shit," I said.

"I don't want to have to call nine-one-one because you can't keep your nipples in your blouse."

I stuttered a laugh, and Jacob smiled.

"Fine. I'll be less…ostentatious."

"Thank you."

* * * *

I ended up feeling good about Jacob taking me aside, because it helped me to get a grip on things…for about twenty minutes.

I couldn't help wondering what Alastair and his boy toy were doing in the Bordello. I was driving myself crazy picturing the implements I knew were in there and visualizing Alastair using them on his boy toy, when I finally fucking realized why I was so upset.

It wasn't simply that I wanted another sexy hookup with Alastair. It was possible that I was jealous of this random dude getting to see the kinky side of Alastair, when I hadn't — at least not yet.

I'd never thought of myself as kinky, but now I was starting to wonder if maybe I was, or could be, with someone like Alastair guiding me through it. Because the thought that it was another random hookup in there with Alastair right now was *killing me*.

Every server got a tour of the Bordello during their interview. Jacob and Sebastian were very clear on exactly what Maverick Molly's was and what it wasn't. After seeing that ornately decorated and kinked-up space, it was hard to forget it. I'd thought it was pretty cool and definitely detailed. Part of me had been curious about it, but I'd always thought the kink aspect of some people's sex lives was simply an add-on — like those bonus questions you could answer on a test. Sex was sex, and kink was extra. I'd never seen it as something independent of sex itself. And now that I was thinking about it philosophically, I wanted to know more about it — and I wanted Alastair to teach me.

The Bordello had become a kinky Disneyland in my imagination. And the secretly stern and gentlemanly Daddy who had treated me so well at the Chateau had taken another boy there to play.

Hanging and displayed everywhere were items for use to discipline and punish, according to different themes. Sebastian had shown me the hidden Bluetooth speakers that could connect to the user's cell phone.

I wondered what music Alastair was playing in there right now, and what toys he was using on the hot guy he'd brought with him.

Goddammit, I needed a smoke.

I ducked outside and lit up, standing exactly where I'd been the night I'd met Alastair, inhaling the soothing smoke into my lungs. After a few long puffs, I felt better. I did want to quit this stupid habit completely. Just, not yet.

If Alastair fucking Kenney wanted to play around with half the men in Ottawa, that was his business. He was damned lucky he'd got that one night—*er, morning*—with me at the Chateau. Even though it had been *vanilla*, it had rocked my socks, and I knew it had rocked his. He'd even said as much. We'd had an incredible connection, and maybe that was worth more than all the kinky shit in the world.

I was standing there smoking my ciggy, explaining to myself why there wasn't anything to feel insecure about, when someone shoved the door open and stomped down the steps, almost crashing into me.

"Oh sorry," I said, because I was Canadian, and it was instinct to apologize for being in someone's way. Then I realized it was Alastair's boy toy.

He turned and scowled at me, then went on his way, as I stared after him, wondering what had happened. Had Alastair used the wrong paddle?

The air out here was frigid, but I didn't want to go back inside until I'd finished my cigarette. Since I didn't smoke all that much during the day, I wanted to enjoy it when I did. I was curious now, but I just stood there, holding my coat closed with my free hand, listening to the ambient sounds of the city.

I heard the door open, and the edges of my lips tipped up even before I turned to see Alastair coming down the stairs. He was coatless and frowning, with worry marks etched into his forehead.

"I was looking for you," he said.

I gazed at him and took a leisurely puff on my cigarette. Once I'd exhaled, I said, "Last I heard you were taking a pretty boy into the Bordello to spank into submission."

Alastair cleared his throat and shoved his hands into his jean pockets, looking like he wished he'd stopped to grab his jacket. "Well, he left."

"Yeah. He passed me. He looked pissed."

Alastair sighed, and the worry lines on his forehead faded. "He *was* pissed."

"What happened?"

"Nothing. That's why he was pissed."

I gaped at Alastair. "Nothing? You took him to the Bordello and nothing happened?"

Alastair looked embarrassed. "Well, it started to happen. We tried to get things going."

I could just imagine.

"But I was distracted," he admitted, gazing at me almost shyly.

"Really," I said, taking another puff on my cigarette. I thought about offering it to Alastair, but I was still kind of mad about the boy toy, even if he'd left in a huff. Alastair wasn't having much luck tonight, and that thought made me happy.

Alastair looked at his feet and nodded. He nudged a pile of slush with the toe of his boot. "I couldn't stop thinking about undressing a gorgeous man in a chemise," he said, suddenly breathless. "And how much I wanted to do it again."

I rolled my eyes, even though his words pleased me more than I wanted to admit. "Oh, yeah?"

"Look… Can we go inside? It's fucking freezing out here."

"You should have worn your coat," I said.

"Why are you so angry? You knew I brought men here."

I shrugged, dropping the butt of my cigarette to the pavement and grinding it out with my heel. "I don't honestly know."

"Well, it seems you've ruined it for me…after one fucking night."

"It was morning," I reminded him.

He glared at me, and a frustrated Alastair Kenney was a sexy Alastair Kenney, even though I hated to admit it.

"I'm going in. But we need to talk," he said.

"We probably shouldn't do that here."

"Why?" He cocked his head.

"Because at the club, I'm an employee and you're the client. Remember?"

"Dammit."

I looked down at the remains of my cigarette. "Oh, sorry… Did you want a suck?" I asked benignly.

He stared at me, opened his mouth as if to speak, then closed it. He shook his head and gazed at me with meaning. "Not of your cigarette."

We stared at each other for a long moment.

"Anyway," Alastair muttered, "it's fucking freezing."

"You keep talking about the cold. I didn't make you come out here."

"Toby, for fuck's sake. Can we get together after your shift? We need to talk."

"Talk?" I asked, with a quirk to my lips. I figured it was time to let him know I wasn't a complete dick.

"Yes. Talk. That's all."

"Not at the Chateau," I said, with firmness.

"No. We can go to my place," he suggested.

I raised my eyebrows and thought about the implications of that.

"If you're uncomfortable doing that—"

"Okay," I said.

"Okay?" He seemed incredibly pleased.

"Sure."

* * * *

I sent a text to Esther letting her know I wouldn't be back until the next day. It would be midnight when my shift was over, so I'd sleep at Alastair's. I sent her his contact info as a safety measure.

Alastair Kenney lived in a picturesque historic townhome on Cameron Avenue, a couple of blocks west of Bank Street. The Uber he'd arranged dropped us off in front, and I followed him up the steps and onto the porch. The door had one of those fancy touchpad locks. Alastair put in his code and opened the door, muttering about the cold as we went inside.

I was trying to get a look at Alastair's digs when he turned and hemmed me in against the wall.

"I need to kiss you," he said.

I thought about denying him, because I was still resentful about the boy toy, but that didn't last for one heartbeat before I gave him my consent. He sighed with relief and planted his mouth on mine. The kiss was a little bit desperate, a little bit frustrated and a little bit precious, a combination that just about laid me flat, especially because I responded in kind without even thinking about it.

We stood there, in the tiny entryway, kissing like we were already an established couple, until I forced myself to end it.

"I thought you wanted to talk."

He was staring at me as if he couldn't even fathom his own behavior. He blinked, and remembered the plan.

"Yes. Talk. Sorry." He stepped back and started unbuttoning his coat. "Please come in."

I smiled. "Now, that's much more gentlemanly."

He gave me a shaky smile as he hung up his coat.

"What the fuck have you done to me, Tobias Dunn?"

And…that was a cold splash of water in my face.

"Please don't call me that," I said in very controlled tones.

"Isn't that…I assumed that was what Toby was short for."

"It is," I admitted. "But only my mom calls me that. And, uh, she's not exactly my favorite person."

"I'm so sorry."

"It's okay. But please don't do it again."

"No, of course not. Here… Let me hang up your coat."

"For fuck's sake, I can hang up my own coat," I scowled.

Now I was pissed. It had been an emotional roller coaster of a night, and I was tired. Maybe I should have gone home and agreed to talk with Alastair another time.

He didn't say anything, but he gestured to a hook and backed off, toeing off his boots and opening the inside door to his home. Christ I was in *his* home. I needed to be nicer.

"I'm sorry," I said. "I'm a little on edge."

"It's all right."

I hung up my coat and toed off my boots, then padded into the main part of the house. He shut the glass door behind me.

"I keep it closed in the winter. It helps keep the warmth inside."

"It's very cozy in here," I said, gazing about.

"Thanks. It's small, I know."

"But it's yours. That's what's important." Spoken by a guy who would kill to have his own place. "Do you own it or are you renting?"

"Own. Well, I'm still paying off the mortgage." He flicked on the lights in the kitchen and switched on a table lamp by the sofa in the living room.

The plaster walls were white, but the wood trim was stained dark, and it kind of reminded me of the way that European pubs looked. The décor was decidedly masculine—lots of leather and darker pieces—but there were some soft touches, like a vase of flowers on the dining table and throw pillows in bright fabrics on the couch. Bookcases lined two walls in the compact living area.

"You like to read."

"Yeah. Little bit." He laughed. "Do you?"

"Yeah. But I don't have as many books as you do."

Alastair smiled, and I thought we were gonna be okay.

"Make yourself at home. Would you like a drink?"

I blinked. "Do you have Coke or something?"

Alastair eyed me. "Oh, right. I think so? Hold on."

"Or tea?"

He laughed. "Sure. I'll have some, too."

I sat down on the sofa and watched him through the archway as he went about filling the kettle and putting it on the burner of the stove.

Hmm, old school. I liked that. I had a gross old electric kettle at my mom's, but I liked the idea of boiling water on the stove.

"How long have you lived here?" I asked him.

"A couple of years. I got a good deal on the place, but it needed fresh paint and a bit of renovating. My parents helped me with a down payment, but the place is mine. It's a good investment for the future and, for now, it suits me."

"I like it. It's very homey."

"Thanks. You said you live at home, with your mom?"

"I'm staying with a friend right now," I said. "It's complicated."

Alastair tossed teabags into two mugs. "Complicated?"

I sat back and stared at the ceiling.

"Technically, I live with my mom. Or, at least, that's where most of my stuff is."

He frowned. "But you're not staying there now?"

"Not if I can help it, no." I lowered my gaze to his. "I'm looking for a room to rent because I can't stay with Esther longer than a few weeks. She has roommates."

He didn't say anything, just continued making the tea. I took a second to relax, lounging on Alastair's leather sofa and staring at the darkness out of the window.

"You can shut the curtains if you want."

I walked to the window and pulled the navy drapes closed. It made the room seem smaller, but I was happy with the privacy. I felt cozy and safe.

"The remote for the fireplace is on the mantel if you want some heat."

"Thanks," I said.

I got the remote and pressed the power button. There was a hiss as a blue flame reared to life.

"You have a really nice home, Mr. Kenney."

He laughed. "Oh, for fuck's sake, Toby. Call me Alastair."

Chapter Ten

Friends

When the tea was ready, he asked me how I took it, so I made a dirty joke because, hey, it was me. Alastair laughed but he told me to behave myself, which gave me a bit of a thrill, to be honest.

He brought the mugs out and put them on the narrow coffee table.

"This looks like a bench," I said.

"It is a bench. But it's the perfect size for the space."

"It's nice."

"Thanks."

"Your place is really cool."

It wasn't a lie. He'd decorated it with traditional furniture but there were modern touches as well, such as metal-legged plastic chairs around the dining table and modular bookcases.

"Thanks. The rooms are small, but these old homes have so much heart. I'd rather have a cozy home like this in the city, than a spacious new build out in Barrhaven or Kanata."

I looked at him strangely. "So, why did we go to the Chateau the other night? This place is closer to Molly's."

He shrugged. "I wasn't sure you'd be comfortable since we'd only just met. And the Chateau is" — he blushed — "impressive. And, maybe, I wanted to impress you?"

"Oh," I said, charmed once again. "Well, you definitely did — and not just with the accommodations."

"The feeling is mutual."

I grinned and sipped my tea. "Huh. Did I impress you with my astonishing flexibility?"

He laughed. "With everything. And the Molly's outfit was a very nice touch."

"I figured you'd like that. I'm not really supposed to take it with me, but…it was worth the risk."

"It certainly was." Alastair met my gaze with a frankness that made me pay attention. "We need to talk about what's going on," he said, "between us."

Oh, okay.

"Right. Which is…what exactly?"

He laughed and shook his head. "I don't know. This is uncharted territory for me."

"In what way? You said you have hookups all the time."

He frowned. "I didn't say *all* the time."

"Uh, you kind of did — or at least, that's how it sounded."

He cleared his throat. "I've never been so distracted by someone that I couldn't engage physically with someone else. That's a first for me."

I raised my eyebrows. "Congratulations?"

He laughed. "God, I sound like an asshole."

"Kind of. But do go on."

"Look, Toby. I've been having casual sex since I was your age." He held up a hand. "*Safe* sex. I get tested every six months, and I use condoms religiously when there's penetration."

"That's good," I said. It felt weird, having this conversation. "You know, I didn't plan to let you seduce me."

Alastair's eyes narrowed. "Is that what I did?"

I rolled my eyes. "Don't act all innocent. The thing with the shoelace? You're telling me that wasn't a calculated seduction?"

Alastair blinked. "It wasn't...*exactly* calculated. I suppose I wanted to touch you, but I knew I wasn't allowed. And those shoes are so...delicate. And the way you were lying there, in your molly-boy clothes." He stood, as if he was seeing me like that again. "Fuck, Toby. How could I resist?" He made a strangled sound and put a hand to his lips. "I couldn't."

"Wow," I murmured. "I had no idea..."

He gave me a look.

"Okay, fine. Maybe I was trying to seduce you, too. I don't know what came over me. Honestly. It wasn't planned."

Alastair sat down again and sipped his tea.

"I know that the understanding was that it would be a one-time thing."

"Yeah," I admitted. "Absolutely. You didn't make any promises, and neither did I."

"But, Toby, that...experience...with you was more than I'd bargained for, in a good way. A really good way."

"Yeah, it was pretty awesome."

He raised his eyebrows.

"Okay, fine, it was epic. I felt it, too. I didn't want to admit it, because I was trying my best to stay detached."

"You were?"

I gave him a frank look. "I don't hook up with guys very often."

He looked a bit skeptical.

"I don't. And I was way more into you than I wanted to be."

He shrugged. "I thought the best thing to do to get over you was to take someone to the Bordello."

I bristled. "Uh-huh. Right in front of me. That was super sweet."

"Well, I wanted you to know what the deal was. At least, I thought I did," he said. "But when I saw you flashing your nipples at the guy playing cards, I wanted to walk over there and punch him in the fucking face."

My eyes went wide, and I couldn't stop an amused smile from landing on my face. "You *were* glaring at us fairly aggressively."

"That's never happened, either," he said, taking a sip of his tea. "I didn't think I was the possessive type."

"You're the possessive type now?"

"Felt like it. With you," he said. He ran a hand through his hair. "It was…unexpected."

"Huh." I gazed at him, contemplatively. "So, you took the fuckboy upstairs to get kinky and you…couldn't do it?"

He puffed out some air and shook his head, as if he was embarrassed. "I froze. I don't know. I mean, he —" Alastair raised his eyebrows. "Do you really want to hear this?"

Did I?

"Yeah." I leaned forward on my elbows.

"Okay. Well, he got naked and, fuck, he had a nice body. And I got him buckled in. And he was there, all trussed up and waiting for me to start, and I kept thinking about you downstairs, in your sexy little bloomers, and remembering the other night..."

"Did you touch him?" I'm not sure why I was torturing myself, but I wanted to know.

"I couldn't. I picked up a flogger and...he was waiting for me to use it."

A flogger. *Fuck.* I didn't really know what a flogger was, but I knew it was a member of the whip family, and boy, did it sound intense. I was getting hard just thinking about it. I was getting hard imagining Alastair holding something like that.

I remembered the look on Fuckboy's face when he left. I felt kind of smug about it, to be honest. If that was wrong of me, too bad.

Alastair continued. "But...I knew it wasn't going to work. And more than that, I didn't want to continue, so I safeworded."

"You...used a safeword?"

"Yes. To end the scene."

"Oh. Is that what happens? Sorry... I don't know much about this stuff."

"That's what's supposed to happen, yeah. If anyone safewords—the sub or the Dom—the scene ends immediately."

"Oh. I see."

He splayed his hands out. "In theory, neither party is supposed to show anger or irritation in such cases—but he wasn't happy."

"I could tell. He almost ran me over on his way out."

"Sorry."

"Not your fault."

"Anyway," he said, rubbing his palms on his jeans and looking troubled. "It was embarrassing, and I felt bad for him, but I was glad when he left."

"I mean, I can't say I'm upset about it," I said softly.

Alastair gazed at me. "You weren't too happy about me bringing him."

"No."

"But...we didn't make any promises."

"I know. Well, my brain knew that. My body was being a little bitch, though."

"Yeah?"

"I was *trying* to be cool. I don't have any claim on you."

He stared at me with the sweetest, most lost look I'd ever seen on anyone. "I don't know. I think maybe you do."

I smiled, because that thought made me happy, and I couldn't pretend it didn't.

"I can see you're not overly concerned about that," he muttered.

I laughed. "No. I guess...the other night affected me, too."

He put down his tea and leaned back in the leather chair, his gaze on me.

"So...what do we do now?" he asked.

He seemed so adrift and confused, when I knew exactly what I wanted.

We stared at each other in silence for a few beats, the current between us as strong as ever. He'd said he wanted to talk, but we had talked, and now I wanted to do something else. I had a feeling he might want to do it, too.

I put down my tea and stood, taking things slow so he had plenty of time to object. But his gaze tracked me as I moved forward and straddled him where he sat on the couch. He inhaled a breath, and his hands came to rest on my hips as I leaned in and held his gaze, our lips inches apart.

"This is what *I* want to do," I said, my voice a whisper as I gazed at his soft lips and his wide, dark eyes that shone with intelligence and need. So much need. I traced the silver ring in his eyebrow with the tip of my finger, then touched a wayward curl of hair. "But I don't have my bloomers or corset to seduce you."

His breaths came quick as he stared at me. "You don't need them."

I brought my hand up to cup his furred chin and pressed my lips to his. He gripped my hips as if he were afraid of what I might do, but he was languid under my tongue.

The kiss deepened, our connection a perfect storm of arousal and desperation.

I worked the buttons of his shirt, unwrapping him as I kissed him with relentless need. He let me take control, even though I knew he could turn the tables at any moment.

I got his shirt open and found a nipple with my thumb, pleased with his reaction when I rubbed at it then pinched it. He groaned and pressed his covered erection against me, opening his mouth wide and snaking his tongue along mine.

"Oh fuck," I said. "You taste so good."

He panted like he'd been running, his eyes wide as his hands went higher and he wrapped his arms around me, pulling me close.

"Toby…" he gasped. "Fuck."

"I know," I said, as breathless as he was. "I don't know what the fuck is happening, but it's so good, so good."

He laughed and found my wrists with his hands, holding my arms down and curling forward to take my mouth aggressively as I arched my back and pressed myself against him.

"God," I moaned. "Damn."

"You like that," he panted, his fingers like iron on my wrists. I squirmed against his hold, my arms straight at my sides.

"I like it," I admitted, the sensation of being held down by him almost euphoric.

"Make me come," he whispered between kisses.

"What?"

"Rub against me. I'm so hard. I can come like this."

Oh, hell yes.

"Can I unzip you?"

"No," he said, and my pulse increased by tenfold.

What the fuck was wrong with me? Who knew being denied was such a huge turn-on?

I whimpered and pushed my hips forward, rubbing my cock—hard as rock in my jeans—against him, feeling the strength of his desire under me. He groaned and pushed back, keeping my hands immobile as I wiggled against him.

"Fuck, fuck, fuck," I whispered, dizzy with arousal as I ground myself against Alastair's covered cock. The look on his face was something I'd remember. He looked pained and desperate as I rubbed against him, his erection pushing against the front of his dress pants as I drove my hips back and forth, my wrists pinioned against the leather of the sofa.

"Oh my God," I panted, my forehead furrowed with concentration as I rocked. Alastair's face became a picture of bliss as he groaned, went rigid then let out a curse as he gasped mouthfuls of air.

I rode him like a bucking bronco, my cock so hard in my skinny jeans it was torture. I almost came in my pants, watching him lose control, but instead I simply whimpered and begged for assistance.

In a moment he had released my wrists and had my cock out of my jeans.

"Put your hands on my shoulders," he mumbled, sounding shattered and stunned.

I watched his face as he licked the palm of his hand and wrapped it around my cock, pulling with firm, relentless strokes until I gasped and came in thick spurts all over his chest.

"Fuuuck, fuck, fuck," I groaned, amazed at the intensity of the fumbling, desperate joining. We were like two high school kids in the basement after school before anyone's parents were due home.

I rested my forehead against his, eyes closed, as he stroked me through the aftershocks. Then I made a choked gasp and pushed his hand away.

"Too much. Stop, *stop*."

He let me go and we breathed together, coming down from the high of climax and whatever it was that had taken hold of us. When I opened my eyes, he was smiling and looking down at where my spunk had landed — right in the middle of his beautiful chest.

"I, uh, made a mess," I said. "Again."

He swiped his finger through my jizz and sucked it into his mouth.

"Jesus," I hissed as my dick twitched. "I thought you were safe."

He grunted, withdrawing the finger, licked clean. He held it up in front of me. "You're twenty years old. You said you don't have casual sex."

"Yeah, but..."

"Should I be worried?" he asked, frowning.

"No. I would have told you if I had anything."

"Well, then, let me enjoy my kinks, Toby."

I held his face in my hands and kissed him again. He was pliant and relaxed.

"I need a shower," Alastair murmured. "You want to come with?"

"Is there room?" I asked.

"We'll make it work."

* * * *

Alastair's main bathroom was at the top of the stairs, and the shower was more spacious than I'd expected. For a heritage home in Old Ottawa South, it was modern and swank. There was a walk-in shower surrounded in black and white retro-style tiles, an antique wood vanity with glass-bowl sink and waterfall faucet, and a modern, rectangular, stand-alone tub.

"For fuck's sake, Alastair!" I said.

"What?"

I glared at him, raising finger quotes. "*Not much but we'll make it work?*"

He shrugged, but blushed. "I mean, it's not massive."

I narrowed my eyes. "It's the size of my bedroom."

"Shut up. It is not."

I laughed sardonically. "Oh, you have no idea how the rest of us live, do you?"

He smiled. "Stop making fun of me and get naked, please. I need to take these pants off."

"Yes, Sir!" I said.

It had been a joke, but the look that came over him — halfway between his O-face and the expression of a startled pigeon — made my dick twitch.

"Oh, you like that."

He tried to brush it off. "Well, I like it when my partners do what I tell them. Yeah."

"Hmm. I liked the way you looked when I said it."

"Just get in the shower."

We gave each other surreptitious glances as we undressed, curious to see the other completely naked. Kind of funny that we'd had sex twice now without taking our clothes off. Alastair bent to turn on the tap then the showerhead. I ogled his fine-as-fuck ass and the muscles of his thighs.

God, he was a good-looking man, just the right amount of body hair and muscles with the definition of a swimmer or a runner…strong, but not bulked up. Not that I cared — okay, fine, I did. I liked my men on the sleek side.

Being in the shower together felt incredibly intimate but also seemed completely normal.

"Here… Turn around," Alastair said.

I gave him a suspicious look, and he laughed.

"I want to wash your hair."

"That's what they all say," I quipped.

I turned, and he took a bottle of shampoo from the shelf and started lathering my hair. It felt…nice. Really nice. I stared at the tiles and let myself feel cherished and cared for. It was a strange sensation, and one I don't remember having experienced often. Although there had been one time, years ago, after a particularly heated argument with my mom when Esther had looked after me, taking me to the clinic where I'd lied and said I'd got hit during a baseball game.

"I never asked what your pronouns are," Alastair said, out of the blue.

"Oh," I sighed as my body relaxed in the warmth under Alastair's care. "Any are fine. I don't care."

"So, I could use 'she'?" he asked.

"Sure." I knew he was fishing for an explanation of my gender, and I decided to take it easy on him. "I'm gender fluid."

"Oh," he said. "Cool. My sister's gender-queer."

He rubbed the shampoo into my scalp while I tried not to show how good it felt.

"Is there a difference between being gender fluid and being non-binary?" Alastair asked.

"They're close, for sure. It really depends on the person," I said. "I guess I kind of feel male some of the time, and female at other times. Whereas someone who's non-binary might not even feel one way or another. The non-binary folks I know seem to be questioning the entire idea of gender."

"Huh. Interesting. Okay, time to rinse," he said, nudging me to turn around. While I was leaning my head back with my eyes closed so I could rinse the shampoo out, he leaned in and gave me a sweet kiss on the cheek.

"What was that for?"

I kept my eyes closed because I really didn't want to get soap in them.

"For being so adorable."

I laughed, but it sounded like a schoolgirl's giggle.

Alastair gasped. "Did you just giggle?"

I did it again. "Maybe."

"Stop being so fucking cute. I can't keep my hands off you," he said, circling my waist with his hands then reaching down to squeeze my bum.

"I am entirely okay with that."

I finished rinsing and opened my eyes to see that Alastair was lathering his own hair now.

"I'd offer to do that for you but you're taller than me, and my arms would get tired."

"God forbid. Thanks for letting me do yours."

Something was niggling at the back of my head.

"Hey, you know when you, uh, tasted my, uh, spunk? Before?"

"Oh yes."

How to ask this without seeming rude or overly paranoid.

"You sort of implied that it was your kink."

"One of them, yes."

"So, do you do that, like, a lot? With the guys you hook up with?"

He nudged me aside so he could stand under the stream of water to rinse his shampoo out. He gave me a sober look.

"Nope. Too risky."

Which sent a wave of relief through me.

"Okay. Yeah," I said. "So, it's not risky with me because supposedly I'm only twenty and don't generally have a lot of sex?" *Oh, that doesn't sound right.* I frowned. "I mean, casual sex?"

"I know you're not a virgin. But, yeah, you don't really scream 'using Grindr every weekend' to me."

I laughed. "Okay, fine. Well, you're right. I don't hook up with guys very often. Not *never*, though."

"Are you safe when you do?"

"Yeah...always."

He finished rinsing his hair and gazed at me. "Well, swallowing is a low-risk activity for HIV transmission."

"Really?"

"Yeah. But don't just take my word for it. Look it up when you have a chance."

"But you don't do it with casual hookups?"

"No."

"So, what are we then?"

"Huh?"

"Well, you swallowed my semen. Does that move me up from casual to, oh I don't know, maybe dating?"

"Maybe dating. I like that. Okay," he said, my gaze tracking his hands as he soaped up his body in all the right places. "Anyway, I don't have any open sores in my mouth, or I wouldn't have kissed you. And it was only off the tip of one finger. I'm not worried."

"Okay," I said. "But if it's a kink, how do you indulge it with the fuckboys? Or do you just...not?"

He smiled and there was a lot behind that grin. "Oh, Toby. There are a lot of ways to indulge a jizz kink without swallowing it. Trust me."

"Trust *you*?" I said with a mocking, skeptical look. "I don't know."

He laughed. "Well, you should, because I'd like to get to know you...more than just what your jizz tastes like."

"Whoa. You are such a romantic."

It was a very nice shower, and neither of us tried to get up to anything. By the time we were toweling off, I was starting to feel that electric boogaloo thing again.

"I want to try out the Bordello," I said.

Alastair eyed me strangely. "Yeah? With who?"

"With you...duh. Who do you think?"

He didn't say anything, and I wondered if I'd shocked him. But how could I shock him? He was the one who had all the experience. Wouldn't he want to take me there?

"Is that something you'd want to—?" I asked.

"Yes, Toby. It is something I want to do," he said, so quickly it took me by surprise.

"Oh, goody."

"Are you sure, though? I don't want you to do it just to please me, because you think I need it or something weird like that."

"You don't need it?"

"No. I like it. I don't need it."

"Well, I'd like to see what it's like, being in that room. With you…telling me what to do. And…you doing things to me because you want to do them—and I'm letting you." I smiled. "Is that how it works?"

"Yes, Toby. That's *exactly* how it works."

Chapter Eleven

It's a Thing

"I'm glad you want to do that. In fact, it's making me think of all kinds of things I want to—" He took a steadying breath. "I don't think we should rush into it, though."

"Oh," I said. "Why not?"

He shrugged. "I'm just...I'm really enjoying—" He laughed, as if he was surprised by his own feelings. "I'm enjoying being vanilla with you, more than I ever thought I'd enjoy that with anyone."

"Hold on. You said you didn't need the kink. But you didn't think you could be vanilla?"

He sighed. "No, I—I figured if the right person came along..." He shook his head. "Never mind."

"Wait! Am I the right person?" *What the fuck am I doing?* That was *not* a question to ask the super-hot man you were having super-hot but still pretty casual vanilla sex with. Even though we were dating—maybe—it was only the second time we'd been alone together.

"Toby, it's too soon to tell, don't you think?"

"Nah, I think I *am* the right person." I couldn't help getting excited because it seemed as if he really liked me, and I was here for it.

"Hold on," Alastair said, clearly regretting what had slipped out.

"The right person to have vanilla sex with, but also the right person to Dom the fuck out of in the Bordello."

He snorted. "'*Dom the fuck out of,*' huh?"

"You know you want to."

"Don't get so excited. We're still in the beginning stages of" — he waved his hand around between us — "whatever this thing is."

"But you admit it's a thing."

"Sure. I mean, it's *something.*"

"It's something all right," I said, dropping my towel and walking toward what I hoped was Alastair's bedroom.

"Toby, Jesus."

It was his bedroom. It was the same size as the living room, so not huge, but there was a queen bed onto which I climbed and lounged in what I hoped was a seductive way.

"This is… I mean, it's like an adult lives here," I said.

"I'm thirty-five."

"It's a state of mind that you obviously have. I'm just not used to being sexed up by adults." I frowned. "Oh, that sounds wrong."

I turned over onto my stomach, gazing at him and waving my legs in the air, propped up on my elbows. I cradled my chin in my hands.

"The guys I've dated are so immature," I admitted. "You're in a totally different league."

"Am I?" Alastair said. It seemed he liked that idea. He stood there, with a navy towel wrapped around his hips, his skin glistening, damp curls going every which way.

His gaze skimmed my skin as he licked his lips. "Am I the oldest guy you've ever been with?"

"*Ding!* Why, yes, you are! I never thought I had a thing for older men, but come to think of it, I do like working at Molly's — and it's not just the tips."

Alastair regarded me with a dreamy look. "God. You must get massive tips."

"They're all right. Most of the regulars like me."

"I'm sure."

"Why do you say that? Because I fill out my bloomers well? I'm not the only one. Have you seen Patrick?"

"Is he the new guy? The redhead?" Alastair asked, sitting on the edge of the mattress.

"Duh."

"Yeah, he's cute," Alastair agreed.

I narrowed my eyes at him.

"In a very basic way. Not like you, obviously."

"Obviously."

Alastair put a knee on the bed and crawled toward me. "They like you, Toby, because you're sweet." He kissed me on my nose. "Sexy." He planted a chaste kiss on my mouth. "Smart." He kissed my forehead. "And sincere."

I frowned. "Sincere?"

He nodded, hovering beside me, his gaze consuming me as he waited. "You are unabashedly yourself. People notice that. I did."

"Huh. Cool, I guess."

"Some people go their whole lives pretending to be someone else."

"I suppose," I said. "Anyway, back to the Bordello…"

He laughed. "Wow. You're really curious about that place."

"I've seen it, you know. I know what's there. I just don't know what…people do there. I mean, I've got an idea."

"I'm sure you do."

"I've got a few ideas, actually."

"Really."

We stared at each other, that electric current urging us together. We let it build, enjoying the hum of energy. Alastair yanked on the tuck of his towel. My gaze followed it to the floor but then snapped back to…

"Oh fuck," I said, staring at Alastair's erection. His dick was almost as big when it was soft as it was now, but boy did it look good standing for me.

Alastair blinked and let his gaze linger on my ass. "I want to fuck you."

"You do?" I said, playing dumb.

"Duh," he said, with an impish smile.

I laughed. "Well, that's good, because I've been dying for it since you took a drag off my cigarette that first night."

"Really?" he said.

He splayed his fingers along my throat, and I tilted my head back as he dragged them down my neck and over my chest, languorously sliding them over my body as my desire ballooned and collected in my groin. When his fingers reached my pubes, he played with the soft curls before finally, *finally* wrapping around my erection.

"Oh, hello," I breathed, pushing into his grasp as he stroked and touched me with the lightest pressure.

"So pretty," he sighed, then found my mouth with his and kissed me hard and deep. "God, you taste good."

I moaned into his mouth as he urged me onto my back and let go of my cock. He pushed my thighs open. Before I knew what was happening, he located the wrinkled skin of my hole and touched me there.

"Oh, hell yeah. Goddammit." I bit my lip as he teased me with a gentleness that made my knees tremble.

"Mmm. Hold that thought," he said.

He reached for the side table and tugged the drawer open, finding what he needed. He put a condom on the pillow and popped the lid off the lube, pouring some into his hand, then rubbing his hands together like a cartoon villain.

I gazed at the condom and raised my eyebrows.

"For later. I want to have some fun first, get you ready."

"Oh, I'm ready, whenever you want."

"Oh no, Toby. You're nowhere near ready."

"I'm not?"

He shook his head, delving between my cheeks, finding my hole again.

"No," he said, circling with the tip of his finger, spreading the lube around. "I want you crying for my cock before I fuck you."

I took a shuddery inhale and made a surprised sound as he pushed a finger inside. When he took my cock into his mouth, I cried out as my brain exploded.

"Alastair," I gasped, as my head fell back. But I needed to see, so I lifted up and watched him.

I wove my fingers into his black curls as he sucked and licked and teased me, and explored me with his finger, hitting spots that made my vision blur.

"More," I moaned, ever the greedy lover.

Alastair popped his mouth off my dick and grinned at me. "Settle down. You'll get more when I'm ready."

"Bastard."

"Oooh, now I'm going to make you wait even longer."

"Fuck. Is this what you do in those rooms? Is this the kind of torture I can expect, only with toys and bondage?"

He smiled wider, and the dimple appeared. "Oh, Toby, you have no idea."

My eyes widened. He bent to my cock again and I made the most ridiculous noise of desperation. It sounded like I was being legit tortured – and I was – but with pleasure and the frustration of enduring it without release.

After a while, he added another finger then a third, and by the time he was ready to fuck me, I was almost sobbing. So, mission accomplished.

"Now I'm going to fuck you," he said as he sat up and ripped the condom package with his teeth.

"Fucking finally," I muttered, wiping my trembling fingers over my brow.

"Watch your language, Toby. You might be young but you're not a child."

Oh, I was enjoying bossy, Dommy, toppy Alastair Kenney.

"Yes, Sir," I said in a shaky, desperate voice. Maybe I should have minded my manners earlier, because Alastair started getting serious.

He sheathed himself in two seconds flat and crouched over me, guiding himself into position and glaring like a lion in heat.

"Fuck!" I said, my mouth gaping at the look in his eyes and the sensation of penetration as he breached me with the steady motions of a pro. "Oh God. Oh *God*!"

He held my gaze as he pushed in all the way, and I whimpered with the sheer possessiveness of it. Then he just rested there, gazing at me, watching me like I was a curiosity or a specimen, and for some fucking reason that was a massive a turn-on.

I tried to move, but he held me still.

"Uh-uh. Don't move."

"Come on, Alastair," I whimpered, and he laughed. I smiled, because he was so utterly calm and in control, and I fucking loved it. And I tried to wriggle again.

He sighed and gave me a pitiful look that only inflamed me more. "Oh, Toby. Am I going to have to pound you to make you behave?"

"Yes! Pound me. Please, please, *please*."

No one had ever rolled their eyes while they were buried to the hilt in me, but it did crazy, wonderful things to my brain. I moaned and pleaded and begged and finally, *finally*, Alastair started to fuck me.

"You are such a pretty little thing," he muttered as he rocked against me, leisurely at first, then with purpose. "I'm going to wreck you and break you, my pretty little bird. I'm going to make you scream my name when you come."

"Yes, Sir, yes, Sir, yes, Sir," I mumbled between gasps as he pounded me into the mattress.

"So pretty. So, so, pretty and sweet and dainty, little Toby, the molly boy. So fucking lovely," he grunted in time with his thrusts.

His words were caresses as he fucked me, his cock a welcome ramrod, brushing my prostate again and again. This was it. I was going to come.

As if Alastair had heard me say it out loud—I didn't—he wrapped his fingers around my cock and jerked me, fast.

"Alastair!" I yelled, the orgasm barreling through me in a burst of ecstatic pleasure.

He said my name and bent his forehead to my shoulder, his motions becoming quicker and shallower until he froze, groaning and shuddering in my arms.

We lay there, breathing hard, for long moments. Alastair had collapsed on top of me, and I welcomed his heavy ballast. He was still deep inside me as I drew my fingers along his beautiful biceps and kissed the top of his head.

"Wow," I said, truly shaken.

Alastair finally lifted his head and gazed at me with emotion. Then he reached down and held the base of the condom as he eased himself out and lifted off me.

"Well. That was…" he said.

"Uh-huh," I commiserated as I stared at the plastered ceiling and tried to decide if I'd seen Jesus or the Dalai Lama at the moment of climax. It was one of those two, I was sure.

"You okay?" he said, turning toward me.

"Fuck yeah. Oh, I mean, yes, Sir, I'm just fine. Thank you, Sir."

Alastair grinned. "You're good at that."

"I know."

"You don't have to call me that."

"I know."

Alastair laughed. "Oh my God. You are so damn cute. I hate you for it a little."

"Whaaat?"

"Only because I like it so much. You see, I had built this very strong fortress of 'only in it for the kink' around myself. And you've broken right through that façade."

"Huh. Go me," I said, bumping my fist in the air. "To be honest, I'm a little pissed that the vanilla sex with you is so good, because I want to try the kink but you seem to be having some kind of vanilla awakening. I'm worried you're going to abandon your kinky side forever," I said, with a dramatic and forlorn look.

And he laughed, his face the picture of innocence and mischief combined.

"Ah, Toby. I don't think you have anything to worry about."

* * * *

I woke up alone in a strange bed. I couldn't remember where I was until I saw the framed photo of Alastair's childhood dog on the bedside table, because we'd had a conversation about it before we'd gone to sleep. Everything came back to me then, and I was overwhelmed by vivid memories.

I'd been properly fucked by Mr. Alastair Kenney in his own home. We were sort of dating. And he thought I might be the right person for...something. I tried not to let it go to my head.

His bedroom was pretty in the daylight. There wasn't a lot of furniture, but what he did have looked expensive. I could hear him moving around downstairs.

I turned onto my back and touched my nipple, where Alastair had sucked and teased me before jerking me off onto my own stomach. He'd played with me like I was a special new toy, and I'd soaked up the welcome attention.

The stairs creaked, and in a moment, Alastair came in with a cup of coffee.

"Good morning!"

I squinted and propped myself on my elbow, reaching for the mug.

"Good morning, Sir."

Alastair's eyes widened, and he smiled.

"You look so fucking sexy in my bed."

I blew on the hot coffee, holding Alastair's gaze, then took a sip. It was strong and rich, like him. Okay, maybe he wasn't rich rich, but he seemed to have a lot more money than I did.

"Do I? I feel like I fucked ten guys last night."

"No, it was only me."

"Are you sure?"

"Pretty sure. Do you see any dead bodies lying around?"

I laughed but made a good show of checking. "Nope."

He sat on the edge of the bed. He was wearing gray sweatpants, for fuck's sake, and I could see the outline of his dick under the material, all relaxed and sated but still very sexy — and a white T-shirt, which made him look delectable. I liked him in his suits, don't get me wrong, but I could get used to this, too.

"So...listen. It's Sunday. Do you have to work today?" he asked, his gaze landing on my lips as I sipped the coffee.

"At Molly's? No."

"Hmm. How convenient. I also don't have to go to work today."

"What a coincidence!" I exclaimed.

"Listen, Toby," he said, with a serious frown. "I have a very important question to ask you."

My blood went cold. He sounded so somber.

"Uh...sure." *Oh my God, oh my God, oh my God.*

"Do you want pancakes or waffles for breakfast?"

The breath caught in my throat, and I realized I'd been had.

"Hardy, har, har. Pancakes all the way…if you're offering."

"I am offering."

"Then I'm accepting."

The smile that filled his face was the happiest I'd seen him.

"Get dressed and come downstairs. I'll have a plate ready."

I narrowed my eyes at him. "Hold on a second. Are you my fairy godmother, by any chance?"

"Not yet. But if the position is vacant, I'll fill it."

"Huh. I like the way you say 'fill it'."

He grinned. "Just get dressed and come downstairs."

* * * *

When I keyed myself into Esther's apartment at three-thirty, she was lounging on the sofa with Lev, watching TV.

"Heya," I said, as casually as I could. I put the takeout container with half my sandwich from the Royal Oak in it, on the counter.

"Well, well, well," Esther drawled.

"What are you watching?" I asked.

"Oh, no, no. I'm the one asking the questions. Where the hell have you been?"

"Didn't you get my text?"

"Yes, but— Wait! You've been with that guy this whole time?" She gave me a disbelieving look.

"Yeah. We had a lazy morning then went for lunch," I said, as if I hung out with hot guys all the time.

"Toby, that's awesome!" she exclaimed. "Wait! He could have murdered you! I should have texted! I'm so sorry!"

"It's fine. He didn't murder me."

"Cute. I can see that — and thank God. Some friend I am."

"Esther, stop. You're the best. You would have known where to find the body."

She glared at me. I grinned.

"Anyway," I continued, "Alastair is... Well, he's all right."

My unrestrained look of happiness must have belied my casual words.

"Uh-huh. You look like you've just had the best sex of your life."

"Well..."

"Congratulations!" she said, jumping off the couch and running over to hug me.

"Calm down. Jeez." I hugged her back politely and tried not to get caught up in Esther's excitement. I didn't want to jinx things.

"So? What's the story? Are you dating him now?"

"I guess." I shrugged. *Yes. Yes, we were dating.*

"Cool beans," Lev said from the sofa, giving me a thumbs-up.

"When do I get to meet him?" Esther said, jumping up and down.

"Esther, come on. Do you really think he's ready for that?"

"Very funny. But I want to meet him after the two weeks' mark. Please?"

"We'll see. Maybe."

She frowned and put her hands on her hips. "What are you worried about?"

"I just...I don't want to ruin it."

"Letting him meet *me* will ruin your relationship?"

"No, no, no. That's not what I mean. It's just, I don't even know if it's a relationship." *Maybe the beginning of one?*

She stared at me with confusion.

"No comment. Now listen… I need to work on a couple of things this afternoon, but I can go to the library if you and Lev…"

"I'm going out," Lev said, standing up and throwing the remote to Esther. "You can use my room if you need some peace."

"Really? Thanks. That would be super helpful," I replied.

"Yeah, no worries."

Lev's room was plastered with pride stuff. They had a trans flag and a pride flag and a non-binary flag, which did a good job of covering most of the walls. There was a bulletin board full of news clippings. They had a rainbow comforter on their bed.

Everything was neatly put away and tucked in. A light-blue plush shark perched on their pillow, looking like it was guarding their sleeping spot.

The desk was tidy and neat, so I put my laptop on it and sat in the ergonomic, cushioned desk chair. My phoned dinged.

I pulled it out to look and saw it was a text from Alastair. My heart leaped in a way that would have embarrassed me if anyone else had known of it.

You forgot your gloves. Smiley face.

I replied back.

sorry Pouty face.

I'll keep them safe for you. Wait! Do you need them?

no, no
got more here
thank u

I'll stop bothering you. Smiley face. Except, if you're off tomorrow, did you want to have supper with me?

have a class until five-thirty.

After that?

sure.

I'll pick you up from school?

i want to change.

I gave him Esther's address and arranged a time. Were we dating then? It might be too early to call it a relationship, but it was more than a hookup if we were going out to dinner.

I got to work with a smile on my face and the start of a boner in my pants. Weird how just texting the guy could get me worked up. Anyway, the schoolwork I had to do took care of that.

Lev's room was quiet and organized, but it was their space, not mine. I needed to get off my ass and try to find a proper living arrangement. Esther and I had a good thing going, but if I stayed here longer than a week or so, things would go downhill. I didn't want to risk it.

Chapter Twelve

Safe Haven

Alastair and I spent the next few weeks dancing around the idea of a relationship and getting to know each other, and I tried to find a room to rent in a not-so-sketchy part of the city that was affordable and not far from my job at Maverick Molly's.

Alastair had three brothers and two sisters, and he was the second youngest. His oldest sister was married and an accountant in London, England. His other sister ran a bakery in Toronto with her two girlfriends/partners. His older brother was an artist, supposedly straight, and teaching high school in Ottawa, while his younger brother was currently touring Europe with his band. I didn't recognize the name of the group, and Alastair said they weren't well known yet but were hoping the tour would help.

They were having a blast, last he'd heard, staying in hostels and cheap Airbnb's and enjoying being young. He had a feeling his brother was bi or pan, but they'd never talked about it. There was quite a difference in their ages. His baby brother had just turned nineteen.

I pointed out that that was only a year younger than me, which made Alastair curse and stutter and caused me to grin at his awkwardness.

Alastair had come out to his family at the age of sixteen. His mother and siblings had been supportive, but his dad had needed a little time. They were good now, though.

We hadn't gone to the Bordello yet, and I was itching to try it.

Alastair was a solicitous lover, but I was getting tired of being treated with kid gloves, and I craved something more. I appreciated that Alastair thought of me as delicate and feminine—the part of me that felt that way appreciated the tenderness and care. But I was tough under this pliable exterior, and I wanted Alastair to wreck me.

I was managing to get my schoolwork done, despite work and sexing Alastair, so that was a triumph. The last thing I wanted to do was compromise my studies because of really good sex and a new boyfriend.

As far as I knew, we were being exclusive. We hadn't said anything definitive, but I figured after the debacle with the boy toy at Molly's he hadn't tried to hook up with anyone else. I'd slept over at his place often, because by the time I finished work it was already midnight or one, and even later if we got up to anything, which we often did.

It also meant I didn't have to crash at Esther's. Neither she nor her roommates had given me a deadline to be out, but I felt like a moocher, and I hated that.

So, when I had time, I scoured the internet for a room to rent. I had just seen the most depressing fucking pad in a basement apartment in the Byward

Market that cost more than I wanted to pay but was cheaper than anything I'd found so far. And the guy renting it out had seemed okay—not a serial killer or a homophobic A-hole. I didn't think so, anyway. I'd have to take my chances.

I was supposed to meet Alastair at the Starbucks in Old Ottawa South and I was late. By the time I got there, he was sitting at a table all by himself, nursing what was probably a Tall Macchiato, when I arrived.

"Hiya," I said, grabbing the seat opposite. "Sorry I'm late."

"Don't worry about it," he said with a smile. "I've been people watching."

"You mean eavesdropping?"

"It passes the time." He narrowed his eyes. "You look exhausted."

"Yeah. What with work and school and homework…and you, it's a lot."

"Me?"

I shrugged. "You're distracting."

"I am?

"Yeah."

I didn't know if it was because I was so tired or so demoralized from looking at rooms for rent that didn't measure up, but I gave him a frank look. "I'm having lots of fun, but I need to know if this thing with you is worth my time."

He laughed, but then saw the sober look on my face.

"Oh, you're serious," he said, sitting up straighter.

I held his gaze and tried to see into his soul. It didn't work, so I thought words would be better. "Are we being exclusive? I mean, I am."

Alastair didn't say anything.

Ah fuck.

"I really need to know," I said. "Are you my boyfriend, or my sugar daddy, or my Dom or what?" I said, looking at the table. "I have no fucking idea."

He blinked, looking like a confused rabbit. Then he reached for my hand. I hesitated, but I gave it to him. "Toby, I'd honestly like to be all those things."

His words and the hand-holding tipped my already precarious emotions over the edge. I blinked back tears as I gazed at him, then cursed with embarrassment and took my hand away.

"Sorry. I'm sorry," I babbled, wiping at my face.

He furrowed his forehead with concern. "Hey. What's going on?"

"Nothing. I'm just— I'm trying to find a room to rent. And I just saw an apartment that would be perfect, if the other guy wasn't a total stranger and the room was bigger than a postage stamp and not underground." I took a deep breath. "I can't stay at Esther's forever."

I put my head in my hands and closed my eyes.

"Has Esther asked you to leave?" Alastair asked.

"Not yet," I said, "But I think she's starting to wonder when I'm getting off her couch."

Alastair was silent. I opened my eyes to find him regarding me with serious contemplation.

"What?" I asked.

"You know, I have a spare room," he said.

For a long moment I wondered why he was bragging about his swanky house in Old Ottawa South when I was sitting here almost homeless. Then I clued in—and I felt dizzy.

"What?" I said.

He shrugged. "You could move in with me."

I stared at him. Had I heard him correctly?

"*What?*"

"Look, Toby. You need a room. You want to get out of this temporary situation, and you don't want to go back to your mom's, I take it."

"Right but—it can't be so simple."

"Why not?"

"Alastair," I said, putting a hand on his forearm and finally noticing his leather jacket. "Hey, is this new?"

"No, but I haven't worn it in a while."

"But it's so cold out. You must be freezing!"

He shrugged. I think it was his signature move.

"I wanted to look sexy."

"For me?" I said, fireworks exploding behind my eyes.

He gave me a look. "For everyone. Obviously."

I laughed.

"Alastair," I said. "Sweetheart— Can I call you that?"

"Yes, please?"

"Sweetheart, I just don't know if it's a good idea for me to move in with you when we've only known each other for three fucking weeks."

"You just said you were thinking about moving in with a total stranger."

"But I'm not *fucking* that guy!"

"I'm very glad to hear it."

I gave him a look. "Alastair, I can't move in with you."

"Why not? It's close to where you work."

"Yeah, but…what if it wrecks everything?"

His eyebrows pulled together. "What do you mean?"

I blinked. Was he seriously this dense?

"If we're living together, you're going to see me at my worst," I said.

"Bring it the fuck on."

I tried to stay angry, but it was impossible not to laugh. "You have no idea what you've started."

He smiled, like he was *super* happy about what he'd started.

"I'm going to see *you* at *your* worst, too," I pointed out.

"Well," Alastair said, sitting straighter and grinning with glee, "I am an absolute joy, so there's nothing to worry about."

My smile widened, but the relief I felt didn't completely erase the fact that this was probably a stupid idea.

"This is the stupidest idea," I said, staring into his eyes and grinning like a fool.

"Maybe...maybe not," he said, covering my hand where it lay on the table with his own. "Let's find out."

* * * *

I thought Esther would be happy when I told her about our plan.

"What the fuck, Toby? You don't have to move in with Alastair! You can stay here for as long as you need to."

"I know I don't have to move in with him, Esther. But I want to."

Esther was in the kitchen making Kraft macaroni and cheese, and I was sitting on the sofa that I'd used for a bed for the past few weeks.

She gave me a steady look, to assess whether or not I'd lost my goddamned mind. "Have you lost your goddamned mind?"

"Look… It makes sense. It was his idea."

"But it's too early! Are you sure you want to risk your relationship with Alastair by moving in together?"

"What other choice do I have? You know what rent is in this city. Alastair said I could have the room for a couple of hundred a month. That's a huge savings. And he lives in Old Ottawa South, for fuck's sake."

"But you can stay here until you find a place, Toby."

"I'm not staying on your couch anymore. It's too much of a disruption for you, and it's not much fun for *me*."

Shit. I hadn't meant to say that.

She looked devastated all of a sudden. "Wow. I'm sorry we weren't making things nice for you."

"Esther, I know you guys were doing your best. I'm so grateful for the safe haven. You have no idea how much. But…I like Alastair, and his house is lovely. I know it's a risk, and you can believe that I've told him how ridiculous this whole idea is. But it solves two problems, y'know?"

"Does it?"

"It's a place for me to live that's warm and comfortable and cheap, and it means Alastair and I can fuck in two different rooms, and I don't have to go home to my mom's at night." I grinned cheerily.

"Oh, for fuck's sake. You always did think with your dick, Toby."

"That's a fucking lie, Esther."

She laughed, then, and rolled her eyes. "Fine. Move in with your hot boyfriend. See if I care."

"Oh, come on. Won't it be nice not to have a fourth person in the way all the time?"

She gave a pout. "But it's *you*, Toby! I'll miss you. You're awesome."

"Well, hopefully Alastair feels the same way."

"Just know you can come back if things get too intense. And even if everything's going great, I want to see you now and then." She looked at me funny. "Wait! Why are you looking at me that way?"

"What way?"

"Like a unicorn on happy pills."

"Um, because I need to ask you a favor," I said, smiling even more sweetly.

She put her hands on her hips and raised her eyebrows. "Another one?"

"Can you help me move out of my mom's? You know she's gonna be pissed that I'm taking off, and she's already mad that I haven't been back there for so long."

"I will, under one condition."

My smile faded somewhat. "Which is?"

"That you get Alastair to help, too. I want to meet him," she stated.

My happy expression vanished. *No, no, no.*

"But…Esther! Then he'll see what my mom's like."

"So? Maybe that's a good idea."

Oh no. When Esther got like this, there was no changing her mind.

"It's fucking embarrassing!" I protested.

"Everyone has skeletons in their closet."

"*And*, he's already helping me by letting me move in!" I pointed out.

"That's the deal," Esther said, her voice firm. "Take it or leave it, Toby."

"Fine," I said as I caved. "For fuck's sake. We'll do it when she's at work. Hopefully she's on the same schedule."

* * * *

Alastair was more than happy to help me move out of my mom's place. The guy was a fucking trooper and seemed to be gaga for me at the moment. I hoped it would last after he'd lived with me for a month. I had my doubts. I still thought this whole thing would end in disaster, but I didn't have a lot of options in terms of living arrangements, and sharing space with the hot guy I currently couldn't get enough of seemed at least entertaining. If we didn't end up hating each other, it would be a fucking miracle. But maybe there was room in my life for some divine intervention.

Alastair still hadn't taken me to the Bordello, and I was becoming more and more impatient. I knew the cost wasn't an issue, since Alastair had entertained multiple men there in the past, and Sebastian and Jacob would give us a discounted rate—I'd already inquired. I wasn't exactly sure what the issue was.

I had arranged with Esther and Alastair to go get my stuff on Tuesday, because that was when my mom worked all day at the salon. That was, if her schedule hadn't changed. I still had my key, so there wouldn't be a problem getting in. None of the furniture in my room actually belonged to me, which my mother had pointed out on numerous occasions, and it was too bulky to worry about, anyway. I'd empty my drawers into garbage bags or boxes and take it all to Alastair's. It wouldn't take long, because there honestly wasn't much. I'd leave the shit I didn't care about, and she could do what she wanted with it. We'd be quick and gone before she even knew I'd been there.

But I was dreading it.

The weekend before that, I had a rare Saturday night off. Alastair suggested a movie, but I begged him to take me to the Bordello.

I gave him my most winning smile. "As of an hour ago, it hadn't been booked. I texted Sebastian."

"I don't know," he said, looking worried. "Are you sure?"

"Yes. Oh, my fucking God, Alastair, I've been begging you for three weeks." I narrowed my eyes. "Why don't you want to take me?"

Alastair shook his head. "I do want to. It's only…" He looked everywhere but at me.

"What? What *is* it?"

He shrugged. "It's because…I like you so much."

"Okay?" I failed to see the problem.

He frowned. "I'm nervous about sharing that side of myself with you."

I took a deep breath because that was not what I'd expected.

"You do remember I work at Maverick Molly's?"

He seemed aghast. "Not in the Bordello, though. Right? *Right*?"

"For fuck's sake, it's a kink club, not a whorehouse. Jesus," I said. "But I've seen all the stuff. I know what goes on there. Mostly." *Do I? Do I really?*

"Really?"

"Hey, I watch porn. I'm not some little innocent girly-boy. I don't even think I'm vanilla, if you want to know the truth."

He gazed at me, then folded his arms across his chest and licked his lips.

"You watch porn?"

"Oh, for fuck's sake. Duh."

He searched my face. "What kinds of porn?"

I cleared my throat and looked at the floor. So we were going to have this conversation, were we?

"I'm extremely partial to looking at gigantic cocks, so it's mostly that. But lately" —I flashed my gaze to his then back to the floor— "I've been searching out a lot of kinky stuff."

"Huh," he said.

"Yeah, huh. And I like watching it."

He smiled. "Do you?"

I sauntered over to where he was sitting on the sofa.

"Maybe you should tell me about the things you like to do to your boy toys in the Bordello, and I can tell you if I'm interested," I said, straddling his lap and kissing him on the corner of his lips. "Please do go into detail."

He went beet red and squirmed under me, swelling beneath his trousers.

"Suddenly shy, Mr. Kenney? My, my, I wonder what you like to *do* to those boys."

"Oh fuck," he sighed, staring at the ceiling.

Chapter Thirteen

Negotiations

"Fine."

I sat up. "'Fine' you'll tell me, or 'fine' you'll show me?"

"I realize that it's a losing game to deny you."

I grinned. "Yup."

"So we can go, if it's still available."

I reached for my phone but Alastair stopped me.

"But...I'm going to answer your question."

"The one about..."

"The one about what I like to do with my"—he looked me over—"boy toys, so you can figure out if you like the sound of it or not." He took my hands in his and laced our fingers together. "If you must know, I like to put my boys on the spanking bench as an introduction to the space."

I like to put my boys on the spanking bench. The sentence reverberated in my brain, lit up in neon.

His breathing sped up and his gaze met mine with the most adorable expression of reticence.

"The what-now?" I whispered, eyes wide with desire at the words he'd spoken.

Alastair smiled. "The spanking bench. Don't you know what that is?"

"Well, I...I guess I can" — I swallowed — "extrapolate."

Alastair smiled, his dimple showing. "That's a big word."

I stared at him, blinking and letting the waves of lust crash over me. "I'm a big boy," I whispered.

I didn't feel very big right then. I felt small and safe and cared for. It was heady and everything I wanted. Well, maybe not everything.

"You could put me on the spanking bench," I said, gazing at Alastair's chest as I toyed with the buttons on his shirt.

"Could I?"

"Yes," I said. "I would like to try that."

My cheeks heated, and I glanced up to see how Alastair was reacting. He looked like he wanted to rip my clothes off right then, the way his eyes were drilling me.

"Toby, I-I—" he stuttered, but I already had my phone out, and I was calling Sebastian.

Alastair's lips parted as he watched me. I wriggled to get more comfortable, and he groaned and closed his eyes. I think he cursed.

"Sebastian, hi. I'm calling to find out if the Bordello is still available this evening?"

"Hi, Toby. You can have it from eight to ten."

I looked at Alastair. "It's available from eight to ten."

He nodded. "Book it."

"Sebastian, we'd like—"

"I heard him. See you at eight, Toby."

"Thanks."

I ended the call and slid my phone back into my jeans pocket.

"We should talk about limits," Alastair said, putting his hands on my hips and keeping me still.

"Okay. Sounds reasonable."

"Reasonable?"

"I was gonna say 'fuck yeah!', but I'm trying to act like an adult, so you'll realize I am one and do all kinds of very *adult* things with me."

He rolled his eyes.

"So your boy toy is…strapped to the spanking bench. Then what?"

He raised his eyebrows. "Don't you want to know what position I'd have them in?"

"Yes, please."

This might be hotter than actually doing it. Wait! No, it wasn't. But it was very fucking hot sitting there discussing bondage and kink with Alastair fucking Kenney.

His now-sedate gaze drifted over me. He'd gotten himself back under control somehow, while I was a taut wire of expectation.

"Can we stop pretending I'm talking about someone else and just admit I'm thinking of you?"

I took a sudden breath, then let it out. "Yes."

"Okay, then. I'd want you on the bench on your belly," he said, placing his hand flat against my lower half. "Facing down."

I whimpered and leaned in to his touch.

"Yeah," he murmured. "God, you'd look so pretty being good for me."

I whimpered. Then I said, "Duh," but it came out like a sigh.

His breath hitched. "Fuck. You'll need a safeword. And we haven't talked about limits. My hard limits are blood play, scat and body modification. What are yours?"

I blinked. "Body modifications! What the *fuck*? Blood play?" My voice had gone up two octaves.

He let go of my hands. "See? You have literally no idea what you're getting into."

"Wait! You said those are your hard limits, so things you *don't* want to do." I took a breath. "I don't want to do those things, either."

"I didn't think so."

"I'm a little scared to ask what your *soft* limits are," I said.

He smiled, and it was an evil 'I know so many kinky things you haven't even thought of yet' smile.

But I kind of liked it. Scratch that. I *definitely* liked it.

"Well, Toby, my soft limits are piss play—"

My eyes widened and so did his smile.

He continued, "—flogging, paddling or whipping—"

I frowned.

"—*past* the point of leaving visible marks."

I nodded, appeased.

"—and *extreme* ass play."

"Hmm," I said. "What counts as 'extreme' ass play?"

He smiled, as if he were asked that question every day. "You know. Gigantic toys, gaping, that kind of thing. I'm not into that."

"Okay, fair. I don't think I am, either."

He raised an eyebrow, but I charged ahead.

"But what about *non-extreme* ass play? Like 'just the right amount of fun' ass play?"

"Oh, sweetheart. That's one of my specialties."

"Fuck me," I whispered.

* * * *

We could hardly keep our hands off each other in the Uber.

I had made use of Alastair's washer and dryer to clean the clothes I'd brought with me to Esther's, but I didn't have much. I wore my black ripped jeans, and a gray button-up that was too small for Alastair but fit me pretty well. I'd put on black eyeliner and gelled my hair.

He wore a pair of relaxed straight-legged jeans that showed off his angles and curves in a subtle but effective way and a white button-down under his wool coat. Going to Maverick Molly's as anything but an employee was a bizarre experience. I hung up my jacket and headed into the games room with a swagger before Alastair had a chance to follow me.

The patrons regarded me with curiosity. I didn't think they recognized me out of 'uniform'. However, you could always count on Robin.

"Toby, what the fuck? What are you doing here? You're not on tonight..."

"Shhh, I'm here with my boyfriend," I stated as I passed by and headed for the bar. His chin dropped, and I noticed several of my regular customers tracking my ass in the snug jeans.

Sebastian stood at the bar, in the clothes of a Victorian gentleman, his blond hair in a ponytail, tapping the screen of the tablet used for orders and payments. He looked up as I approached.

"Well, hello! You don't work until Monday, Toby."

"Knock it off. We both know why I'm here," I said.

A familiar pair of hands landed on my shoulders.

"Please excuse Mr. Dunn's rudeness," Alastair said benignly from behind me. "He's very excited."

"Hello, Mr. Kenney," Sebastian said to Alastair. "Mr. Dunn." He gazed at me with amusement.

"Hello, Sebastian," Alastair said. "Good crowd tonight."

"Saturdays never disappoint."

"I was surprised the Bordello was free," Alastair said.

"Were you?" Sebastian glanced at me, then met Alastair's gaze. "You've reserved it at the last minute before."

"Oh, good one," I said to Sebastian, turning to throw a smug glance at Alastair. "He got you there."

Alastair looked chastened, but he smiled and tipped his head to Sebastian. "Yes, he did."

"I saw that you filled out and signed the electronic consent forms, Mr. Dunn. So you're aware that there's video surveillance that will only ever be accessed if there is a legal complaint resulting from your use of the Bordello?"

"Yeppers. I guess that means you and Jacob can't watch the footage for kicks?"

"Yes. It's a darn shame, but, you know…ethics and all that." Sebastian grinned. "Of course, I already have Mr. Kenney's forms on file."

"Of course, you do," I muttered. "Hmm. How *long* have you had them?"

"I'm afraid I can't tell you that," Sebastian said with a conspiratorial glance at Alastair.

"Bummer."

"Knock it off," Alastair told me.

Sebastian smiled.

"Don't forget. You promised me twenty percent off the regular rate," I said.

"Huh. Did I actually?"

"Yes, you did *actually*."

"I'll get the key."

"Thank you, Sebastian," Alastair said. "You can give it to Mr. Dunn."

Sebastian got it from its place under the bar and handed it to me. The weight of the rusted antique keychain felt different in my palm.

"You've got your hands full with this one," Sebastian said to Alastair.

"Don't I know it," Alastair muttered.

"Hey, what's that supposed to mean?" I said, but Alastair took my hand and pulled me along like I was five years old and, hell, I did not hate it.

He led me out of the games room and down the hall, past the kitchens and along the familiar corridor to the door of the Bordello. The surroundings were familiar, but my role was so different.

I enjoyed being a server at Molly's. It let me fulfill my fluid gender identity and tendency to exhibitionism in a way that was safe and appreciated. But walking down the hall with Alastair as his — well, as his boy toy, I supposed — felt very different.

"Last chance to back out," Alastair said as we stopped in front of the door.

I rolled my eyes and slipped the key into the lock, twisting the handle to push the door open. We stepped inside, and Alastair stretched to pull the cord of the antique floor lamp by the entrance.

The Bordello was a fantasy — a pretend space that wanted to be a Victorian parlor, dungeon and school room all in one. Walking into it was like entering another dimension. My gaze flitted from object to object as Alastair shut the door and locked it. He held his hand out for the key, and I gave it to him. He hung it on the hook by the door.

A notice on the wall stated what we already knew and had signed off on, that the room was monitored by CCTV cameras at all times, but that the footage would only be reviewed if an issue was encountered. A list of rules followed that emphasized consent at all times, no high-risk activities, such as breath or blood play or unhygienic play involving bodily fluids beyond semen.

I felt like a kid at Disneyland for the first time— although I'd never actually been to Disneyland. But I didn't really care, because this was better. Watching my boyfriend move about the large space as if he owned it, checking things over and no doubt coming up with ideas of what to do to me, made my cock hard and my brain explode.

"Okay," I said, taking a deep breath and letting it out. "Fuck."

To the left of us stood an antique settee, similar to the one in the gaming parlor, but larger and more ornate. Alastair strode to it and stopped. He touched the polished wood frame, turned to me and smiled, showing his dimple. Then his expression changed into something sterner, in a transformation that sent bolts of lightning through my insides as he tilted his head.

"Pardon?" he said. "A good boy doesn't use curse words."

His voice had gone low, and his expectations were clear.

My smile vanished as a tingle rode down my spine then back up.

"I'm sorry, Sir," I whispered, blinking like a kid caught with his hand in the cookie jar. "I would like to thank you for bringing me to this amazing and wonderful den of depravity where we can explore some seriously kinky and fun vibes...finally. Sir."

Alastair threw his head back and laughed. It might not have been extremely Dom-like, but it was very Alastair-like, and my smile returned. Despite my eagerness to experience all of *this*, I was nervous, and Alastair's relaxed and confident attitude was definitely helping.

He stared at the low couch, stroking the frame with his long fingers. "I want you to stand by the settee, Toby."

My knees wobbled as I made my way over. It was only a few feet, but it felt like a mile. I stood there, biting my tongue because it wanted to be a smart-ass, but something told me that wasn't a good idea.

"Good boy," Alastair said.

I smiled. He didn't smile back.

"I want you to look around this room and tell me what you see."

"Oh," I said. I'd expected him to tell me to kneel or to get on all fours and suck him off or something. I'd been watching all the kinky gay porn I could find over the last couple of weeks, and in none of them did the Dom make the sub look around the room and tell him about it. "Okay."

But I started talking.

"So, the floor is wood, dark wood. And there's a settee." I sidelined a glance at Alastair, whose lips twitched.

"Go on."

"And there's a rack of clothes...like, old-fashioned stuff."

"Victorian and Edwardian. Yes."

"And there's a vanity with a mirror and a cushioned stool."

I wondered why that was here—in case a Dom wanted to threaten a sub with a makeover? I would be so lucky!

I shifted my gaze and took a breath. "There's a bed? Kind of a platform, really, with what looks like a leather mattress?"

"It's vinyl. Easy to clean."

"Ah. Anyway, it's got um...lots of places to...attach someone."

"Mmm. Very practical," Alastair murmured, his voice like velvet. "What's on the other side of the bed, against the wall, Toby?"

"Well, that's a...that's a St. Someone's cross. I can't remember the saint," I mumbled.

I glanced at Alastair. He was struggling not to laugh. "St. Andrew. A St. Andrew's cross."

"Yeah. That. Which looks pretty crazy but also kind of fun."

"*Fun*. Interesting."

"And there's a...spanking bench? Is that what that is?"

"Yes, Toby. That's a spanking bench."

"Yep. A spanking bench. For...spanking."

"For being spanked," Alastair corrected.

I side-eyed him. "That's what I meant, Sir."

"Good. Go on."

"There's what looks like a student's desk and a blackboard over there." I nodded toward the other side of the room. "And maybe a teacher's desk?"

"Yes. For teacher-student roleplay. Does that interest you at all?"

I swallowed. "Um…yeah."

"Perfect. Keep going. There's lots of stuff here. Good thing it's a large space."

"I don't know what that thing is. It's made of wood. It's triangle-shaped…"

"It's a Berkeley Horse."

"Oh," I said. "It doesn't look like a horse. Sir."

"It's not that kind of a horse."

"Oh. Beg pardon, Sir. I barely know what I'm doing or saying."

My breathing rate had increased as my brain had absorbed my surroundings and Alastair had explained them.

"Well, it's a good thing I know exactly what I am doing and saying," Alastair said, stepping close to me from behind. "Isn't it?"

"Y-yes. Yes, Sir," I breathed, feeling the energy of his closeness and also something suspiciously hard poking me from behind.

"Put your hands on your head."

I did as he'd asked and waited.

Alastair's hands appeared from behind me, and he undid the button on my fly then unzipped it with his competent fingers as I tried to breathe properly.

He reached into my jeans and cupped the lace that stretched over my swelling cock. "So pretty."

I moaned and shifted into his touch.

"Easy, there. Hmm, already so hard."

I moaned, going nuts with having to keep my hands on my head and Alastair fondling my bits through the panties.

He took his hand away and backed up. "Settle down, boy. We're just getting started."

I whimpered, and Alastair laughed.

"Turn around, and stay still. Keep your hands up."

I obeyed, watching as he went over to the clothes rack. He sorted through the items on the hangars, taking things off and folding them over his arm — white cotton and lace, red and black satin, robes in all kinds of fabrics. We were going to play dress-up.

There was a wooden chest by the settee. Alastair opened one drawer after another, pulling items out and placing them on the velvet couch.

There was a pair of black stockings, a black leather corset with buckles and straps, white lace panties — designed for men like the ones I bought myself, with an ample pouch in the front — a pair of off-white bloomers that looked shorter and more delicate than the ones I was used to, and a royal blue silk kimono like the black one Robin owned, but embellished with butterflies instead of dragons.

"Strip."

I blinked, wondering if I was allowed to say anything or if he still wanted me to be quiet. I lifted my hand tentatively.

"Yes?" he asked.

"Are you going to dress me up, Sir?" My voice sounded rough and soft at the same time.

"Would you like that, Toby? It doesn't matter, because I'm doing it regardless."

"Yes, Sir. Are you going to — undress me, like, after?" I said, gazing at the loaded settee.

"Maybe. Or maybe I'm going to punish you while you're wearing those pretty things," he said, as he bent to remove his shoes and socks.

I swallowed. Nodded. *Fuck.*

My trembling fingers went to the buttons of my shirt. "What am I being punished for, exactly, Sir?"

Alastair walked toward me as he rolled up the sleeves of his shirt. "For being criminally beautiful."

"But…there aren't any laws against being beautiful, Sir. And…" I laughed, gazing down at myself. "I'm really not."

"There should be," he said. "And don't contradict me."

I felt dizzy and full of desire as I stared at him and finished with my buttons. I shrugged the shirt off and lifted my chin.

"No more questions. Just do what I say."

"Yes, Sir."

"And, Toby?"

"Yes, Sir?"

"You are stunningly gorgeous. If you don't start thinking of yourself that way, you're going to spend a lot of time over my lap."

Oh. *Oh!* Well, then. Okay. I swallowed hard.

"Yes, Sir."

I got the rest of my things off and stood before Alastair, completely buck-fuck-naked, which seemed strange in this mock-up of a fancy Victorian parlor, especially since Alastair stood there looking at me, his gaze caressing me in my nudity.

I waited, trying to control my breathing and temper my embarrassment, as my cock stood to attention like it was under his command and eager to perform.

Metal buckles rattled as Alastair picked up the corset. It wasn't exactly Victorian but it had a steampunk vibe to it.

"Hands on your head," Alastair said.

I did as I was told, gazing at him with blatant desire. Fuck, this was so exciting already and we'd barely done anything. I couldn't help imagining Jacob and Sebastian and my co-workers in the gaming parlor where it was business as usual, while I was here about to get sexed up and disciplined by my dream of a boyfriend, who had stopped bringing casual fuckboys to here so he could be with me.

"Eyes down."

"Yes, Sir," I whispered as I obeyed.

"Good girl," Alastair said, the unexpected designation landing like a swat with a riding crop.

I gasped, as the word bounced around in my head and made my insides liquefy with pleasure. I'd had no idea that being called 'girl' in a situation like this would affect me so strongly, but it did.

I wasn't picky about pronouns, and I hadn't changed my name. Toby was a decently androgynous name and I liked it. As long as nobody but my mom called me Tobias, I was fine with having it on my identification cards. Words didn't define me and couldn't possibly express everything about me.

On the other hand, I'd had no idea that one word used in this context by a man I was intensely hot and possibly starting to feel deeper things for would be this mind-blowing.

I fought a smile as Alastair walked around me with the casualness of a man in total control. The touch of cold leather on my skin made me gasp as Alastair wrapped the corset around my middle.

"A little chilly?" Alastair whispered, close to my ear, as he fastened the straps and buckles that ran all along the front of it, pressing into me from behind.

I didn't say anything in reply, because I was trying to focus on breathing. Watching Alastair's fingers at work, securing each buckle so that the corset hugged me tight, was a religious experience. I could tell from the steel-like pressure against the top of my ass crack that I wasn't the only one who was really into this already. I swallowed the smart-ass sexy comment I wanted to make and channeled my submissive side, which seemed to emerge naturally in this space under the skilled handling of Mr. Alastair Kenney.

Alastair groaned. "You. Look. Edible."

I am edible. You can totally eat me.

The straight edge of the corset crossed my chest just below my nipples and shoved them upward in an entrancing way.

"Yes, Sir."

Alastair walked to the settee and picked up the lacy panties. He returned to me and knelt.

"Lift your foot," he said, as he glanced up. "You can use my head to steady yourself."

I was honestly happy to be allowed to touch him. I rested a hand on his curls to balance as I lifted one foot then the other. Alastair slid the white panties up my legs and tucked my balls and swelling cock into them as I tried, unsuccessfully, not to moan.

Next, he drew a stocking up each leg and attached it to the garter straps that hung from the corset. Then he helped me into the delicate little bloomers. When he'd finished, he stood and admired his handiwork.

"Oh, fuck, Toby," Alastair breathed, pursing his lips in a way that made me wonder if I was about to get that spanking.

Chapter Fourteen

Shenanigans

In his faded jeans, with his shirt untucked and half unbuttoned, the sleeves rolled to his elbows, Alastair looked hotter than I'd even imagined when I'd pictured him here with one of his boy toys.

Being in a formal position of dominance brought out a fascinating and arousing confidence and competence in Alastair that I ate up. He seemed at home, with me at his service in my lacy panties and corset. I'm sure his fuckboys had appreciated it, too, but I knew by now how sweet Alastair could be, how vulnerable and kind and thoughtful he genuinely was. Still, there was something absolutely irresistible about the way he assumed control and went about the business of dominance in a singularly casual and pragmatic way.

I realized I was staring at him in a dreamy way when he cocked his head and said, "What?"

"You're...you're more at home here than I expected, Sir."

"Meaning?"

"You know what you're doing."

Alastair only smiled and brought me the kimono.

"You can lower your arms," he said.

He helped me into the robe and tied the belt in a casual knot.

"There," he said, and stepped back.

I stood there, feeling beautiful and outrageously feminine in my finery.

"Toby, you look totally fuckable," Alastair said, eyeing me up and down. "I wish we had your little brown shoes." He sighed with regret. "Arrange yourself on the settee, please. Look seductive."

I tried to be graceful as I did my best to lounge in an alluring way on the velvet cushions of the settee.

"With your permission, I'd like to take some photos," Alastair said.

"Uh...I'm not sure I'm comfortable with that, Sir," I said, hating to disappoint him. But it was one of the rules I had and maybe I should have put that in my hard limits. I never let anyone take photos of me without my clothes on—or with very minimal clothes on. Basically, in sexual situations. Definitely not in *this* room.

"All right. Thank you for telling me," he said. "Can we pretend?"

"Yes, of course, Sir," I said.

"Thank you. Just pose for me. That's all."

Alastair stepped forward to arrange the folds of the kimono. Then he stepped back and stood with his arms crossed as my heart beat frantically and my cock bubbled with anticipation.

He'd barely touched me, and I was dripping like a leaky faucet.

"Mmm, that's nice. Put your chin in your hand. Yes, like that. Perfect."

I did my best to model for him, despite the fact that I was a touch away from an orgasm. I smiled and primped and tried to look saucy. Alastair egged me on with encouraging words.

"Okay. Now get on all fours," he said, tapping his chin with a finger.

I did as he'd asked, going up on the cushions and posing like a good puppy, as if we really were engaged in a photo shoot. Alastair stopped talking and examined me with a frown.

"Stay still," he said, his voice rough.

I gazed down at the velvet cushions as Alastair moved forward. They sank beneath his weight. The warmth of Alastair's hand landed softly on my behind as he inhaled a shaky breath.

"Fuck, you're beautiful," he said as he drifted his palm over my rear end. He shoved the fabric of the kimono up and over, so that my ass in the white bloomers and garters was there for his pleasure. He gathered the material of the ornate robe in one hand and held it at my waist then pushed the elastic edges of the bloomers up. Then there were fingers running along the garters, touching the skin of my thighs and pushing up under the edges of my panties.

"Fuck, fuck, fuck," Alastair muttered, as he examined me. "So fucking soft. How are you so goddamn soft?"

I couldn't answer. I was beyond making words.

"You're as soft as a girl, Toby, and just as pretty. But you've got this," he murmured, as he slipped his fingers around the front to stroke my balls and up the bottom of my cock. I was hard as a rock, and the panties were wet with my lust.

I thrust against his hand, moaning like the desperate slut I was. I shuddered and whimpered as he touched me.

"So very pretty, baby...just for me."

I gasped and lowered my chest to the cushions, so that my ass was in the air. He could have it.

"Good girl," he said, and slapped me with his other hand.

I cried out in surprise and pleasure, and he did it again, his palm landing against my buttock over the thin white cotton and silk with a satisfying thwack.

"Oh fuck," I said, unable to stop myself. "I'm sorry, Sir," I whispered.

"Such language from something so pretty and dainty," he murmured, stroking my cock with the lightest pressure — a deliberate tease. "I should punish you properly for that."

He withdrew his hand and stood. He came around in front of me and urged me to my knees, holding my hand to help me. Then he sat down on the settee and pulled my upper half across his lap, and I knew what he was going to do.

My eyes went wide as he settled me, adjusting my body so that I was in the position he wanted. Something about being manhandled sent a spike of desire through me, and as my trapped cock bumped his thigh, I thought I might die. I made a desperate sound.

"Good boy, Toby. Just stay there. That's all you have to do. Oh, and don't come. It's not allowed. Only when I say."

I made a choking sound.

"I know, it's going to be difficult to control yourself. But good boys and girls wait until their master gives them permission."

"Yes, Sir," I whispered, staring at the imperfections in the velvet as Alastair stroked his palm over the panties. "Yes…Master," I murmured, just to see how it felt.

"Sir will do just fine, Toby."

I could feel his cock, hard as hell under the soft material of his jeans.

"Yes, Sir." I pressed my forehead against the cushions, overwhelmed. The physical sensations were one thing, but the mental mindfuck of bending over another man's lap for a spanking was something else. It was exhilarating and terrifying and embarrassing and humiliating all at once.

"I'm going to spank this pretty bottom now."

I nodded, unable to speak.

"Good boy. My pretty, pretty boy," he said, and I squirmed, pressing my cock into his thigh as the first spank came. The shock of it, the sound of it, startled me almost as much as the stab of pleasure that accompanied the pain. I gasped and cursed behind clenched teeth.

He went back and forth between each buttock, laying his hand on me like he owned me, and I fucking loved it. It hurt, sure, but not much. And it felt so…deliciously possessive and corrective and *yes, Daddy, I deserve a spanking because I've been a naughty, naughty boy* and I didn't even know where my mind was going.

He stopped and rested his hand as I tried to scramble my thoughts back together. I panted hard as the sting spread out and warmed me like a small, cozy fire. If this was how it felt overtop of cotton and silk, I wondered what it would be like on my bare skin.

"Have you ever been spanked before, Toby?" he asked suddenly. I felt like we'd been over this, but I couldn't remember my name right now, let alone a previous conversation.

"Not like this."

"Explain."

It was hard to form a coherent thought, even more difficult to form words. But he'd asked me to elaborate.

I craned my neck to look at him. "You think nobody's given this ass a quick slap? Of course, they have. But nothing like this." I swallowed thickly and my cock throbbed. "I've never been spanked over anyone's lap like I was a—"

"A what?"

"A...a bad boy. A naughty boy."

Alastair huffed a laugh.

"Even when you were a kid?"

"Nope. Thank God, because if it felt like this it would have been really fucking embarrassing."

He laughed harder.

My breath hitched when he tugged the bloomers down, then slipped his fingers under the waistband of the panties and dragged them to my thighs, exposing my skin to the air.

"Oh fuck," I whispered.

"Not yet," he said. "You need to be spanked properly, Toby, so that you'll learn to watch your language. Such a pretty, sweet femme-boy shouldn't be cursing like a sailor all the time."

I hoped he was joking, but I ate it up like wanting to behave was my truest desire. I'd honestly do whatever he said if he kept treating me like this.

"Yes, Da— I mean, Yes, Sir."

"I beg your pardon?"

"Nothing, Sir," I said, my face on fire, making me way too hot all over.

"It sounded like you said something else."

"Nope."

"Hmm."

"I'm ready, Sir," I said, to distract him.

"We'll talk about that later. For now, I'm going to spank my sweet slut for cursing and being a brat."

Yes, yes, yes!

"Okay!" I squeaked.

He brought his hand down on my bare ass. I jerked, moaned then cursed, almost at the same time.

"Shit. Sorry. Oh fuck. Goddammit."

My face burned with embarrassment.

"I'm so sorry, Sir," I gasped.

He was laughing so hard the vibration went through me.

"It's okay. Well, it's not okay, but I understand that this is all very new for you."

"Thank you, Sir," I said, breathing hard and wondering when the next spank was coming.

"You have no idea how much I'm enjoying this."

"I think I do, Sir." I wiggled myself over where I could feel his cock jutting up against me.

"Fair. But it's not just that. It's not just physical."

"Yes, Sir."

He stroked the bare skin of my bottom.

"Ready for more?"

"I think so, Sir."

It turned out that I was not prepared for anything that happened next.

Alastair disciplined like a pro. He went harder than I'd expected, and it was an eye-opener. Gone was the easy, playful technique he'd used when I'd still had my bloomers on.

It hurt. It stung. It became a roar of pain and heat under my skin in a matter of seconds. I was beginning to regret my decision to submit, to be honest, but not enough to use my safeword. Because at the same time that I was suffering and my ass was burning and my skin was screaming, my heart was beating like a drum and my insides were gooey with emotion and lust and the joy of being *handled*.

I squirmed and tried to get away, thinking I had a chance, because Alastair Kenney was a nice guy. I forgot that in this room, Alastair Kenney was something else.

"Uh-uh. Stay still," he said, without an ounce of sympathy.

Dammit.

"Yes, Sir. I'll try." My voice was weak and shaky. The only part of me showing perseverance was my cock as it shoved at Alastair's thigh like a firebrand.

"You're doing great," Alastair purred, the kindness in his voice contrasting with his current treatment.

Yay me?

"Here, give me your hand."

I moved the arm that wasn't confined by Alastair's body and reached behind me.

Alastair wrapped his fingers around my wrist and bent my arm at the elbow so that it lay across my lower back, effectively keeping me in place. He kept me firmly trapped as he soothed my spanked cheeks with the palm of his hand, crooning soothing words. I dared to think it might be over.

But then he started again—slaps so hard I yelped and begged for leniency.

"Say your safeword if you want me to stop. Do you remember what it is?"

"Yes," I said, sounding so small and scared.

"Ready for more?"

"Oh, come on. It hurts!"

"It's supposed to. I thought you'd like it."

I took a breath. "I do. It's just…I'm scared. I don't know how much more I can take."

"All right. Thank you for being honest with me. We're almost done, anyway."

I felt relief at those words, but also a strange disappointment. My cock was hard and leaking, there was a fire in my belly and I liked being held so firmly. The only thing not happy about everything going on was my poor lily ass.

Alastair started spanking again, and I tried to take it. I struggled to be good, but I couldn't help squirming and begging. Then I realized I was crying—sniffling like a little kid, and I didn't know what had happened.

He rested his hand on my bottom.

"Toby? You okay?"

"Fine," I said. My voice trembled, and I couldn't stop snuffling.

"Are you crying?" He didn't sound shocked or upset, just curious.

"Maybe?" I admitted.

Yep, I was crying like a little baby over Alastair's lap. Again, I didn't hate it. But I kind of hated that I *didn't* hate it. What the hell was wrong with me?

And he laughed. He actually laughed, which made me sniffle harder.

"*You bastard,*" I mumbled.

"You can't talk to your Dom that way. Didn't anybody tell you?" he said.

"I'm sorry, Sir. It just…hurts. But…" *Sniffle.* "That's not why I'm crying."

"It isn't?"

"I don't think so. I think it's because…it's over?"

It was so strange, because I had struggled to get away and now all I wanted was to stay like this forever. I didn't understand it.

"Oh, honey," Alastair murmured, cupping my chin with the hand that wasn't spanking me anymore. "It's not over."

I blinked. *Sniffle.* "What?"

"This part is over, that's true," Alastair said, letting my wrist go so I could bring my arm around. "But there's a whole room of delights to explore."

I rubbed my face, feeling ridiculous and silly. Alastair helped me stand and placed me between his spread legs as he held both my hands in his. He gazed at me with concern.

"You okay?"

"Yeah. Are *you* okay?"

He blinked, then laughed. "You know, I don't know if a sub has ever asked me that before."

"Huh."

"Or cared, frankly," he admitted. "Do you know how stunning you are?"

"Even like this? With the tears and the snot?"

"Especially like this."

I squinted at him.

"That's kind of fucked up," I said.

"Oh, I know. I'm hoping we can be kind of fucked up together," he said, motioning me closer. "Let's get these off."

Alastair helped me out of my bloomers and stockings and peeled the panties the rest of the way off, leaving the corset and robe. Then he stood and took my hand, leading me to the vanity. The stool made a scraping sound on the wood floor as he pulled it farther out and laid the bloomers flat over it.

It felt strange to be only naked from the waist down.

"Sit."

I stared at the stool. I mean, thank God it had a cushion.

"I..."

"Yeah, it's gonna hurt. But I want you to do it."

I took a deep breath. "Yes, Sir."

"Good girl."

Well, that helped. I carefully sat my sore ass down, not without a wince and a whimper.

"Does it hurt?" he asked, sounding more curious than concerned. And kind of excited.

Beautiful, adorable, pervert.

"Yes."

He smiled. "Good. That will add to the experience."

The experience of what? Was he going to do my makeup?

He went to his knees in front of me.

"Oh," I said, staring at him and realizing again how fucking attractive he was, especially with flushed cheeks, his curls disheveled and that devilish goatee. He gazed at me for a moment, then placed his palms on my knees. He took a deep breath and slid his hands along my thighs until they landed at my waist where the corset hugged me close, eyeing my standing, leaking cock.

"Oh, fuck," I said. Then my eyes went wide. "Sorry, Sir. I'm sorry."

He didn't say anything. He was staring at my cock like he wanted it so bad it hurt.

"Toby?"

"Yes, Sir?"

"I'm going to suck your pretty cock."

Okay, then.

"Okay." It sounded like a sigh.

"But I want you to keep your eyes open and watch the mirror. Don't look away. I want you to see yourself come undone," he said, his voice low, measured and hypnotic. "Can you do that for me?"

"I think so, Sir," I said. I gripped the edge of the stool and my heart pounded.

"Good."

I stared straight ahead and watched myself in the gold-framed mirror. My cheeks were flushed, glistening from the tears, and my kohl-rimmed eyes were wide with sudden anticipation. I hadn't expected him to go down on me. The spanking had been strange and exciting and fucking painful, and my throbbing ass was a sexy reminder of it, but I didn't know what to think about *this*.

Alastair moved forward, sliding his head into my lap as I watched the reflection in the mirror. His tongue slid up the bottom of my cock and swiped the bubble of moisture from the tip, as my mouth opened on a gasp. Then he did it again.

I tried not to look down at the top of his head, but it was hard. Instead, I focused on the mirror. Watching the wide-eyed femme-boy in the reflection gave me a strange feeling of being simultaneously outside of my body and within it.

Alastair seemingly savored every curve and ridge of my penis with his tongue and lips and teeth, while I held onto the stool and my sanity for dear life, watching my responses in the mirror. The pain of my spanked bottom made the pleasure more nuanced and reminded me of my debasement. Alastair made sweet noises of pleasure as he sucked me, mingling with my gasps and moans to provide a scintillating soundtrack.

"Oh...God...Sir..." I moaned louder. "I'm close, Sir. I'm close."

He changed his pace and went back to the slow, soft teasing, driving me mad as I waited with my hands on the stool for him to give me permission to come.

It seemed to last forever. I walked a tightrope of desire as Alastair brought me to the brink and back a dozen times. I almost started crying again.

He must have noticed my distress, because he told me I could come, then swallowed me down and sucked like his life depended on getting me off right the fuck now.

I came hard and long, with embarrassing noises. When the shudders and gasps subsided, he pulled off, and caught me as I relaxed into a pile of goo and slack muscles.

C h a p t e r   F i f t e e n

Aftercare and All That

"Mmm," he said as he held me, kissing the side of my face with the utmost care and tenderness. "You taste good."

"You still have your clothes on, Sir." My voice sounded far away and wiped out.

"True."

"That doesn't seem fair," I said.

"Toby, nothing in this room is supposed to be 'fair'."

He had a point.

"Also, you didn't come," I said, with a pout.

"That's entirely true, although it was close at a couple of points."

"So," I said, taking a rejuvenating breath, "do you want me to suck you off while you call me nasty names? That's a Victorian kink thing, isn't it?"

He leaned back against the vanity, contemplating me, his eyes sparking interest.

"It's not necessary," he said. "We can stop now, or I can take care of myself."

I narrowed my eyes. Sure, I was tired and sore, and completely fucking sated. But I also wanted his dick down my throat.

I slid off the velvet stool, whimpering due to my smarting behind, and kneeled at his feet. In only the corset and kimono, I must have made a pretty picture as I gazed at him with my mouth open.

I gave a cheeky grin and summoned my best Oliver Twist impression.

"Please, Sir. Can I have some more?"

Alastair cursed and took a breath. His fingers went to his belt then his fly, working with tortuously measured movements. Finally, he offered his cock to me, leaning back against the vanity with a curve of his luscious lips.

"Come and get it," he breathed.

I braced my hands on his thick thighs, the denim of his faded jeans soft under my palms, and leaned forward. I stared at his cock, recalling all of our encounters, but realizing that we'd only ever breached the surface of what we could be together. Here, in this room of fantasies, Alastair had taken me somewhere I'd never been. I felt renewed and invigorated, even though I'd been treated with such strictness, and Alastair's implacable will as a Dominant was everything I'd hoped for.

As I used my extensive skills to show my appreciation, Alastair cupped my face and watched with half-lidded eyes, until he couldn't hold back anymore and came with a swallowed groan. He lost his precarious perch on the vanity and sank to the floor, taking me with him. I laughed and tried to keep his dick in my mouth, chasing all the remnants of his release with my tongue and lips as he sighed and muttered endearments.

"Jesus fucking Christ, Toby. I think I could die right now."

"Don't you dare. I need to rent that room from you."

He gazed at me and smiled. "You're moving in this week."

"For better or for worse," I said, then realized how that sounded. "Oh fuck, that's not what I meant. That sounds like—"

But he laughed, thank God.

"Fuck, I need a cigarette," I muttered.

"You need to quit for good," Alastair said. "You're going to get cancer."

I sighed. "I know."

"Come on," Alastair said. He tucked himself away and led me to the platform bed. "Here, lie down. I need to make sure you're okay."

I lay down with my head in his lap, pulling the kimono around me, even though the room was comfortably warm for a half-dressed, thoroughly debauched, femme-boy. Alastair stroked the sweat-damp hair from my forehead.

"Did you have fun?"

"Duh."

"Can you be more specific?"

"Well, the spanking was painful, but that was the point, right?"

"How so?"

"It hurt like fuck, as I'm sure you could tell..."

"Yes," he said, in a dreamy way that pissed me off but also made me happy.

"But at the same time, you doing that...the way you did...? I don't know. I felt...cared for? It was weird, but I guess I loved it...even though I kind of hated it at the same time." I glanced up at him. "Does that make any sense?"

"Sure. In the land of kink and discipline it does."

"The Land of Kink and Discipline. Is that where we are?" Somehow, Alastair had dimmed the lights. The rest of the room became shadows and vague outlines as I drifted in a state of pure relaxation and… contentment?

"Maybe Jacob should change the name of the club."

I laughed. "It doesn't have the same ring to it as Maverick Molly's. What time is it, anyway?"

Alastair looked at his watch. "Nine-thirty. We have the room until ten."

"Then I turn back into a pumpkin?"

"Your ass already looks like one."

"It better not be orange, Alastair. Jesus."

He laughed again, the sound of it adding to my happiness. He reached under the robe and placed his palm against the tender skin of my bottom, making me gasp as pain radiated out.

"Your skin is hot to the touch."

"Goddammit. How long is it going to feel like this?"

"Hmm, I don't know. A few days?"

I turned my head and gazed at him. "A few days? What the fuck, Alastair? You know I have work! And classes I have to sit through."

"Yes, and you'll remember what happened in this room."

I sighed. "You've ruined me."

"Oh, come on. It's not that bad."

"It's not the pain. I kind of like how it feels, to be honest," I said.

"Good."

"You've ruined me for vanilla sex."

"Oh, I hope that's not true, Toby. Vanilla sex with you is…it's wonderful. I don't want to give it up."

"Fine," I said. "We don't have to. But I want to come here again."

"I want to bring you."

Oh, thank God. Now that I'd had a little intro to the pleasures of this kinky world and Alastair as a Dom, I didn't want to leave it.

We lounged together on the bed, Alastair tracing the skin of my backside with a fingertip and saying soft things to me as my cock tried to get hard again and I almost fell asleep.

"Come on," he said, finally. "Up. We need to go home."

Home. Alastair's house was already starting to feel like home, which was equal parts weird, scary and wonderful. And I hadn't even fully moved in.

We tidied up and put the clothes I'd worn into the laundry bin. I was sad to get rid of the kimono and clutched it in my arms for a moment before adding it to the rest of the laundry.

Maybe I could swing a deal with Jacob and buy it.

Taking the key back to Sebastian was interesting. Alastair told me to do it, and I was still in submissive mode, I guess, because I didn't argue. I was sure my recent debasement was written all over my face, and Sebastian gave me a smug sort of look, but he was a professional, as always.

"Thank you, Mr. Dunn."

"I'll see you tomorrow."

"Sure."

"Do you think you can get someone to cover my shift on Tuesday?"

"Probably. I know Patrick's looking for more hours."

I nodded. "I'm…moving."

He smiled, his eyes going wide. "Finally getting out, huh?"

"Yep," I said.

The entire club knew I'd been desperate to move out of my mom's house.

"Toby's going to stay with me."

Alastair had come up behind me in that stealthy way he had. He put his arm over my shoulder and across my chest, pulling me snuggly against him in a way that felt both proprietary and comforting.

"I have an extra room, and we've been getting along, so…" Alastair shrugged.

"He can't keep his hands off me," I said.

"Clearly," Sebastian said, grinning. "I'm glad you've figured something out."

Alastair spun me around and took my hand, leading me out through the dwindling crowd in the parlor.

As we passed Robin, he mouthed the word 'slut'. I gave him a big grin and a thumbs-up. Then he rubbed his bottom and made an expression of pain, and I changed my thumbs-up to a middle finger salute.

His cackle was all I heard as we made our exit.

* * * *

Our Uber driver was remarkably talkative for the late hour. Alastair took pity on me and made small talk so I could stare out of the window as snow drifted down from the cloud-filled sky. When we got home, Alastair sat on the sofa and cuddled with me as I came down from the high. The heat of my ass and the throb of pain there kept me grounded in reality, and a sense of being in good hands pervaded me.

"That was," I said, glancing at his profile, "not exactly what I'd been expecting."

He glanced my way with a smile. "Me neither. I had bigger, more adventurous plans for you."

"What? Really?"

He nodded. "Yes. But once I got you decked out, all I wanted to do was put you over my knee."

"Huh. What were you going to do to me?"

"Well, I had plans for the spanking bench."

"Jesus. Is that worse than an over-the-knee spanking?"

He shrugged. "I don't know. I think over-the-knee is more humiliating and debasing personally, but some subs really get off on the bench and the whole objectification thing."

"I want to try the bench next time, if I have any say about it."

"Of course, you have a say about it," he said. "I want to make you happy, Toby. And expand your horizons."

"Good. Great."

"The nice thing about what we did tonight, though, is that"—he threw me a devilish look—"we don't actually *need* the Bordello for stuff like that, although the ambience is very sexy and cool. I can just as easily pull you across my knee at home."

I blinked at him. "Oh."

It was entirely possible that Alastair had an ulterior motive for asking me to move in with him, but I can't say I objected to it.

* * * *

Alastair dropped me off at Molly's for my shift on Monday, then went back to his place to clear some things out of the guest room, which would be my own space while we lived together. It still seemed kind of surreal, but I couldn't wait to get my things in there and clear the stuff I gave a fuck about out of my mom's place.

I'd texted her that I was just having fun and I'd be back soon, only to placate her. *All lies.* I didn't actually know why she cared so much. From all the things she'd said about me being a hassle and a mooch, you'd have thought she'd be happy I was gone. But I don't think my mom actually knew how to be happy.

I hated to think of the state the place would be in when we got there on Tuesday, since I was the only one who ever did any cleaning. Huh, maybe that was why she was mad. She'd lost her live-in maid service and errand runner.

I hadn't had a cigarette since Alastair had spanked my ass over his lap in the Bordello. I had thrown the rest of the pack in the trash bin outside the club. I was done with that, and now that I wasn't living in a home filled with someone else's second-hand smoke, I had an actual chance of kicking the habit. I was trying to be a good boy. For once I had an older person in my corner who actually cared about me, and I wanted to please him. And I actually didn't want to die of lung cancer like my mom probably would, unless she OD'd first.

It wasn't easy, and I found my nerves on their last edge a lot of the time. Alastair assured me that my body would settle down after a while, and in the meantime, he'd distract me enough that I'd be able to stick to my decision. He'd told me to text him if the urge to smoke got too strong to manage by myself, and we'd figure it out together.

Robin and Patrick were in the staff room at Molly's. They stood and applauded when I came in and dropped my bag by my locker.

"Oh, fuck off," I said.

"Oh no, Toby. We are not going to do that. You need to tell us what that gorgeous hunk of a man did to you in the Bordello," Robin stated.

"Uh, that's confidential intel, don't you know," I said, getting my stuff out and dumping it on the bench.

Robin put a hand to his chest. "Confidential intel! Have we not been servers together for over a year?"

"So?"

"So, Toby, I think that I deserve at least a soupçon of information about your tryst with Alastair Kenney."

"Why?"

"So I can live vicariously through you, of course."

I stuck my tongue out at him, and Patrick laughed. By now, Patrick was used to the irreverent atmosphere at Molly's and also to Robin's antics, and he was much more relaxed.

"That's very mature," Robin said. "Fine. Have it your way. I don't care what the fuck you did up there."

"Yeah, you do."

His face fell, and he folded his hands together in a begging gesture. "Oh fuck, Toby, please? Just tell me one thing! You're living the fucking dream, you know!"

"Oh, as if. I'm sure you've been to the Bordello, and probably with one of the regulars. Or all of them, maybe?" I said, thinking of all the times Robin had hinted that he'd done exactly that.

He played his fingers along the edge of the settee. "Actually, I haven't."

I stared at him, while Patrick's gaze went back and forth between us. "But…you've told me—"

"I have a big mouth—and an even bigger imagination."

"Huh. I always thought those stories were true," I said, regarding him from a new perspective.

He shrugged. "Well, I had to say something. You all think I'm a huge slut. I didn't want to disappoint anyone."

"Robin," I said, "trust me. Nothing about you is disappointing."

He nodded and didn't say anything. But he almost smiled.

"I wouldn't mind hearing what you guys did back there," Patrick said in a hopeful voice.

I sighed, because although Robin could be disingenuous and annoying, he was also kind of hilarious and I loved him in a weird way, and Patrick was unbelievably sweet. The two of them seemed to be forming a bond, and Patrick might be a calming influence on the flamboyant server.

"It was nothing. He dressed me up and spanked me, then sucked me off. Then I sucked him off. No big deal."

"But you could have done all that at home," Patrick said, sounding disappointed.

"Well…" I smiled, remembering the details.

"Never mind, Patrick. He's not going to tell us," Robin stated, ushering Patrick out of the room.

It really did sound like nothing.

But it had been everything.

* * * *

Alastair's phone alarm woke us at eight-thirty on Tuesday morning, which was later than Alastair got up on a workday. He'd booked the day off, so he was cheerful when he got out of bed. I wished I felt the same.

"It's fine. I don't need any of that stuff. Let's forget it," I mumbled, turning over and closing my eyes.

The mattress dipped.

"Toby."

"Shhh."

"Get up."

"Nope."

The bedclothes flew off of me, and a hand cracked against my backside.

"Fuck! Ow!" I said, my hand shooting back there to protect my skin.

"Get up. I didn't book a day off work to sit here and argue with you."

Ooh, he sounded pissed. I cracked an eye open. He was smiling.

"Fuck you," I said.

He raised his eyebrows and lifted his hand.

"I'm up, I'm up. Fuck," I said, pulling my legs around and sitting up. "You're an asshole."

"You knew that before you moved in here."

"Yeah, but I didn't know how much you liked to smack my ass back then."

"It's my favorite thing."

I ran a hand through my hair. "Goddammit. I need a cigarette."

"No, you don't."

"Alastair," I said patiently. "If you knew what I've been through with my mom, you would understand. And you would go out right now and buy me a whole pack. You'd even light it for me."

"No, I wouldn't."

"Yes, you would."

"You can do this, Toby. And you can do it without caving in to your smoking habit."

"But, Alastair, I really just need one or two ciggy's today then I'll quit. I promise."

"Nope. Not happening."

I stared at him. He stared at me.

"You can't tell me what to do."

He sighed. "Really? You usually like it when I tell you what to do."

"That's different. That's...playing. And it's fun. But...it's *my* life."

"It is your life, and I can't tell you not to smoke. But, Toby, if you can get through today without caving, you'll have this thing beat."

I mean, he had a point.

"But if you threaten to put me over your lap if I smoke a cigarette, that's just a win-win for me."

"Hmm. Really."

"Yes, really."

"Well, what if I say that every day you *don't* smoke a cigarette, I'll put you over my lap?"

I laughed. "And punish me for what, exactly?"

"Oh, it won't be a punishment."

My mouth went dry. "Huh?"

"I gave you something close to a punishment spanking the other night in the Bordello, only because I wanted you to know what you were getting into with me. But, I, uh...can make a spanking something else entirely."

I narrowed my eyes. "Why are you only telling me this now?"

He smiled with a mischievous tilt to his head. We gazed at each other for a long moment.

"Get up, darling," he said. "You can use the shower first, if you want."

I raised my eyebrows, my heart warming to his use of the endearment.

"Darling, huh?"

He shrugged. "I call all my roommates 'darling', especially the ones who let me fuck and spank them."

He gave me a look that was all self-indulgent and smug, and I couldn't help laughing.

While I showered, I prayed to a God I didn't even believe in to make sure my mother wasn't there when we went. I figured we could be in and out in about thirty minutes or less, so I was really hoping we didn't have to deal with her. She wasn't someone I wanted to introduce to Alastair, and Esther would be even less thrilled to see her.

While we were drinking coffee and Alastair was eating his requisite piece of toast with apricot jam, Esther texted me that she and Lev were outside.

i hope you don't mind.

they wanted to help.

"Esther is here," I said to Alastair, as I got up and headed for the door. "And she brought her roommate, Lev."

"Great! The more the merrier, right?" he said, stuffing the last bite of his toast in his mouth as he stood and brushed the crumbs off his shirt. He was in jeans and a black Henley, looking hot as usual.

"Sure," I said, not convinced.

Now I regretted asking Alastair to help. If I'd known I could rely on Esther and Lev, the three of us could have done it on our own. If Mom found so many strangers in her house, she was going to lose it, and the woman didn't have much left, to be honest. I only wanted out, not to be the reason for her nervous breakdown.

"Hi, guys," I said, holding the front door open for them to come in from the porch.

"You really got the golden ticket, didn't you?" Esther said as she stepped inside and looked around. She lasered in on Alastair. "And you must be Alastair. I'm Esther."

"Hi, Esther," Alastair said, shaking the offered hand. "I'm pleased to finally meet you. We're glad you and Lev can help out today."

She shrugged. "Nice place." She gave Alastair an assessing look. "Toby's my bestie. I'm always there when he needs me."

"Okay, okay," I said, holding up my hand. "Down, girl."

"What? It's true."

"Yeah, but you don't have to have a pissing contest with my boyfriend."

"That's not what I—" She frowned and squinted at Alastair. "Oh, hey, maybe it is."

"Alastair, this is Lev," I said, introducing our friend, who was wearing leggings and black jean short-shorts, motorcycle boots and a gray tweed hip-length coat.

"Hi," Lev said. "I'm Lev, and my pronouns are they/them."

"Hi Lev," Alastair said, then pointed at himself. "Alastair. He/him."

Lev nodded, then turned to me.

"Are we doing this now?"

Chapter Sixteen

Getting Out

I sat in the passenger seat and gave Alastair directions, silently cursing myself for asking for his help, even though Esther had all but made me, because even if my mom wasn't there, he'd see where I'd been spending my life before we'd met...and it wasn't pretty.

Why I'd ever thought it was a good idea to show my brand-new boyfriend, who had a beautiful heritage home in Old Ottawa South and a job that paid him really good money, the ratty bungalow that my mom and I had shared for eighteen years, was anyone's guess. I supposed I hadn't really considered what it would mean, Esther's demand notwithstanding.

A huge wave of relief hit me when I saw the empty driveway.

"This is it," I said, a blush of shame and humiliation creeping into my cheeks. "You can probably wait in the car, though."

Alastair gave me a strange look.

Esther said, "Toby…"

As soon as the car stopped, I got out and headed to the front step. I felt weird and sick to my stomach. I'd been living in a different world the past few weeks, dating Alastair, and enjoying the kinky life. But this was what I'd known for too long to think about. This was what I was used to. My two separate lives crashing together made me queasy, and I wondered which was the real one.

My fingers shook as I slipped the key into the deadbolt and turned it, relieved that she hadn't changed the locks. She was a very unpredictable person, and I was nervous just being here.

I closed my eyes for a second, praying that the house wasn't the disgusting shambles I thought it might be. Then I pushed the door open.

The others had followed me without a word, but they waited as I went in and took a look around.

It wasn't as bad as I'd imagined. At least, the living room wasn't too gross. It looked like she had tidied it up to an extent, or at least maintained what I had done when I'd last gone through it. There was a glass half filled with either water or vodka on the coffee table and a couple of candy wrappers, but that was it.

My panic subsided, and I looked back at my crew. "I don't know how much of a mess this place is gonna be."

Alastair gave me a sympathetic look. "It doesn't matter. You're leaving."

I nodded curtly. "Right. Come on."

I led the way past the kitchen but glanced in as we passed. Sure enough, dishes were piled up beside the sink, the faucet was dripping, and there was a smell like soured milk suffusing the place.

It's fine. It's okay.

If I kept repeating that to myself, maybe I'd believe it.

I hadn't worried about my room, because I'd left it in a tidy state. The thought that she might have gone in there and fucked with my stuff hadn't even occurred to me until I opened the door and saw the bed unmade, the pillow on the floor and papers and books strewn around.

"Fuck," I said.

I stood there, embarrassed and angry and hopeless as I looked at the disaster my room was now. A hand landed on my shoulder and Esther spoke.

"His mom did it. Toby's room never looks like this. Toby is neat and clean and responsible with his things, for your information. His mom, on the other hand, is a selfish, slovenly bitch with a drug problem." I glanced back at Esther, my savior. I was so thankful that she was explaining everything, so I didn't have to. But also super embarrassed and ashamed of where I was from.

She held up her hand to forestall comments. "And I know she needs help and so does Toby, and we've begged her to get help so many times. But she won't, and she continues to deny there's any problem at all, because in her messed-up mind, the problem is Toby."

I didn't know if I really wanted Esther to lay it all out like *that* in front of Alastair, but by this point I'd stopped caring — or I'd pushed the part that cared so far down into the pit of my stomach I couldn't feel it anymore.

"I need to clean up," I said, because it was an automatic response to a mess, and how the hell was I gonna find anything I needed with it like this?

"No, you don't," Esther said, pushing past me and going into the room. "Alastair, why don't you and Lev go to Tims and get donuts and coffee? Toby and I'll figure this out while you're gone."

I could have kissed her for taking charge, because there wasn't anything left in me to do it. I felt lost and confused and unsure about everything. I was, technically, still living here. Maybe my mom was right, and fucking off without a word to her had been irresponsible and immature.

I sat on the bed and put my head in my hands.

"We'll be back soon," Alastair said. "Lev?"

Then he and Lev were gone, and it was just me and Esther.

"Okay, let's figure this out. What—"

"Maybe I should just stay."

Esther was silent for a second, then the mattress dipped, and her comforting and familiar scent filled my nostrils. She put her arm around me.

"No. Toby, come on. You can't do it anymore."

"What?"

"You can't save her. You can't look after her. You need to get out...*now*."

I nodded, because she was right. But all of a sudden, I didn't have the strength.

"Fuck, I need a cigarette," I said, looking at the room around me. Those walls I'd stared at for twenty years trying to figure out what to do.

"I wish I had one for you," Esther said, and I knew she meant it, even if she didn't approve of the habit any more than Alastair did.

I took a deep breath. "I promised Alastair I wouldn't smoke today."

"Huh. That seems...overly ambitious."

I looked at her. "What?"

"Toby, *I* want a cigarette, and I don't even smoke."

"Well, I'm sure we could probably find some..." I said, my gaze frantically sweeping the room.

"No, come on. We're not wasting time looking for smokes. I've got an idea," she said, covering my eyes with her hand. "Picture your room the way it was, okay? And tell me what you want to bring to Alastair's." She put her other hand on my back and rubbed it soothingly. "And just breathe, okay? It's going to be all right."

So that's what we did. I sat on my bed with my eyes closed and told Esther what to get and where she might find it. And somehow, by some miracle, she was able to locate everything I needed. And when I opened my eyes, there was a pile of stuff outside the door to my disaster of a room of the things that meant the most to me.

And the rest could stay. The rest of it could be damned.

"Thank you," I whispered, wiping a tear from the corner of my eye.

Esther sank to her knees in front of me and kissed my cheek. "It's going to be okay."

And that was when I heard voices in the driveway.

"Oh fuck. Oh fuck, fuck, *fuck*," I muttered, as one of those voices sent chills down my spine.

Esther and I ran toward the front of the house.

Two cars were in the driveway…and three people.

Alastair's car was closest, and he and Lev had got out, Lev carrying a tray of drinks and a box of donuts. They stood there as my mom, who had pulled her ratty car in behind Alastair's, yelled at them from the rolled-down window.

"Who the fuck are *you*, and what are you doing in *my* driveway?"

Great, Mom. Keeping it classy.

As sad and sorry and embarrassed as I'd been before, watching my mom being a bitch to the best people I knew, made me really fucking angry.

Esther and I charged forward.

"Mom, calm down. This is Alastair and Lev. They're helping me get some stuff from my room."

My mom pressed down on the horn, startling everyone. Lev almost dropped the drinks.

"Get out of my fucking driveway!" she yelled.

I ran a hand through my hair and narrowed my eyes, passing Alastair and Lev without a glance as I made my way to her car.

"Mom, how are they supposed to get out of the driveway if your car is blocking them?" I asked, in the calmest voice I could manage through my irritation. One thing I knew from dealing with my mom — if *you* lost it, *she* lost it. She'd probably lose it anyway, but if I did, too, things would get ten times worse.

"Who the fuck are all these people, Tobias?"

"They're my friends. They're helping me move out." I might as well lay it out for her.

"Looks like you're having a party," she said, staring at Alastair and Lev and Esther.

"Hi, Mrs. Dunn," Esther said with a little wave. "How are you?"

"You remember Esther, right?" I said, through gritted teeth. We'd only been friends for like…always.

My mom stared at Esther and didn't say anything.

"Mom," I said, somehow keeping my voice steady and firm. "I'm getting some of my things and I'm moving in with my boyfriend. Can you give me half an hour?" I dug in my back pocket for the four twenties I'd been planning to use to order a pizza later, as a thank you to them all for the help they'd given me. "Here. You can go get an early lunch or something...on me."

She stared at the money. I could see the wheels in her head turning. She *wanted* the money. She always wanted the money. But she also wanted to punish me. She stuck her head half out of the window.

"You all need your heads examined. Tobias isn't moving out. Why would he? He's got it good right here with me, and he knows it."

I hung my head as someone approached. I hoped to God it wasn't Alastair.

"Hey, Mrs. Dunn? Toby has been sleeping on my couch for the past few weeks, so he didn't have to come back here. We just went to his room, and it's been completely fucked over by someone – and my guess is, it was you."

My mom stared at Esther like she was garbage. "You always were a piece of shit. No doubt it's been you telling my son lies about me."

"And what lies would those be, Mrs. Dunn?"

"That I'm a shitty mom and a drug addict and he's better off nowhere near me."

Esther stared at my mom, and actually looked happy, as if she'd been waiting years for this moment.

"All I know is that Toby is miserable living here with you. And he's old enough to decide for himself where he wants to be." She leveled a stare at my mom and held her hand out to me, palm up. I gave her the eighty bucks. She pocketed two of the twenties and waved the rest in my mom's startled face. "I suggest you take this money and go use it for whatever... I don't care. Come back in half an hour and we'll be gone, and you can have your fucking driveway back." She glanced at the rest of us, then back at my mom. "Or I'm calling the cops."

My mom looked nervous when Esther said that. Esther and I both knew there were drugs in this house, probably a few different stashes.

"You can't prove anything."

Esther smiled then, and I mentally prepared myself for what I knew she had kept in her back pocket all these years, ready for a moment like this.

"Hey, you remember a while back when you were on a cocaine bender, and you broke Toby's nose?"

My mom didn't say anything. I was sure she remembered that. I know I did.

"I took pictures. Toby didn't want to press charges. I didn't make him, even though I thought he should have. But I still have the pictures. He was fourteen when that happened. You want to go to jail for child abuse, Mrs. Dunn?"

For the first time, my mom looked less than confident. "I didn't mean to break his nose. I said I was sorry."

"Take the money."

My mom stared at the money, then she looked at me, and I knew the waterworks were coming.

"Tobias, I'm sorry. You know I never meant to hurt you…"

"Just. Go," I said. Two distinct words. "If you really are sorry, just go — and I'll never bother you again."

She stared at me, then glanced at the others, then turned to Esther and grabbed the money from her.

"Fucking bitch," she said, as she put the car in reverse and squealed out of the driveway, taking the turn hard and accelerating down the side street like it was the Grand Prix.

"Jesus Christ," Esther said. She turned to me with the most apologetic expression I'd ever seen on her face. "Are you okay?"

I didn't say anything, but I guessed she could tell that I wasn't exactly okay, because in a minute she had stepped close and gathered me into a hug. I collapsed against her, not crying, not saying anything, just glad to borrow someone else's strength for a moment.

"Hey, it's okay. But we'd better get your things."

I nodded against her jacket, preparing myself for the look on Alastair's and Lev's faces when I turned around.

They were standing in the same spots they'd been in before. Alastair looked furious. In fact, I didn't think I'd ever seen an expression like that on his face before.

"I'm sorry you had to see that," I stuttered, my voice trembling, as Esther handed me the forty bucks she'd confiscated and walked to Lev so she could take the drinks from him.

"We'll be inside," she said, as they walked to the door. "Take a minute, okay?"

I didn't want to take a minute. I wanted to run inside, grab my stuff and get the fuck out of here. But instead, I just stood there while the anger on Alastair's face turned into something close to pity, and I couldn't take it.

"Let's just get out of here," I said.

"Toby."

I cleared my throat. "So that's my mom." I tried to laugh but it came out like a choked sob, because that was what it was.

Alastair put his hands on my shoulders. "Toby, it's going to be okay," he said. "I promise."

It was exactly what I needed to hear, and I nodded. "I know. But thanks for saying it."

He moved forward but I couldn't handle that right now. I was barely holding myself together and we didn't have time for me to collapse in tears, which is what was going to happen if I let Alastair hug me. I held up my hand to stop him.

"Can I get a raincheck on that?"

He lowered his arms and smiled, so I knew he had me, even if I didn't want physical contact. And it was in that moment I knew he was a keeper.

"Sure, you can. Let's go get your stuff."

* * * *

We were quiet on the drive back. Alastair dropped Esther and Lev off, and Esther made me promise to call her later. Lev gave me a commiserating look, and I knew their family situation was at least as fucked up as mine.

When we got to Alastair's place, we pretended nothing weird had happened, but were subdued and quiet as we hauled my things inside and figured out where to put stuff. Like I'd said, I didn't have much.

"I'm just gonna get settled in my room," I said, desperately needing some time alone but not wanting to be rude to the man who'd given me this refuge in the first place.

"Okay. I'll leave you to it. When you're ready, we can order takeout for lunch, okay?"

"I only have forty bucks," I said.

"It's fine. It's on me."

"Okay…sure."

And he was gone. Probably just downstairs, so that was good. I didn't want him to *leave,* and besides it was his house. I just needed some space to process everything. The fact that he'd accepted that without argument was a good omen for our living together.

I dragged my box of books and miscellanies up onto the bed and sat down beside it, grabbing my dog-eared copy of *Zen and the Art of Motorcycle Maintenance* and starting to read it for the umpteenth time. I just needed to get out of my head and into someone else's for a bit. Then I would be able to think clearly.

* * * *

I must have dozed off from the exhaustion and stress — and knowing I was in a safe place. I woke up to knocking at my door.

For a split second I thought I was in my bedroom at my mom's, and I wondered why she was being so nice for a change and not yelling at me to wake up and clean the kitchen. Then I realized it was Alastair, and the pressure in my chest vanished instantly.

"Just a second," I mumbled as I sat up and put my feet on the floor, the book tumbling to the carpet. I grabbed it and shoved it onto the bedside table.

When I opened the door, Alastair was standing there with a bouquet of red and yellow flowers.

"Welcome to your new home," he said, with the brightest smile I could have asked for.

I grabbed the bouquet and threw it on the bed, then launched myself into his arms, holding him tighter than I'd ever held anything before.

Chapter Seventeen

A Change of Scene

Living with Alastair wasn't that big of a deal.

I mean, in some ways it *was* a big deal, in terms of me finding somewhere to live other than my mom's toxic home. But it wasn't a big deal when it came to moving in with someone I didn't know well but with whom I had amazing sexual chemistry. We shifted into being roommates and lovers in a way that seemed strangely easy.

Technically, I was *renting* the guest room for two hundred a month—a ridiculously cheap price, but it worked for me, and Alastair was resistant to charge me more. He said it was the 'student rate'. Our schedules didn't match, which worked out, because I got the place to myself all day during the week, and he got some time to chill on the evenings I was working. I had my own code for the door, and it was great not to have to remember to take a key with me whenever I went out.

Old Ottawa South was one of the swankiest neighborhoods in Ottawa, so I found myself well-situated. There were tons of places I could walk to during the day — coffee shops, bakeries, even a paint-your-own pottery place called The Mud Oven. I felt a bit out of place at first, but there were a couple of shops I frequented where the staff got to know me, and that made all the difference.

Of course, I still had my classes to go to, and papers to work on, but having a quiet, clean space of my own felt like a triumph. There was a little desk in my room, and I sat there to do my schoolwork, with the door open and the ticking of the clock my only companion while Alastair wasn't home.

The offices where Alastair worked were located farther north, in the central downtown part of the city. This made it easy to see him between classes, since the University of Ottawa campus was downtown, too. If I had a morning class, I could meet Alastair for lunch. Sometimes he met me after class and drove me home. I didn't have a full course load this year. I'd opted to take an extra term next fall rather than overload myself with work and school and see my grades suffer. I'd only have to take two more courses, and I was saving up to pay for them.

I generally had five shifts a week, and I always worked Fridays and Saturdays, which were the busiest evenings at Maverick Molly's. I made a shitload in tips on those nights. But that meant that if Alastair and I wanted to go out together, we had to go Wednesday or Thursday — or whichever other day I had off. And if we wanted to reserve the Bordello, those were the days available, which was a little hard on Alastair because he had to get up early to go to work.

But maybe I could change that. Maybe I could ask Jacob to switch me from Fridays to Wednesdays, which would give me Thursdays, Fridays and Mondays off. I felt like that would make having a boyfriend a little easier and give Alastair and me more time to have fun together.

"Hey, Jacob," I said that Friday night, sitting on the stool at the bar and crossing one leg over the other to dangle my foot in its little brown shoe.

"Yes, Toby?"

I smiled, touching a finger to my throat. "I'm, like, one of your best servers, right?" I said, fluttering my eyelashes.

He laughed and nodded. "Sure."

"Well…I was wondering if you really needed me here on Friday nights?"

His face fell. "You want me to cut one of your shifts?"

"No, no, no. Not cut it. Just switch it?" I said, pleading with my eyes.

"You don't like working Fridays?" he said.

"Okay, here's the thing. You know Alastair and I are a thing."

"Yeah."

"And he has a Monday-to-Friday day job."

"Ah," Jacob said, understanding dawning.

"And, uh, we kind of want to get kinky in the Bordello on a more…regular basis," I said, remembering the fun we'd had in there a few weeks earlier. We hadn't had the chance to come back, mainly because it was difficult to find a night that worked.

"Oh. But you could come on a Thursday, like you did last time…"

"Yeah, but it was brutal for Alastair to get up for work on Friday. Also, I'd kind of like to have two days off in a row. I've worked here long enough."

"I'll have to ask one of the other guys if they'd mind switching," Jacob said, eyeing me with caution. "But I should be able to swing it."

"Yay, thank you! Plus, even though I won't be working on Fridays, the plan is to spend money on the Bordello most weeks, so it'll be a win-win."

He smiled. "I take it you enjoyed it the last time?"

"Oh my God, Jacob. You have no idea what a pro that man is."

"Well, he's certainly had lots of practice," Jacob said with a laugh.

I frowned. Jacob sobered.

"Honing his skills with meaningless hookups until the right man came along is what I mean."

I smiled.

"Exactly. I'm not too proud to acknowledge my benefit from those" — I waved my fingers carelessly — "little flirtations."

"All right. Next week I'll put you on Wednesdays, and you can have your little meet-up with Mr. Kenney. Might I make a suggestion?"

Oh, saucy Jacob.

"You may," I said, flashing him a coy smile.

Jacob leaned forward onto his elbows as if he were sharing a secret with me.

"You and Alastair might enjoy making use of the schoolroom set-up in the Bordello. I assume you've seen the desk and blackboard?"

I pictured Alastair as a strict professor worried about his student's wandering eye. I didn't hate it. "Can you book us for next Friday? Say, ten to twelve?"

"Done. Glad I could help," Jacob said, with a devilish smile, his teeth sparkling in the lamplight.

I clapped my hands. "Thanks, Jacob. You're the best!"

I couldn't wait to tell Alastair. I hoped he had something to wear that would make him look like a professor.

* * * *

Alastair liked to come to the club on the nights I worked. He teased that it was to make sure I was good and didn't get up to anything with the clients, but he knew how strict the rules were at Molly's.

He liked to watch me prance around in my 'uniform' and see to the needs of other handsome men, while knowing he would be taking me home afterward and fucking me silly, worked up by the voyeuristic pleasure of it all. I definitely reaped the rewards of his little pastime, and I didn't mind him being there. It fulfilled my exhibitionist and acting temperament, which was why this job suited me so well.

It was near to eleven one Tuesday when he showed up just as I'd stepped onto the stage. He looked tired but fine, in dark jeans and a tan linen shirt. When he saw me, his face brightened. He found a spot at the back, where he could watch.

"Well, gentlemen," I said. "I'm going to tell some jokes."

There was applause all around. Alastair joined in and whistled.

I gave him a saucy nod. "Okay, so three old ladies are sitting on a bench, feeding the pigeons."

"Is that a euphemism?" someone yelled.

"Maybe," I said. "Anyway. A guy in a trench coat comes along and flashes them. The first old lady has a stroke. The second old lady has a stroke. But the third old lady *can't quite reach.*" I grinned as groans and laughter erupted.

"What does a robot do after a one-night-stand?"

"What?" the audience shouted.

"He nuts and bolts," I replied, smoothing my chemise and widening my legs.

"Okay, okay, last one. Then I have to get back to serving you delinquents."

More laughter.

"A doctor walks into the room and tells his patient, I have some bad news for you. You really have to stop masturbating."

Horrified gasps.

"The man looks aghast and says, 'Oh my God, Doc, why?' The doctor replies, 'I'm trying to examine you.'"

Groans and chuckles.

"Ba-dump-dump," I said, wielding imaginary drumsticks. "That's all folks. It's getting late, and I need to save my energy for later."

Several men gazed after me knowingly as I waltzed offstage, picking up my empty drinks tray and making my way to Alastair.

"Hey, guess what?" I said, leaning in for a kiss and smiling like the Cheshire cat.

"Your lace panties are riding up?"

"Cute. I'm wearing a thong."

His eyes widened and he shifted in his seat. "Fuck. Why did you tell me that?"

"So you can picture it. Duh."

"You are a nasty little minx."

I grinned. "I booked the Bordello for next Friday."

He smiled with pleasure, then gave me a look. "But, you work Fridays…"

"Not anymore," I said, pleased with the surprise.

The smile returned. "Really?"

"About the Bordello or about not working Fridays?"

"Well, both. I've been dying to get back into that room with you."

"Oh, really?" I said, folding my arms over my chest and lifting my chin. "I'm working Wednesdays instead of Fridays now."

"Great!"

"Yeah, I said we needed a night to get super kinky without you having to go to work the next day."

"It does take a lot out of me."

I nodded with a naughty lick of my lips. "Oh, I know just how much it takes out of you."

He laughed. "Naughty thing."

I had to get back to work, but I gave him a saucy wave and noticed him ogling my ass, so things were going to plan.

I hadn't had a cigarette in three weeks, but I did miss it. I didn't think having one cigarette once in a while was a big deal, but Alastair was convinced if I smoked one more, it would lead to one more after that, and I'd be back in the thick of it.

Anyway, by the time my shift ended, I was craving one bad. Alastair was deep in conversation with Jacob, so I told him I was going to get changed. After I had my street clothes on, I rifled through my backpack for the almost-empty carton I'd stashed in the deepest pocket. I slid a cigarette out, and my lighter, put the carton back then made my way outside.

It was a mild night for a change, and I barely needed my jacket since I was warm from working hard all evening. I stared at the cigarette between my fingers instead of lighting up right away. Was this actually a good idea? I'd done so well over these past few weeks. I wanted it, sure. But I also realized how nice it was to have gotten free of the hourly, then daily, cravings. If I smoked this now, maybe I'd be right back into the lure of the addiction, like Alastair predicted.

I flicked my lighter on, then off again...then back on. I lifted the cigarette to my lips, but before it reached them I heard scuffling. When I glanced up, I saw a man in a torn and dirty coat standing on the sidewalk a few feet away, staring at me. He looked like he was in his forties and was the kind of skinny you got when you lived off booze and drugs—ask me how I knew—and he watched me with a weird intensity.

I regarded him cautiously as I lowered the cigarette and flicked the lighter closed. I felt vulnerable and alone, even though the door to the club was steps away, and Alastair should be coming through those doors any minute.

"Can I help you?" I asked.

"Are you Tobias Dunn?" the man said, with a hollow-eyed stare.

What the fuck?

"Who wants to know?" I asked, slipping the lighter and cigarette into my front pocket. I narrowed my eyes at him.

"I need to give you a message."

"Oh, for fuck's sake. Are you one of my mom's loser boyfriends?"

He gave me a creepy smile and looked me up and down, like he was sizing me up for a casket or about to rape me. A chill crept down my spine.

"You watch out, Tobias. Janice has a lot of friends in this town, don'tcha know. You'll go back if you know what's good for you."

I heard the door of the club scrape open and familiar footsteps behind me as the chill spread, but I schooled my expression so as not to show how freaked out I was as the guy stepped closer, and Alastair brushed past me with casual confidence.

"Can I help you?" Alastair said to the man, who took a step back now and scowled with displeasure.

"Fuck you. Both of you," he said, before he hocked a wad of spit that landed right in front of Alastair's boots.

Alastair threw a startled look my way but I simply stood there, watching the guy amble away down the sidewalk.

"Who the fuck was that?" he asked

I didn't say anything for a minute.

"Toby? What's going on?"

I took a deep, steadying breath, and let it out, trying not to succumb to the panic that wanted to grip me.

"My mom's not ready to let go just yet."

* * * *

Back at Alastair's, I retrieved the cigarette from my pocket and the two that were left in the carton and flushed them down the toilet. Then I crumpled the carton, buried it in the bin and put my lighter in the medicine cabinet.

After two cups of tea, I told him what I knew.

"But why? Is she that possessive of you that she's sending some weirdo to scare you into coming back?"

"I don't know," I said. "She's a little messed up, you know?"

He snorted. "A little!" He shot me a guilty glance. "I'm sorry. She's your mom. I don't mean to be insensitive."

"She's got problems. I figured she could do with one less. But she doesn't seem to agree."

"That guy made me nervous," Alastair said. "I'm glad I came out of the club when I did."

"Yeah. He's probably a drug dealer...or a sex trafficker."

Alastair gave a little laugh but sobered when he saw the look on my face.

"Oh fuck. You're serious."

"I'm dead serious, yeah. She's not exactly on the PTA committee. Never was."

"Well, this sucks," Alastair said. "Maybe we should call the cops?"

I stared at him. "And tell them *what*?"

He spread his hands. "That this man *threatened* you."

I shook my head. "That's not how it works."

"What do you mean? That's how it's supposed to work."

I didn't say anything, just sipped my tea and put my feet in Alastair's lap. "I could use a foot massage."

I think he realized I was changing the subject deliberately, but he could probably see how much I didn't like this conversation. He peeled off one sock, then the other. Since I wore stockings at work, my socks were pretty clean and probably didn't stink.

I wasn't so sure about my feet.

"You don't have to," I said, pulling away, but he grabbed my ankles and held them fast, stroking the soles with his thumbs and just about making my eyes roll back in my head.

"Tell me about the time she broke your nose," he said, as he squeezed and rubbed.

Alastair's hands were literal works of art, bigger than mine and smooth—the hands of a man who worked on a computer all day. I agreed that there was something about a guy with calluses, but I liked my white-collar man. He was my first, and I hoped to keep him. But that meant that this wouldn't be the last conversation we had about my past. I came from a different world than he did.

"I was fourteen, and I had a smart mouth. I called her a bitch, and she hauled off and punched me. Told me I was a dirty faggot and a useless son, and she couldn't stand the sight of me. I mean, she was drunk out of her mind."

"Jesus. Toby…" Alastair's hands froze for a second but then resumed.

I shook my head because that wasn't the whole story.

"I should probably tell you that I punched her once, too — and it wasn't in self-defense."

Alastair was silent. He watched me with sad eyes and rubbed my foot like it was his job.

"I was sixteen, so she could have charged me with assault. She's been holding that over my head for years. I don't know why she didn't mention it when Esther brought up the nose incident."

"Does Esther know about that?"

"About me punching my mom? Yeah. She always says she had it coming. Which, yeah, she did, but it was still assault. She wasn't attacking me at the time."

"What made you…lose your temper?" Alastair asked.

His soothing motions on my muscles were putting me into a kind of a trance, and I didn't answer right away.

"You don't have to tell me, Toby. It's okay."

"She let my kitten out," I mumbled.

"What?"

"I had this kitten. I knew my mom wouldn't approve, but I kept it in my room, with its litter box in my closet. I changed that damn box like three times a day so it wouldn't stink. In those days she was hardly ever home anyway and out of it when she was there. I know I shouldn't have done that. It was her house." I shrugged. "I was sixteen, lonely and having issues at school. And this guy on my Instagram was giving away free kittens, so I got one."

Alastair just watched me. I kept my gaze on his strong fingers as he rubbed my foot with the care and strength that I needed to absorb more than anything at that moment.

"She was all black, with a little white spot on her chest. I named her Star, and she was the—" I choked on an inhale and pushed the emotion down. "She was the sweetest thing." My voice was barely a whisper. "I never let her outside. They tell you not to, because they kill birds and get run over, shit like that. But I came home that day, and she wasn't in my room. And when I asked my mom if she'd let her out, she said, yeah."

"Jeez."

I nodded. "Except I thought she meant she'd let her out of my room, so I spent half an hour wandering the house and calling her name, tamping down my anger at my mom, looking in every closet. Then my mom started laughing. So, I said, what is your problem?" I swallowed thickly. "And she said, '*You are. You're so fucking stupid. I didn't let it out of your room, I tossed it out of the front door.*'"

I met Alastair's gaze.

"I wanted to kill her, Alastair. I legit wanted to slam her head into the wall, again and again. I was sixteen. I *could* have. I'm stronger than I look."

"I know."

"She kept laughing, I punched her right in the chin, and she fell down. I think she was in shock, because I'd never raised a hand to her before. It was always the other way around."

We were quiet for a long time. Alastair put down my foot and picked up the other one. I closed my eyes.

"I'm surprised you didn't leave right then," Alastair said.

I opened my eyes and stared at him, wondering about his childhood and if he'd ever hated his parents so much he'd wished the worst things on them. Maybe all kids did at one time or another.

"Where would I have gone?" I asked.

"Did you ever find your kitten?"

An image flashed in my head of seeing something in the middle of the road on my way home from school two days later that looked like a dead squirrel but wasn't.

"No," I said.

"I'm sorry," Alastair murmured, soothing the muscles of my foot with practiced movements. "That's awful."

"I probably should have left. But what the fuck was I gonna do? I didn't have a job. Esther was still living with her folks, and I didn't want to ask if I could stay *there*, even though they might have let me."

Alastair was silent. His strength and calm confidence were exactly what I needed.

"She never touched me after that. Her anger became cruel words and manipulations—and holding that punch over my head every time I got mad at her for something or complained about her drinking."

"She broke your nose, Toby."

"That day she was only standing there, and I'm a guy. You know what the courts see, right? An angry man and a victim."

"You were sixteen!"

I shrugged. "I still think they would have sided with her."

"I'm not so sure. Anyway, it doesn't matter now. You're here, and she's there—and you never have to go back."

Chapter Eighteen

Writing Lines

I kept my eyes peeled for any sign of the dude who'd approached me, but he didn't make another appearance.

Alastair had insisted I share my location with him so he could keep tabs when he wasn't with me. It should have been an imposition. Maybe a couple of weeks ago I would have laughed and told him I was an adult and he didn't need to babysit me, but I truly didn't mind. It was nice to know he cared enough about my safety to risk pissing me off. I'd never shared my location with anyone before, even Esther.

Anyway, I didn't care how many strangers threatened me. I wasn't going back.

For the first time, I felt like I could breathe. I probably would have felt the same if I was renting any old place, but having Alastair in my corner and in my bed was a real benefit.

By the time Friday night came around, Alastair and I had managed to 'forget' about the weirdo and his message. We were out for a date and feeling good about having the time and space to get kinky.

* * * *

When Sebastian handed me the key to the Bordello on Friday, he had a weird smile on his face.

"Okay, you have to stop looking at me like that," I said. It was bizarre having a boss who knew just how kinky you were — or wanted to be.

"Sorry," he said, blushing. "Have a great time."

Robin looked like he'd give anything to be in my place as Alastair and I exited the gaming parlor. I was thrilled to finally have something that made Robin jealous.

Alastair had dressed the part of sexy professor, wearing brown corduroy slacks, an off-white button-down and a tweed blazer. When he'd come into the living room I'd just about swallowed my tongue.

I'd put on my sexiest pair of ripped skinny jeans and a snug Twenty-One Pilots T-shirt. Alastair had taken one look at me and grabbed his coat. In the entry hall at Molly's, I'd switched from my boots to a pair of beat-up Converse sneakers with rainbow laces that I'd had for years and would make me look a lot younger.

"Nice touch," Alastair had said.

I keyed us in and turned on a lamp.

The smell of furniture polish hit me, and I suddenly knew what Jacob had been grinning about. Had they given the antique desks some extra attention because they knew Alastair and I would be using them?

When we'd been here before, I'd been so caught up in the experience in one corner of the room that I'd barely paid attention to anything else after cataloging it for Alastair.

A stretch of wall contained a small blackboard and two desks. One desk was a student's, with the chair attached and a sloping top that could open. The wood was marked and beat-up, with initials and other graffiti carved into it.

"Fuck," I said.

When my impressed gaze locked with Alastair's, he grinned with mischief. Then he walked over to stand before the blackboard. He picked up a piece of chalk and began to write something in a neat, cursive script.

"Take a seat, Mr. Dunn," he said, in a stern tone, and it was on.

I swallowed, already feeling like a teenager in detention. "Yes, Mr. Kenney."

He half turned toward me, and I saw the reflexive smile before he became the stern professor again. He finished what he was writing on the board and spun around.

"Take out a piece of paper and a pencil."

But I was reading the words on the board and didn't act quickly enough.

"Mr. Dunn, open the desk and take out paper and a pencil."

I swallowed, but I did what he'd told me to do.

"I want you to copy the sentence that I've written on the blackboard on every line of that paper."

"Yes, Mr. Kenney."

I picked up the pencil, staring at it like it was some kind of strange technology I'd never seen before. I legit hadn't used a pencil since middle school. I didn't even know if I could write.

I raised my hand. "Mr. Kenney?"

"Yes?"

"Is it okay if I print? My cursive isn't very good."

He stared at me like he couldn't believe I was asking for such a thing.

"If your cursive isn't very good, that's all the more reason to practice," he said, sitting on the corner of the teacher's desk. "Isn't it?"

Wow. Okay, then.

"Yes, Sir," I said, suitably chastened.

He gave me a cool smile, and I bent to my task, wondering how long he'd make me work before we got onto more interesting subjects.

I will not send dick pics to teachers.

I almost laughed, because the very idea was mortifying and would probably land a kid at the police station in the current climate. But for our purposes, it was a clever segue into things.

He actually made me fill the page. I couldn't believe it and kept glancing at him where he sat at the desk watching me in quiet contemplation. The sadistic bastard even motioned me to keep working when I raised my eyebrows with the silent suggestion that maybe we could move things along.

My handwriting was as bad as I'd supposed, but by the end of the page, it did seem significantly improved. I had elected to write my own sentence, instead of the one on the board, because I was a shit-disturber in this scenario, and punishment was the name of the game.

I raised my hand when I was done.

"Yes?"

"I'm finished, Sir."

"All right. Put down your pencil and bring the paper to me."

"Yes, Sir."

I put the pencil down in the groove of the wood —
God, how old *was* this thing? — and took the paper to
the front of the room where Alastair perched on the
edge of the desk.

"Here," I said, holding it out.

He flashed me a look of amusement but then got all
stern as he took the paper from me. He looked at it. His
lips quirked then flattened into a firm line again.

"This isn't what I asked you to write."

"No, Sir."

He looked at the paper again, his cheeks flushing
with either anger or lust, I couldn't tell. Hopefully, lust
pretending to be anger.

He passed the paper back to me.

"Read it."

I stared at the words I had written, blinking and
regretting being a badass. Strange that reading out loud
in this situation was just as embarrassing as if Alastair
was actually my professor. I should add being a top-
notch actor to Alastair's many talents.

"Out *loud*, Mr. Dunn."

Goddammit.

I cleared my throat, then whispered the sentence I'd
written all down the page.

"Since the sentence refers to me, I'd like to hear you
read it."

I nodded and licked my lips.

"I want to suck your fat cock, Mr. Kenney."

Alastair stared at me, and I couldn't read his
expression. Surely, he thought that was funny? Or even
sexy? He crossed his arms over his chest and shook his
head back and forth.

"How on earth would you know the girth of my
erect penis, Toby Dunn?" he said, with the most

deadpan acting I'd ever seen. He could have won an Oscar for that one goddamn sentence. And those words landed fucking chills all up and down my body. But wow, this was fun.

I stared at the floor—at my wrecked-up sneakers with their dirty rainbow laces—and fought a smile. I kept my eyes down as I responded to his question.

"Because you had me choking on it last week, if you remember. Sir," I said, shoving my hands in my pockets and smirking like a delinquent.

The sound of our heavy breathing filled the space.

"Oh, I remember, Mr. Dunn. If I recall, you handled yourself pretty fucking well."

"Yes, Sir. I did. So why am I in detention right now?"

"Why do you think you're in detention right now?"

"Because…because you want me to suck you off again?" I said hopefully.

And he laughed. It was a sound that went right to my dick, because it wasn't a 'We're sharing a joke right now' laugh. It was a 'You have no idea what you're getting into' laugh.

"If only it were that simple."

I raised my gaze to his and pressed my palm against the bulge in the front of my jeans.

"Isn't it, Sir?"

I could tell he was imagining every fucking thing he wanted to do to me in this room. I hoped it was a long list. Maybe he should have written that on the board.

"I'm very, very disappointed in you."

"You are?" I blinked like the innocent kid I definitely wasn't.

"Why did you tell Principal McMillan that I sucked you off in the janitor's closet?"

Huh. My brain tried to come up with a good reason.

"Because I wanted to see the expression on his face?"

"Hmm. Do you know how awkward that conversation was? Trying to convince him you were lying?"

"But I wasn't lying."

"Do you want me to lose my job?"

"No, Sir. Of course not. You're a great teacher." I licked my lips and gave him a look to let him know exactly which lessons I'd found most stimulating.

"I'm glad you think so. But you should realize, part of what makes me a good teacher is knowing when one of my students needs extra discipline."

And, there it is.

"Discipline?" I said. Why on earth was that word so hot?

"It's a good thing we have the whole school to ourselves, so that when I strap you over that desk, you can yell as much as you like."

I made a little noise and almost came in my pants. "Oh fuck."

He stood up and straightened his blazer, nodding as if he'd made up his mind.

"Now you can make this easy by doing what I say without argument, or you can make it even more difficult by resisting. It's completely up to you."

"Um, I'll do what you say." At least, I would to begin with. We'd have to see how far that went.

"Excellent. I can see you are trying to be a good...student."

"Yes, Sir. The best."

He grinned at me with a delightful glint in his eye.

"All right then. Best to get this over with." He walked over to the wall, where a selection of wood and leather paddles in various sizes and styles hung on hooks.

Oh, lordy. Help me. No, wait, don't. Jesus.

I remembered being spanked over Alastair's lap. That had hurt a lot. Something told me this would be worse. A thrill of fear coursed through me.

"Hmm." He touched the polished surface of one of them — an oval shaped paddle with a long handle. Then he looked at me. "Have you ever been paddled before, Mr. Dunn?"

"No, Sir." My voice was barely there. I cleared my throat. "Never."

"Hmm," he said again. He turned to the wooden sticks in some kind of an umbrella stand. They were long and thin and made of different materials. They looked nasty. "Caned?"

I shook my head. "No, Sir."

He clicked his tongue. "Well, I find that very surprising, Toby, since you don't seem to know how to follow instructions."

I didn't know what to say, so I simply shrugged my shoulders and prayed he wouldn't decide to cane me. I didn't know much about it, but something told me I did not want a caning.

"Well, maybe it would be better to start with something less…brutal."

I shuddered with relief.

He walked behind the desk and opened a drawer.

"Ah," he said, taking out a wooden ruler. "This will do nicely."

He examined it and touched his fingertip to the engraved markings as I dissolved into a pool of confused desire. Part of me was terrified, even of a wooden ruler. It was better than a paddle or a cane, but

I had no idea how it would feel or whether I'd get off on it.

"Wow, *this* is even an antique," he murmured to himself, though he raised his eyes to mine for a split second.

"Huh," was all I could get out as my pulse hammered in my throat and my cheeks went red.

"Oh, someone is having a lovely reaction to the sight of this instrument of discipline," Alastair said, smiling in a way I had learned meant that he had numerous kinky ideas percolating in that dirty mind of his. "Now, pull down your jeans and lean over that desk, Mr. Dunn."

I inhaled so suddenly and fast that it made a noise. "What?"

"You heard me." He placed the ruler on the edge of his desk as he removed his tweed jacket and started to roll up his sleeves.

Oh fuck. Oh fuck.

"Yes, Sir," I quavered, turning around so I didn't have to look at him as I undid my jeans and pushed them to my thighs. I was super embarrassed, almost as if I were actually a student in a heap load of trouble and hadn't come to this room with my kinky AF boyfriend for exactly this sort of thing.

My breaths came rapidly, and my dick felt like a ramrod.

"Toby Dunn. Are those *lace panties*?" Alastair asked, as if he hadn't already seen me in them numerous times.

"Oh. Yeah. Do you like them, Mr. Kenney?"

"Yes, I like them very much."

I hooked my thumbs under the waistband.

"Keep them on for now. I'll warm you up first."

"Yes, Sir," I said, bringing my arms forward and shaking them out. I wasn't sure exactly how he wanted me, so I glanced at him with a question in my gaze.

God, he looked insanely good. He totally looked the part. His tweed jacket lay on the desk, and he'd rolled up his shirtsleeves to his elbows to expose his muscled forearms.

"I suggest you clasp your hands and prop yourself on your forearms."

"Yes, Sir," I said, starting to turn.

"*Psst.*"

I hesitated and glanced at him, and he had the biggest smile on his handsome face, coming out of his stern professor mode to reassure me that he was still my gorgeous, kinky boyfriend.

"You look so fucking good like that, Toby," he whispered. "I can't imagine you in anything but panties."

I smirked. "Good."

They were the skimpiest ones I owned — a soft baby blue color.

He shook his head, then cleared his throat and went back into the role.

"I don't have all day, Mr. Dunn."

"Yes, Sir. I mean, no, Sir."

I positioned myself on the desk, anxiety and arousal swirling as I leaned onto my elbows and braced myself.

"Oh, hell yes," Alastair breathed. He cleared his throat and resumed his professional demeanor. "Excellent."

He came to stand beside me. His familiar scent helped to calm me as he placed the ruler on the desk where I could see it.

"I want you to look at that ruler while I give you some practice swats with my hand, over these shocking panties. I shouldn't be treating you with kid gloves, but you haven't been disciplined this way before. If you had, your behavior would be better."

He shoved the fabric of my shirt up my back with one hand as his other one rested on my ass cheek. It felt warm through the powder blue lace, and I let out a sigh and girded myself for pain.

The first few spanks were hardly anything, and I had to hold back a laugh, because I knew what Alastair could do with his hand, and I was nervous to provoke him. He leaned over and said my name.

I turned my head to look at him.

"You remember your safeword?"

"Yep."

"Okay. Say it if you need to. I don't want to go too far with this."

I grinned. "Just enough?"

"Just enough."

He grabbed the ruler off the desk and straightened.

"I'm going to give you six over the panties, Mr. Dunn. You can make all the noise you want—just know that it won't deter me."

"Yes, Sir."

"It's my job to teach you to behave."

Chapter Nineteen

Schooled

The impact of the ruler was bearable through the lace of the panties, and I really liked the hiss as it cut the air then slapped against my ass. But once Alastair had me pull them down, all bets were off.

"Fuck!" I hissed. "*Jesus.*"

My eyes went wide, and I stared at the worn wood of the desk as the burn spread from the narrow spot where the ruler had landed on my naked flesh.

"Language," Alastair—aka Mr. Kenney—said, and I almost turned and told him to fuck off and that I wasn't playing this game anymore. But the second hit landed, and I couldn't say anything, then the third after that. I tried to remember my safeword and the reason I had chosen to submit to this.

"Good job," he said, and there was genuine admiration in his voice, which helped with my suffering. I rested there, trembling with the shock of the stinging pain that had become a fire under my skin. I wondered if I'd have bruises from this. I wondered how many he was going to give me.

I lifted one hand from the desk. "Sir?" I asked in a shaky voice.

"Yes, Mr. Dunn?"

"How…how many of those… I don't know if I can—"

"You get ten. You've had three."

"*Ten!* Alastair, come on," I begged. "It fucking hurts."

He laughed—a beautiful, shameless, indulgent sound. "It's supposed to hurt, Toby."

Then he wrapped his fingers around my cock, and I must have been really into the pain, because I was hard as hell. I let out a low groan. The burn spreading over my ass seemed to make the pleasure that much sweeter.

"My ass is so sore. That ruler is fucking evil."

"Awe, methinks he protests too much. Your bottom looks so pretty. It's striped red and white, like a kinky candy cane."

"Holy shit."

"I'm exaggerating. The lines are fading already. You know that I'll stop if you want me to. You just have to say the word."

I thought about it. I stared at my hands where they were clasped together on the desk.

"I…want to know what comes after…"

"After what, Toby?"

"After the ruler. Are you…are you gonna…you know…reward me?"

"Ah. You need some motivation to get through your ten lashes?"

I sighed, imagining Alastair putting the ruler down and fucking me over this desk. "Yes…please, Sir."

Alastair moved. He slid his fingers into my hair and jerked my head around so I had to look at him. It took me by surprise, but it made my cock leak, so I guessed I was a really kinky little slut.

His expression was fierce and full of lust. "You are treading on some serious ground here, Toby Dunn. You know I could be fired for fucking a student."

"Yes, Sir."

"Why should I give you a reward when you've earned every bit of this punishment? Hmm?"

"Because you want to fuck me. I know you do."

He pushed my head away and let go of my hair, as he disappeared behind me.

"Count. We have seven left."

I took a deep breath then strike four landed...hard.

"F-four."

I squeezed my eyes shut and planted my feet.

"F-five."

Three in quick succession had me moaning with the pain, but also caused a release of endorphins that allowed me to float above it.

"Six!"

Seven made me yell. Eight made me bite into my arm so I wouldn't. And nine and ten made me bleat like a tortured animal, but I didn't cry. I blinked back the tears, because I knew if I could get through it, he'd fuck me. He'd promised.

The whole dominance thing was really pushing my buttons. The fact that he had me bent over a desk with my pants down and was disciplining me like I was a delinquent teenager was totally doing it for me. Also, despite my small size, I'm fucking strong. I can put up with a lot.

"Do I get my reward now?" I said, panting and sweating and shaking.

"Oh, you are an eager little bunny, aren't you?"

"Fuck, yes. I mean, yes, Sir." My voice wasn't steady, but I didn't know if that was from suffering or anticipation.

I hissed as Alastair rested his palm on my sore skin.

"Shhh. You're doing so well, Toby."

Those words did something to me. They made it all worth it. I would run through literal fire to hear Alastair praise me. *What is that about?*

He smoothed his palm over my flaming cheeks, causing the pain to come to the surface again.

"You know it's gonna hurt, right? Getting railed after a spanking like that?"

I couldn't explain why that made it hotter. Was I officially a masochist now? Had I always been one? Had Alastair suspected?

"I don't care. Anyway, I deserve it."

"For being good or for being bad?"

"Does it matter?"

He laughed. "No, Mr. Dunn. It doesn't."

I cracked a smile. Now that my brain chemicals were overriding the intense pain of the discipline, I floated in a hazy space of pleasure and warmth and arousal. I heard the crack of a lube bottle opening, then the cool fall of liquid down the crack of my ass.

I moaned with anticipation and at the frigid relief of the cold substance. "Oh my God."

"You want this?" Alastair asked, as he smoothed the lube down my crack and swirled it around my hole.

"Oh my God. Yes. Fuck, yes."

"All right, naughty boy. I'm gonna fuck the fight right out of you."

I wanted Alastair — *this* — so bad. This hot, toppy, dominant version of Alastair was the answer to prayers I hadn't even known I'd made. It was something that had been set in motion the day he'd come upon me having a smoke outside Maverick Molly's and when he'd fixed the laces on my shoe. This seemed like the inevitable result of that initial meeting.

Alastair pushed his finger all the way into me, making a soft sound in his throat.

I grunted and laid my forehead on my arms, lifting my ass for him and giving him access.

"God, you're fucking hungry for it, aren't you?"

"Starving."

I was somewhere out of reality but firmly planted in what was happening this instant. The hunger in my gut was intense, and my cock dripped with the anticipation of a solid fucking. I wondered how much it would hurt, how hard Alastair would pound my burning ass, and shuddered.

"Soon, Toby," Alastair murmured. The finger slipped out, and I almost cried. I didn't want to be empty.

A belt buckle clanged and fabric rustled.

"Just getting sheathed," Alastair mumbled, and I appreciated the info. He could have fucked me bare, and I'd have never realized because I was in such a state of need and desire I didn't even fucking care. But it was good to know he was taking appropriate precautions, even if the idea of forgoing the condom seemed hot in the moment.

"Let me in, baby. I know you can take it."

Those fucking words. He was going to kill me with his words.

I closed my eyes and relaxed. The head of his cock pushed into me—a sudden, perfect intrusion that caused me to whimper.

"Yes. Oh, fuck yes," he hissed, going deeper.

The initial burn of his entry blended with the pain on the outside of my ass and lit me up. And soon it faded so that the outer fire became a counterpoint to the ecstasy of penetration.

"Alastair!" I cried as he sank in all the way, pinioning me against the wood of the antique desk, curling over me and causing the tender skin of my bottom to sing with agony.

"So sweet. You are so fucking sweet," he murmured.

"No. I'm naughty. I'm a naughty, naughty boy," I panted, crazed with the pleasure and the pain and the desperate, outrageous need.

"So fucking naughty," Alastair moaned, fucking me with care. *Too much care.*

"Yes," I said, and it sounded like a sob. "Please fuck me. *Please.*"

I'd never heard myself sound so broken, so desperate.

"Do you think I could deny you anything?" he whispered in my ear as he started to move.

I closed my eyes. My arms ached and my elbows felt raw from the wood, my hands clasped in some kind of prayer.

"Grab the desk," Alastair growled.

I unfurled my fingers. Every bit of me was a mix of sensation — torture and bliss bursting like pop rockets. I hooked my hands over the edge of the desk and held on as Alastair fucked me with powerful and relentless motions that made the desk creak and all sorts of sounds come out of my mouth.

He wasn't quiet, either. He cursed and praised me in the same breath as he lost himself in his pleasure, and I wondered if he'd forgotten about me in its pursuit. Just the thought of it made me love it more — the idea of being used, of being an object that existed purely to be ravished and fucked and enjoyed. I didn't know why, but it made me crazy in a good way. I wanted to reach for my cock, but I didn't dare or I'd slide off the desk and onto the floor.

Alastair was a beast, and I loved him for it. He sank deep and hard, then pulled back and did it again. The third time, he stopped with his cock buried inside me and gave out a yell, giving shallow and staccato thrusts as he filled the condom, his fingers clutching my hips, his hot breath on my back, his soft satisfied groan in my ears.

My brain was a whirl of sensation and desire. I almost came from the mere thought of Alastair's climax. But I didn't need to, because Alastair wrapped slick fingers around my cock and started moving again, fucking me with his still-hard cock and jerking me with rough, merciless strokes.

"Come on, Toby," he murmured, out of breath and wrecked from his recent orgasm.

It didn't take long. I held onto the edge of the desk for dear life as he propelled me over the edge and cursed as my cock pulsed streams of jizz over his fingers and my insides burst with fireworks.

"Oh yeah. Fuck, yeah," Alastair muttered. "You're gorgeous, Toby. Fucking gorgeous. And you're *mine*."

Those possessive words stretched out my climax. I groaned in agreement as the last strains of pleasure wracked me. Alastair supported himself on the desk as we recovered. He shifted and his fingers anchored the condom as he pulled out.

He kissed my shoulder and straightened, giving my ass a slap that made me howl in surprise and agony.

"Sore?" he said, as I hugged the desk and rode the wave of pain until it lessened.

"Don't fucking touch me," I growled, then whimpered.

"Oh, honey, I'm gonna be touching this ass for days, until it's not sore anymore. Then I'm gonna make it hurt again."

Why those possessive and sadistic words sent a thrill through me I'd never know, but I was learning not to question these things.

"Fine. Only lay off the spanking for a couple of days at least. *Shit,*" I said, letting him help me up as my muscles and joints added their complaints. "Everything hurts now."

He smiled with what might have been actual sympathy. "The pain is easier to bear when you're super aroused. Your ass looks amazing, by the way."

I craned my head around to look but I couldn't see it that well. "Oh fuck. I have to pull my panties up…and my jeans!"

Alastair chuckled, the bastard, tucking himself away and fastening his belt. "Well, you don't *have* to, but we'll get some strange looks if you don't."

"Very funny," I said. "Am I officially a spanking slut, now?"

"I don't know. Are you?"

"I think I might be. Yeah."

He grinned. "Well, aren't I the luckiest bastard this side of Saskatchewan?"

"What time is it, anyway? I'm fucking exhausted."

"Yeah, you look a little wrecked," he said, as I tried to pull up my panties with trembling fingers.

"Oh honey, here…let me."

He helped me to do it so the cloth didn't scrape against the tender skin of my backside. The jeans were tougher, because they didn't leave much room. I gasped and made other ouchy noises as he helped me get them up. Then I fastened the fly and tried to ignore the flaming heat and throbs of residual pain.

Alastair turned me around and pulled me into his arms, holding me close and peppering my cheek with kisses.

"That was amazing and beautiful and so much fun!"

"Yeah. It was. My...head is spinning a bit. And I've got the shakes?"

"You're probably coming down from subspace."

"Yeah. What the fuck is subspace? That floaty feeling?"

"Sure."

"Is that a real thing?"

"Did it feel real?"

"Yeah. I feel kind of crappy now, though."

He held me in his arms until I stopped trembling and my breathing evened out.

"It's better now," I said, because it was true. Alastair's strength and confidence helped me to ground myself, although I wouldn't say no to more pampering. "Can we pick up a pizza on the way home? I'm fucking starved."

We'd used Alastair's car this time.

"For you, Toby? Anything."

Walking was another lesson in pain management, and I wondered for a moment if it was worth it. On the other hand, having a reminder of Alastair's stern discipline and expert fucking was not without its appeal. But the focus it took to walk somewhat normally as we descended the stairs was significant.

"Remind me to wear baggy pants next time...and cotton underwear."

Alastair laughed. He handed me my coat. "Here. I'll take the key back."

"Thank you!"

As I was putting my coat on, Patrick peeked around the corner of the games room.

"Hi!"

One of the disadvantages of working at the place where you came to get kinky with your boyfriend was that everyone thought it was okay to be up in your business.

"Hey, Patrick."

"What are you doing here on your night off?" he said.

At that point, Robin pushed past him.

"You mean, *who* is he doing?" Robin said, looking me up and down with a salacious glare. "Well, well, well," he said. "You can stand. But can you walk?"

"Oh, fuck off."

I tried to demonstrate that I was none the worse for wear, but my actions must have looked a little stiff because Robin burst out laughing, and Patrick turned red.

"Huh. Someone got paddled."

Patrick's mouth dropped open. "Like, with an *actual* paddle? *Really?*"

Robin regarded Patrick with an expression of such disbelief that even I laughed. "Oh, my sweet summer child," he said, cupping his fingers under Patrick's chin. "What am I even gonna do with you?"

"Not *paddle* me, that's for sure," Patrick said, his eyes going wide.

"Such a shame," Robin said, shaking his head and giving me a wink. "Enjoy the rest of your night, Toby."

"Thanks." Wow, Robin being actually nice to me was a big shift. "And it was a ruler."

"Same difference. Ask your dear Mr. Kenney if he's got any Arnica," he said, before he ushered Patrick back to the floor.

"What?" I said, but they were gone, and Alastair was back.

"Okay, let's go." He grabbed his coat.

"What's Arnica?"

"It's a topical pain reliever. Why?"

I touched the denim over my smarting backside. "I think I need some. Robin told me to ask you."

"Sure. I have some. I'll rub it on you when we get home."

I smiled at the thought of being taken care of like that.

"Okay. Thanks."

"Oh, Toby?"

"Yeah?"

"I've booked the Bordello for next Friday." He grinned, and I'd never seen him so jubilant.

"Oh, my fuck," I said, wondering if this was my life now.

Chapter Twenty

A Trick of the Eyes

Alastair was good on his word.

We picked up a large pepperoni pizza from our favorite joint and scarfed it down when we got home. Then he ran me a bath, which soothed my muscles and, after the initial pain of contact, settled the ache there too. He rubbed the Arnica gel on my ass while I lay face down on the bed with my arms tucked under my chest, and got lost in the joy of being well cared for, something that still felt very new and precious to me.

While he was doing this, he asked me questions about my childhood, which might have seemed strange after an intense kink scene, but I understood his curiosity and didn't mind.

"Was your mom always like that?"

I sighed, focusing on the delicious feeling of his hands on my body.

"No. Well, she's always been a flake, I guess? But I didn't notice so much when I was really young. I had a lot of freedom, because she wasn't on my case all the time. She ignored me most of the time, which wasn't always bad."

I didn't tell him about having to forage in the beat-up refrigerator for whatever food she'd happened to put in there on any given week. Or how my friends had offered me things from their lunches that they'd said they didn't want, but I had known were given to me on the suspicion that I might not have enough to eat at home.

"Yeah?"

"Uh-huh. I could have gotten into so much trouble. But I guess I'm...not that kind of a person? I don't know. I worried a lot—about her, about *us*. Maybe...I felt more like the parent?"

"God. That's a lot to deal with."

"It felt normal to me." Except on the days it had felt awful and unfair. "It helped having a friend like Esther. Anyway, when I had my growth spurt was when things went downhill. My mom has a lot of issues with men. She doesn't trust them, for one thing, but I guess I can't blame her for that. Then again, when she does trust them, she always trusts the wrong ones. You know?"

"Huh," Alastair said, digging his fingers into my muscles in the most exquisite way.

"Like that guy we saw... He was probably her drug dealer or just another junkie she'd convinced to help her out. I guess she has to be loaded or high to trust a man, but that brings its own problems, right?"

"Right," he said, agreeing with me, even though he didn't understand the whole situation with my mom. But he never would. I didn't even understand it. I knew she'd been through a lot. Her parents had not been the nicest people.

"God. My childhood seems like *Howdy Doody* next to yours."

I craned my head to give him a look.

"Howdy *whaty*?"

He laughed. "*Howdy Doody*. It was some show in the fifties, I don't know. All crazy wholesome and pure, I guess?"

"Was that the kind of childhood you had?"

"Well, it wasn't perfect. My parents both worked, so they weren't around very much, either. But they made sure I felt loved and was cared for, which seems pretty luxurious to me right now."

"Yeah," I said quietly. "It is. You're lucky."

"I'm starting to figure that out."

"My life wasn't *terrible*. I'm sure a lot of kids had it way worse. It made me a stronger person. Although the evidence for that is sorely lacking at the moment."

"What do you mean?"

The man was rubbing cream into the skin of my ass because he'd told me to bend over a desk and I'd let him beat me with a ruler. It didn't exactly make me feel strong and powerful.

"Well, look at me."

He stopped the rubbing and squeezed my butt cheek, making me gasp. He sat on the bed beside me, using a towel to wipe the remnants of the soothing gel from his fingers.

"Toby, you know the submissive has all the power, right?"

I blinked. "Well, I… Really?"

He smiled. "The Dom is the one telling the sub what to do, but the Dom has to work within the boundaries that the submissive has already laid out. And at any time, the submissive can stop everything with one word."

"Well, so can the Dom. That's what you said."

"True. It's important that everyone has a way to tap out."

"Yeah."

"The fact that you put yourself in that vulnerable situation, went to the Bordello with me, submitted to things you had never experienced before because you thought it might be fun?" he shook his head. "It takes a certain amount of courage to do that, Toby."

"Huh."

"And the fact that you persevered through the ruler thing, in order to please me and get a fucking amazing orgasm out of it at the end? That takes a very strong person."

I thought about it and decided his perspective had merit. I smiled up at him.

"It was pretty amazing. And the ruler? I didn't hate it."

He laughed.

"Well, I hated it for a couple of seconds here and there. But I'd do it again in a heartbeat—and, uh, maybe try out some of those paddles."

His dimple was so cute.

"Oh, honey. I have so much I want to show you. But I want to take my time. Do you know why?"

"No," I breathed, getting lost in his eyes and the way they seemed to have endless depths of emotion and knowledge.

"Because watching you experience all this stuff for the first time is...it's incredible, erotically and emotionally." He reached out and cupped my chin. "I've only ever been with experienced players. I've never taken someone on this journey before. I'm honored I get to be the one to explore it with you."

* * * *

The next morning, we lazed around, eating pancakes and drinking too much coffee. I was able to sit down without too much trouble, as long as it was on a softer surface like the couch. The chair at the kitchen table was another story, which I discovered at breakfast. Alastair kindly let me have my lunch and supper on the sofa.

He seemed even more concerned with my comfort now that he'd taken it from me temporarily, and I reveled in his caretaking. I couldn't decide if I liked the *kink* better or the *aftercare*, because it was really nice to know that someone was trying to make your life better. I hadn't had that before. I didn't wholly trust it, but I wasn't gonna sabotage it, either.

I had planned to meet Esther that Monday at a cute little café called Matin for breakfast. Alastair had risen at six-thirty — his normal work wake-up time — and he'd kissed me good-bye when I'd briefly surfaced from sleep.

She was nowhere to be seen when I got there, which was par for the course with Esther. The repercussions of my playtime with Alastair had gone from a six point five on the pain scale to an easy two. When I sat on one of the wooden chairs, there was just enough to remind me of the fun I'd had without impinging on my ability to be comfortable. Although, if we ended up staying for a while, I might have to move to a softer spot. *That* would be a fun conversation.

Alastair was thrilled about the fact that there was still some tenderness, *the possessive fuck*. He kept threatening to take me over his knee and bring the pain level back up, but I'd assumed he was joking, perhaps mistakenly.

Anyway, since I was a newbie to the whole 'beat my ass then watch me squirm' party, I decided to take it easy on myself. Besides, I had to be at zero before we went back to the Bordello on Friday. I was anticipating that with equal parts excitement and trepidation.

I was sitting there, people watching and waiting for Esther, when I happened to glance at the back corner of the café. A guy was sitting in the shadows of a booth there, and he looked kind of familiar. I was confused, then it hit me. It was the man who had approached me and Alastair outside Maverick Molly's the week before.

A slice of fear went through me. He wasn't looking in my direction, so maybe he hadn't seen me yet — or he was trying to go unnoticed.

How had he known where to find me? And what did he want? My mom was probably furious that I'd escaped her clutches but not stupid enough to have me murdered…hopefully.

I turned away and pulled my phone from my pocket. I figured I was relatively safe in this café, with numerous customers and staff about. I wished that Esther would get here. Normally, I could accept that she was never on time and it was all part of her unique charm. But today I was not amused.

I thumbed my phone and pulled up Alastair's contact info. My first instinct was to text him that the guy was here, but then wondered if that was an overreaction. I didn't want to bother Alastair at his job with something that would scare him or make him worry. I probably wasn't in *actual* danger. This wasn't America where anyone and everyone had a gun and people were shot in public places all the time. Right? *Right?*

Esther still hadn't shown up, so I sent a quick text her way with a question mark and a shot of the table where I was sitting. Then I texted an eggplant to Alastair with a winky face, just for fun and to make me feel better. He sent me a shocked face and a water squirting emoji. I put my phone on the table and glanced around casually to check the corner.

He was gone.

I looked to see if he'd gone to the counter or was on his way out, but there wasn't any sign of the guy. The whole thing had unsettled me, and I wondered if I'd imagined it. I picked up my phone and tapped on my mahjong app. Enjoying the solo player game was a good way to settle my nerves and distract myself, which was why I jumped out of my skin and dropped my phone when someone's hands covered my eyes.

"Guess who?"

By the time I'd processed it was Esther, my phone was bouncing off the floor.

"Oh shit. Sorry!" she yelped.

In a second she was half under the table, getting it. She held it out to me with a wide smile. "Here."

Her smile vanished. "Oh my God, what's wrong?" she said, as I took the phone in trembling fingers and tried to calm my racing heart.

"You scared the shit out of me, Esther. What the fuck?"

"Oh damn, I'm sorry," Esther said, getting up and dusting the dirt off her knees.

"You're late," I said, sounding more pissed off than I'd meant to.

Esther's eyebrows scrunched together. "I'm always late," she stated, because it was true.

I sighed and checked my phone for crumbs and dirt, wiping the screen with my thumb. "I know. I'm trying to decide if I love that or hate it about you."

She shrugged and leaned back in her chair, regarding me with blatant curiosity. "You seem a little jumpy. What's going on?"

"Nothing."

"Everything okay with Mr. Alastair Kenney?"

Hearing his name made me feel better in a weird way.

I nodded. "Yeah, everything's fine. Great, in fact."

"Man, I'm so jealous. When am I gonna find my kinky millionaire?"

"He's not a millionaire."

"You said he owns a house in Old Ottawa South. That's pretty close."

I shrugged. "Well, he's got money, enough that he doesn't worry about spending it."

Esther grinned and pointed at me. "On you."

I laughed.

"Seriously, Toby, are you okay? You looked like a startled goat there for a second."

"Thanks."

"I mean that in the best of ways. Goats are adorable."

"Probably not when they're scared."

"*Even* when they're scared. Just don't go fainting on me."

"What?"

"Never mind. What's up?"

I blinked. "It's probably nothing."

"Probably?"

"Can we get some food?" I asked.

"Yes. Absolutely, my lovely baby goat."

I narrowed my eyes but didn't say anything.

"What do you want?"

"A medium dark roast, black, please."

"Anything to eat?"

"Yeah. Something sweet."

"You got it."

While she stood in line, I took some deep breaths and tried to settle my nerves. Nothing had happened. I'd seen some guy who had looked like the creep who had approached us, that was all. It probably wasn't even him.

I started to feel angry. Because how dare my mom try to freak me out by sending her drug dealer or her homeless coke buddy to do her dirty work? If she wanted me to come home, she could maybe ask me the normal way. Of course, I'd still tell her to go fuck herself. But why did she have to do this creepy, weird fucking thing?

Esther brought my coffee in a tray with her tea and a plate of delicious-looking pastries.

"I couldn't decide, so I got one of each. You can have them all, Toby. I'm sorry for being so late."

I took my coffee and popped the lid right off, looking into the swirling darkness of the caffeinated depths. I hadn't had any yet today, because I'd known I was coming here.

Maybe I'd hallucinated that guy. Caffeine dependency was a thing.

Esther watched me blow on my coffee and take some sips.

"You look like you're making love to it."

"I am. Sooo good." After another long sip I was able to give her a smile.

"There's my Toby. Now, come on. What's bugging you?"

I fingered a raspberry Danish off the plate and took a bite. Sweet icing, fruit, and flaky pastry melted in my mouth. I closed my eyes to really enjoy it.

"Wow. If you look like that during sex, no wonder you've got a rich boyfriend."

I snorted a laugh and opened my eyes. Esther was fucking hilarious, and I loved her so much.

I got serious again. "Okay, look. The other night—well, I guess it was last week—when Alastair and I were leaving the club after my shift, this gross guy turned up and basically told me I should move back in with my mom if I knew what was good for me."

Esther's expression turned murderous. "What the *fuck*?"

"I know. It was obviously some drugged-out friend of hers—or her dealer. I don't know."

"Toby, that's messed up."

"I know."

"Did you go to the police?"

I gave her a strange look. "What? No. What was I gonna tell them?"

"Uh, that this stranger threatened you in the street? I assume it was the street. He didn't come into the club did he?"

"No. Jacob would've turfed him."

"Exactly. Wait! You said Alastair was there…"

"Not at first. I was…uh…" I blinked and looked everywhere but at Esther.

She narrowed her eyes. "Smoking. You were smoking, weren't you?"

"I had a cigarette in my hand. But I didn't smoke it."

She looked skeptical. "Why not?"

"Because by the time Alastair got rid of the creepy guy, I didn't want to... I didn't want to be like *her*. I *don't* want to be like her."

"Toby, you'll never be like her."

I shrugged. "Hopefully."

"Definitely. But I won't argue that the smoking habit is sketchy as fuck. I'm glad you ditched it."

"Yeah. Anyway, while I was waiting for you, I thought I saw the same guy sitting in the corner." I nodded toward the booth now filled with a couple and their two kids.

"No way!" She looked legitimately worried, and it was freaking me out a bit.

"I don't actually think it was him. It was probably my imagination."

"Oh man. I'm sorry I was so late, though."

"It's okay. I'm obviously fine. Do I still look like a goat?"

"Not so much."

"Perfect." I took another bite of the Danish. "Fuck, these are good. Have the strawberry one."

We ate and chatted and joked around, like always, and it was so nice to hang out with my best friend again.

"So, things are going good with your man?"

"Sure."

"Sure?"

"He's incredible. And he seems to like me for some reason."

"Toby..."

"Okay, fine. I am awesome — in some ways, maybe."

"In lots of ways." She smiled. "He must like baby goats."

"Oh, fuck off."

She laughed. "I'm thrilled for you, Toby. You deserve to have a sexy man fall in love with you."

I held up my hand. "Whoa, whoa. Who said anything about love? Jesus Christ."

She shrugged. "Maybe not yet. But when you talk about him, you go all gooey-schmooey, and if he has any sense, he'll fall head over heels for you."

"I do not go— Wait, *what*?"

"Toby. I've been telling you for at least five years you're a total catch. When are you going to believe me?"

"I guess when I finally get a ring on my finger," I said, sticking my tongue out at her.

"Hmm. Well. If you look at Alastair like you looked at that coffee and Danish earlier, I bet it won't be long."

* * * *

After the café, Esther and I wandered around Old Ottawa South, popping into several quaint little stores. At Global Pet Foods—which was actually a chain pet store but still cool—we messed around trying dog collars on each other, because it was hilarious and made some of the staff nervous.

"Oh my God. That looks fucking cool on you," Esther said, with a hand over her mouth.

"What? No, it doesn't," I said. I touched my fingers to the soft brown leather and hovered them over the silver buckle.

Esther took a photo with her phone and showed me.

"Oh, shit. It does look kind of good," I said.

"You should get it. I bet Alastair would like it."

"It's for a dog!"

"So? Don't be so confined by social expectations."

I kind of did want to get it. Alastair probably would like it. But that would mean I'd have to take it off, give it to the cashier and pay for it, knowing that the sales guy saw me trying it on myself.

Esther rolled her eyes and held out her hand. "Give it to me, you coward."

"What?"

"I'm gonna buy it for you. Alastair can thank me later."

I blinked in embarrassed confusion, but I unbuckled the clasp and handed it to her.

"Good boy," she said, with a smirk.

My face flushed with heat as she patted her thigh and said, "Come."

I was never gonna live this down, but I wanted the fucking collar.

The sales associate took the collar from Esther and held it in front of me.

"Good choice. Looked amazing on you," he said with a smile, his eyes flashing up at me.

What the fuck?

I blinked. "Thanks?"

He laughed. "Don't worry. Lots of people buy these for themselves."

"Really? Even in Old Ottawa South?" Esther asked.

He leaned in so that the smattering of other customers wouldn't hear. "You wouldn't believe how much of a kinky underbelly this city has. I can point you to a few places…"

Esther directed her thumb my way. "He works at Maverick Molly's."

The sales guy's eyes widened. "Well. Okay, then."

His smile got bigger, and he gave me a once-over, which I was positive was the only time I'd ever been eye-fucked in a pet store.

"Thank you so much..." — Esther squinted at his name tag — "Remington. You've been very helpful."

"No problem." He handed her the paper bag with the collar that he'd wrapped in pink tissue paper. If I hadn't been dating Alastair, I might have asked for his phone number.

When we got outside, Esther dissolved into hilarity.

"Oh my God. You got that surprised goat look again in there. But I think Remington *liked* it."

I rolled my eyes and snatched the bag out of her hand. "Thank you for getting this." I went to get my wallet from my pocket.

"Oh no. Consider it a gift — my contribution to your kinky journey with Alastair."

I raised my eyebrows and put the wallet back. "Should I tell him that?"

"Why not?" She grabbed my hand, and we skipped along the sidewalk in the bright winter sunshine.

Chapter Twenty-One

Nigel

I'd tucked the collar away in my dresser since I hadn't had a chance to wear it for Alastair yet. I figured I'd put it on Thursday, when we'd be home together, as a sexy surprise. But I did try it on a few times, simply to admire the way it circled my neck and gave me a Goth-punk-sex-puppy vibe.

On Wednesday, I was puttering around in my sweats and a crop top doing some cleaning. I wanted to make sure I wasn't taking advantage of Alastair's generosity in housing me so cheaply, so I liked to mop, dust and vacuum during the day. It made my little gender fluid heart happy to play Hazel Housewife for a bit. I even had a little white apron that I'd 'borrowed' from work for just this purpose.

I had turned the vacuum off and was bundling the cord together when the doorbell rang. It startled me. Did people still ring doorbells? I'd thought everyone used text like I did.

I was highly suspicious as I approached the door, especially because of my recent encounter with the stranger at the club. What if it was him? I wouldn't be able to see who it was from the living room window, but Alastair's door had a peep hole. I opened the inside door as quietly as I could and tiptoed into the entry, then leaned in to look through the glass.

It wasn't the guy from outside the club. Instead, a stunningly attractive Black man wearing aviator sunglasses and a navy pea coat waited patiently for someone to acknowledge his presence. He pushed the button again, and the bell rang while I composed myself and opened the door.

"Hello."

Then I remembered that I was wearing ratty gray sweats, no underwear and a *My Little Pony* T-shirt from the children's section of The Gap that worked as a crop top.

Fuck.

My face flushed as the man smiled and took off his aviators, revealing intense blue eyes.

"Oh, hello! Is Alastair at home?"

Oh, fuck me, he has a British accent.

I attempted a smile, but I was feeling self-conscious and caught-out, so I probably looked like a surprised goat.

"Oh, uh, no. He's at work right now."

"No worries, mate. But could you tell him I stopped by?"

I nodded. "And you are?"

"Oh, fuck, yeah. Sorry," he laughed. "I'm Nigel," he said, offering me his hand to shake, which I did. "Just tell him I'm back in town, yeah?"

"Sure." I said, forcing myself to let go of his hand while I blinked in wonder at his beauty.

"Great! Thanks."

He didn't ask who I was or what I was doing at Alastair's home. He simply turned with a wave and strolled down the porch steps with the air of a person assured of their own appeal.

I shut the door and scratched at a spot on my neck, my fingers encountering the leather of the brown dog collar.

"Oh, fuck off. Seriously?" I said to myself, tearing the buckle open and flinging the questionable accessory to the floor, wondering who in the fuck Nigel was and why he wanted to see Alastair.

* * * *

I finished cleaning, my mind turning over the sudden appearance of a gorgeous man looking for my boyfriend. The obvious answer was that he was one of Alastair's former hookups looking for another hot date, which didn't make me feel very good.

Sure, I was cute and seemed to be at least a bit kinky, but this man was fucking stunning and had a history of some kind with Alastair. Alastair had said that he'd hooked up with men for casual sex quite a bit before we'd met. But what if he and Nigel-with-the-British accent had had some kind of arrangement? An arrangement that meant that they'd had sex more than once?

I wasn't sure how I felt about that. Hold on, yes, I did. I didn't like it at all.

But that was in Alastair's past, which was his business and *not* mine, even though we were in a committed relationship now, except that it became my business when a beautiful man came looking for my boyfriend.

I retrieved the dog collar from the floor and changed into some nicer clothes before Alastair arrived home from work. I decided to make spaghetti, since Alastair liked the way I mixed cheese in with the tomato sauce for the finished product—a kind of poor-man's lasagne. Anyway, it was easy, he liked it and we had the ingredients. And I needed to prove that I was a goddamned catch, even if I didn't look as good as Nigel-with-the-British-Accent.

While we were digging into it, I gave Alastair Nigel's message.

"Some guy was looking for you."

Alastair had just shoveled a forkful of cheesy spaghetti into his mouth. He had to chew and swallow before he could inquire further. He wiped some stray tomato sauce from his lips.

"What?"

"Some guy came to the door, looking for you. Nigel? British? *Gorgeous*?"

Alastair's eyes flew wide and so did his smile. "No way! Nigel's back? That's amazing!"

I narrowed my eyes, the green-eyed monster rearing its head, no matter how determined I was to be cool about this.

"*Is it?*"

"Yes, it fucking is. Nigel's wonderful!"

Maybe Nigel hadn't been a sexual conquest, then.

"And an *incredible* fuck as well, but I won't get into that."

I dropped my fork and almost choked.

"*What?*" I asked.

Alastair laughed, his gaze on my angry face.

"Well…we used to hook up, you know." He cleared his throat and sobered. "Occasionally."

"*How* occasionally?"

Alastair's expression went from happy to cautious. "Well…he's never in town for long…so when he was here we'd…"

I leaned back in my chair and folded my arms over my chest. "Do go on."

"Never mind. That's all in the past."

"Unless," I said, trying to keep my voice modulated, "he's expecting to hook up with you again, now that he's *back* in town?" Anxiety swirled in my gut.

"Toby," Alastair said.

"It's fine. If you want to, I mean. God, who wouldn't?" I said, sliding my chair out and standing up. "I'm tired. Good night."

I was being a big, insecure baby, but I couldn't fucking help it. Nigel was so much better looking than I was, probably kinky as fuck and an *adult*, whereas I still felt like a kid half the time. I was getting my shit together, maybe, but I wasn't actually adulting yet — or it didn't feel like I was.

I almost slammed the door, but decided that that would be going too far, especially considering the adulting thing. If I was going to be a grown up, I probably shouldn't be running away in a huff from my kinky boyfriend, but at least I could refrain from making it obvious. I shut the door with a quiet click and threw myself face down on the bed, hiding my head in the pillows.

I mean, who the fuck wanted to be an adult, anyway?

I waited for Alastair to come upstairs to make sure I was okay. But after twenty minutes I realized that wasn't going to happen, which I supposed was totally fair, except it pissed me off. He was all into playing around with our age gap when we were being kinky, but when it really mattered, he wasn't going to buy into my need for a guiding hand?

Well, fuck it.

I didn't know how to go downstairs. I mean, I didn't know how to gather my self-dignity—what was left of it—and reintroduce myself into Alastair's space. Well, *our* space. Should I go down there and apologize for acting like a ten-year-old child?

I swallowed my pride and opened my door, then padded downstairs in my sock feet. Alastair was sitting on the couch watching TV. Usually he loaded the dishwasher when I cooked dinner, but the kitchen was still full of dirty dishes, and that triggered a *ton* of resentful energy tied to my relationship with my mom, and everything I'd planned to say in a moment of maturity flew out of the window.

I stomped into the kitchen and started to clean up in a way that couldn't be ignored. I'd never have dared to act this way at my mom's, because she would have shoved more dishes in my face, but maybe this whole thing was the result of feeling safe. Anyway, I was still mad and jealous and *pissed*, and I didn't know how to deal with those emotions other than to bang dirty pots and pans around.

"Toby."

I ignored Alastair and continued to act out. I couldn't stop now. I was going for the Oscar.

"Toby!"

A chill went through me at the steel in his tone, and I swiveled my head to look at him.

Holy fucking shit.

He was standing in the entrance to the kitchen, regarding me with a 'you'd better get your shit together and answer me, or else' expression, and it wasn't the same as being called out by my mom. Hell, it was *completely* different. He wasn't yelling and throwing things. He was calm and had raised his voice, but he actually smiled.

"Stop acting like a child."

That was something my mom had never said to me, probably because she was the child in the relationship. Oh God, was I acting like her? I looked at the pot in my hand and contemplated what Alastair had said.

I put the pot down very quietly on the counter and straightened, taking a deep breath and turning to face Alastair.

"That's better," he said, and the approval in his words sent a jolt to my cock.

I nodded, wiping a hand across my face. "I'm sorry."

"I know. Come here."

Boy, did I ever feel like a child now. I walked over there feeling like my daddy was disappointed with me.

"I'm sorry. I shouldn't be acting this way," I admitted.

Alastair took my hands and stared into my eyes. "That's true, but I need to tell you something. I met Nigel Farrow through Grindr four years ago." He rubbed my fingers with his own, settling me.

"He's fucking beautiful," I whispered.

"He's a model."

I tried to pull my hands away, but Alastair wouldn't let me.

Figured. A model. I wasn't that surprised.

"Toby, the last time I had sex with Nigel was almost a year ago."

Well, that was a relatively long time, I supposed.

"Yeah, but—"

"Hmm?"

"How—" I cleared my throat and tried to sound remotely like an adult. "How often did you guys hook up?"

Alastair blinked and seemed confused by my question.

I took a deep breath. "It's just that I got the impression you only hooked up once with another guy, then moved on. Like, that you only ever had one-night stands." It sounded like such a petty distinction. "Forget it. Let me finish cleaning up."

"Toby, you're right about my habits. Only…Nigel and I were different."

"Okay. Like, I don't have a problem with that—except he's here now…in town. And he probably wants to hook up with you again…"

"I'm sure he does, but that isn't going to happen."

He said it in such a definitive way that I felt better. "Really? You're sure?"

He laughed. "Toby, do you think I'd endanger what the two of us have found together for a meaningless physical connection with an old friend?"

"Ah. He's your friend."

"Yes," Alastair said. He went into the living room and sat down on the sofa. "We were other things to each other in the past, but that's all done. I promise."

A huge wave of relief hit me, and I moved forward, straddling Alastair where he sat as he enfolded me in his arms.

"Fuck. Thank God," I murmured, snuggling into him and inhaling his scent.

"You were really scared I'd—?"

"*Yes.* Have you seen him? Wait! Never mind. Of course, you have. More of him than I have."

"Toby."

"I'm sorry I'm being so dumb."

He tightened his arms and shushed me.

"It's… I don't even know why you're worried…"

"Oh my God, Alastair. *Look at me*. I'm nowhere near as beautiful as Nigel."

"You're right."

I stiffened and went to pull away.

"You're much prettier."

"Sure, sure," I said with a huff.

I felt his hands like iron grips on my arms, and he pushed me away so that I was still astride him but not collapsed against his chest.

"Do I need to spank some fucking sense into you?" Alastair said with a tone that verged on this side of anger and tipped into major frustration.

Another spike of desire went from my brain to my balls and back again.

"What?" I said in a whisper.

He stared at me. Then he cupped my chin in his hand.

"You don't even *get* how lovely you are. And it's such a *fucking* shame."

"No, that thing you said about spanking. Could you?"

He rolled his eyes and tried to stay mad. But then he laughed. "Do you want a spanking, my self-conscious, insecure, beautiful boy? Do you?"

"Well, yes."

"If I do this, will you understand how lovely you are?"

I shrugged. "Maybe."

He raised his eyebrows.

"Yes, Sir. I will." And I gave him a coy little smile as I felt myself returning to my usual level of confidence.

"All right then. Go upstairs, take off all your clothes and fold them neatly on the chair, then come down here and put yourself across my lap."

He leaned back and folded his arms across his chest, waiting for me to obey.

"Fuck," I said, moving off him and turning to walk away. I swiveled my hips as I walked, giving him a good view, and feeling better about everything. *I bet Alastair never spanked Nigel over his lap.* Maybe they'd done much kinkier things together, but not *that.* I was willing to bet my new dog collar on it.

Oh...

When I came downstairs, the dog collar was the only thing I was wearing.

Alastair was sitting where I'd left him, with his head bent as he tapped his phone. When he saw me, he smiled. Then his gaze locked on my neck.

"Toby Dunn, what are you wearing around your pretty neck?"

I shivered with the absolute bliss of surprising him.

"A dog collar," I said.

"Like, an actual collar...for a dog?"

"Yep." I popped the 'p' and touched the collar with my fingertips. "Esther bought it for me."

"Oh," he said. His gaze traveled over me, seeing me in all my naked glory, my cock half hard and heavy as I moved forward. By the time I got there, it was standing up and pointing at him.

"After I tried it on in the store," I explained.

He blinked and smiled, an expression of surprise and unparalleled joy.

"You little exhibitionist, you. How very cheeky."

I blushed. "We were goofing around."

"But you liked this one so much you bought it?"

"Well, I was embarrassed to go to the counter. Esther bought it for me."

"Hmm," he said, his eyes drinking me in. "Remind me to thank her."

"Do you like it?" I asked, even though the answer was obvious.

"I fucking love it. Come here."

"I am here," I said, suddenly nervous to be spanked.

"Uh-uh. I mean, here, here." He stretched his legs out and pointed at his lap. "Get your ass over my lap, Mr. Dunn. *Now*."

I inhaled a breath of air to steady my nerves. Then I got up on the couch beside Alastair and crawled over his lap like a puppy looking for attention. Maybe the collar was having an effect. I lowered down onto my elbows and surged forward so that my ass was positioned where he needed it.

I groaned as my cock slid over one of his thighs and bumped into the other.

"Oh, God," Alastair said, his hand smoothing the skin of my ass, squeezing and lifting one side, then the other. "Your ass is like a piece of art."

I gave him a cheeky look over my shoulder.

"You think I'm joking? I'm serious. I'm gonna get a mold made and put it on a pedestal by the front door. *Toby Dunn's Incredible Ass*. Michaelangelo would have used you as a model."

I squeaked as he ran his thumb along my crease and tickled my testicles. "I'm...really sorry about...before."

"I know you are. But I think you need a spanking."

"Of course, you do."

"Oh, come on. Let me spank this naughty bottom then fuck it. Pretty please?" he said, sliding a finger along the curve of my ass and around my hip. Then he flattened his hand and slid it up my back to rest between my shoulders. "You know you want it."

"Yeah, I want it. What the fuck's wrong with me?" I huffed a laugh.

"Oh, Toby. Nothing's wrong with you. Everything is just right." He gave my ass a swat, then another. The pain bloomed outward, and I was glad it had recovered fully from the last time. I wondered if Alastair had a plan to keep my bottom in various shades of pink. I couldn't say that the possibility bothered me that much.

I made a show of struggling, only so he'd grab my wrist and keep me still. I was a horny slut with no shame.

He settled in and started spanking me in earnest. He definitely knew what he was doing.

"Hey, have you done this before?" I asked.

"What? Don't tell me you forgot?"

"No, I…only want to know if you've spanked other guys over your lap. I kinda thought that was our thing, but…you're really good at it."

"Am I? That's good to hear." He leaned down and whispered, "Only you. I guess it just comes naturally."

"Or maybe I'm just so naughty it makes it easy?"

"Maybe that, too."

"So…how do you usually spank guys? If you don't put them over your lap…"

"Hmm. Well, sometimes I make them stretch their arms up and grab onto something, and I spank them like that. Or over the bench. It's not so intimate but it's lots of fun."

The very thought made me take a breath. "Yeah."

"You sound interested."

"I am. Only not right now. I like it this way."

"I know. So do I," Alastair said. "Now shush, and take your spanking, little boy."

"Yes, Sir."

He leaned close and whispered, "Or do you want to be my good girl today?"

I sighed, "Girl. I'll be your good girl, Alastair."

It hurt, but not as much as the ruler had, and I loved squirming on his lap, my cock rubbing against his thigh. Plus, he'd stop sometimes and play with my ass, my balls and my dick...until I was a mess and so desperate I could taste it. And he called me 'pretty' and 'lovely' and 'delicate'.

"Do you want to come, Darling?"

"Yes. Fuck, yes."

"Then do it. Show me."

Well, if that wasn't a challenge I was willing to accept. I knew I wouldn't have a problem, because I was almost there.

"Harder," I gritted through my teeth, and Alastair whacked me with more force, alternating between my cheeks and making a staccato beat on my bare flesh.

"Oh fuck! Yes, yes, yes!" I cried, bucking against his thigh as I came hard and fast. I moaned as I soaked Alastair's pants while he laughed and spanked me through it, calling me his 'lovely, messy girl'.

* * * *

Later, after he'd rubbed me with the Arnica gel and we were cuddling under the sheets, ready for bed, he told me that he'd invited Nigel-with-the-British-Accent over on Saturday afternoon, so I could meet him properly.

"But...why?" I asked, feeling like an idiot but wishing I never had to see Nigel again — or think about the two of them together.

"Because he's my friend, Toby. Surely you understand that. You can't keep me to yourself."

"Really? Because that would be super awesome." I was only half joking.

"I don't have those kinds of feelings for Nigel anymore."

I gave him a look that let him know I wasn't buying it.

"Are you telling me that if I wasn't living here, wasn't your boyfriend and so obviously amazing, that you wouldn't jump that train in a second?"

He blinked, and a sly smile crept over his features. "Okay, fine. He is a beautiful man."

I narrowed my eyes.

Alastair narrowed his eyes back. "Maybe you'd like to—? I mean, I'm sure he'd be into a threesome while he's here."

My eyes widened with shock, and Alastair dissolved into laughter.

"I'm kidding. I don't want to share."

I punched him lightly in the arm. "Shut up. I'm trying to go to sleep."

"Want me to sing you a lullaby?"

"What the fuck do you think I am? A child?" I said, with disdain. Then I snuggled up closer and sighed. "Okay, sure."

Chapter Twenty-Two

Initiation

Alastair and I had another appointment in the Bordello at Maverick Molly's on Friday. To say I was looking forward to it would be a massive understatement. He'd insisted on easing me gently into the world of kink, which I did understand and appreciate. But now that Beautiful Nigel had turned up, and Alastair had admitted that he and Nigel had got up to some pretty kinky shit, I wanted to experience something more than a little schoolboy play with a wooden ruler and over-the-lap spankings, as much as I did love them.

And since Alastair had started showing me very specific porn videos featuring a range of perverted things that he liked to do, to get my reaction, he must think that I was ready for it. I hoped I was ready, because I sure as hell wanted it, especially after watching all the delicious and mind-blowing porn. I also had a newfound respect for the range of Alastair's desires and the straightforward way he was able to speak about them. When I'd remarked on it, Alastair had given me a sober look and stated that open communication was vitally important when it came to negotiating a kink scene. And I'd promptly vowed to stop giggling at the phrase 'anal training' — mostly because the way he'd described it to me led me to believe there wouldn't be anything funny about what he was planning to do to me, even though I swore that I'd trained my anus very well myself and had he discovered any issues so far?

He'd simply smiled with a gleam in his eye and moved onto the next item of discussion.

When I walked into the gaming parlor to get the key this time, Sebastian — the less discreet of the spouses — was manning the bar.

"Whoa, the Bordello again!" he said, super loud, so that everyone in the parlor looked over to see who was getting the key. Sebastian shook his head and waved his hand, and they turned back to their games.

"Sorry," he said to me in a low voice. "Jacob keeps telling me not to shout. Sometimes I forget."

"It's fine. I don't care who knows. They're all fucking jealous, anyway."

"Yes," he said as he locked his gaze onto Alastair, who was wearing a pair of brown leather pants and had changed from his winter footwear into a pair of motorcycle boots that gave me a woody just looking at them. He had on a short black T-shirt that hugged his defined curves.

"Good evening, Mr. Kenney," Sebastian said, gazing at Alastair with eyes that wished they were single for the evening.

"Good evening, Sebastian. How's business?"

"Can't complain. Well, yes I can, but not about that."

I took the key and turned to Alastair. "Got it. Let's go."

"Hold on. Can I rent the Bordello for the next two Fridays?" Alastair asked, as my chin dropped. "Same timing."

"Let me see," Sebastian said, reaching under the counter and bringing out his iPad. He swiped and tapped, then smiled up at us. "Certainly. I'll book you in."

"The next *two* Fridays?" I said, with a tremor in my voice.

Alastair gazed at me, and I swear there was an evil glint in his eye. "There's a lot of stuff in that room, and I want you to try out everything."

I swallowed. *Fuck. Me.*

"Well, everything that interests *you*, that is. I'm hoping most of it will."

"Uh-huh."

"Thanks, Sebastian."

"No worries, Alastair."

We walked back through the crowd, and I noticed the Youngbloods and some others eyeing me with interest.

"I feel like I'm being led to the auction block."

"Ooh, now there's an idea," Alastair murmured, taking my hand.

"What?"

He shrugged, climbing the stairs ahead of me. "That would be a fun game."

"Oh my God."

"Red…or green, Toby?"

"Um. Green." My mind spun with the idea, and my cock got harder, also from looking at Alastair's ass in those leather pants and hearing the clunk of his motorcycle boots on the floor. I wondered if sexy Nigel had seen them. *Probably*.

No, no, no, I wasn't going to think about *Nigel!* I used a visualization technique I'd learned from Esther and pictured myself shoving him off a jetty into green water. He didn't die—I wasn't that evil—but he came up treading water with seaweed in his hair and a seagull shat on him.

I smiled to myself as I followed Alastair.

* * * *

Now that the Bordello was beginning to hold some very dear memories, I didn't think of the space as intimidating, except that tonight we were here for *serious* kink, and I supposed the buildup had made me anxious.

The St. Andrew's cross—I remembered the saint this time, so I must be learning—was imposing and made of polished mahogany, with leather padding all along the wood so it at least would be comfortable while you were screaming in agony at the hands of your Dom— or so I imagined.

Every time we'd come into this room on previous occasions, that cross had been there, watching us and waiting.

He led me through the parlor area, past the school desks and the bed and over to the 'serious' side of the room, where the bondage furniture was arranged in ways to make each piece accessible.

"Why don't you have a closer look, Toby? Touch stuff, examine the furniture. Tell me what excites you," Alastair said, leaning against the wall by the door with his hands in his pockets. He seemed unbelievably calm for someone who was about to tie me up and do horrible, wonderful things to my body. But I saw the bulge in the front of those brown leather pants and the intensity in his gaze when he looked at me.

"Sure," I said.

Alastair had told me to dress in something comfortable and easy to take off, as he probably would have me naked for most of our visit. I'd worn a pair of black yoga pants — *yes,* I had yoga pants, *no,* I didn't do yoga — and a baby blue T-shirt with a *Save the Panda* logo on it.

I felt like a virgin as I walked around the space. Alastair had never brought me to this section of the Bordello before, and I wanted to check everything out. There was a leather swing with chain links that rocked when I touched it. And the Berkley Horse that Alastair had explained the first time we'd come to the room. There was some kind of spanking bench that gave me chills — good ones — when I touched its padded top. But the thing that almost made me swallow my tongue when I saw it was the pillory.

"Holy shit," I said, touching the wood and noticing that this piece of furniture did not have padding. It was meant to be uncomfortable.

I glanced at Alastair, who watched me with an intensity that would have alarmed me if I hadn't known him well. He was obviously going into his Dom persona now, and I felt small and out of my depth.

"Do you like the look of that, Toby?"

"Like…is not the word I would use. No."

"Okay. How does it make you feel when you look at it?"

"Terrified."

"Okay."

"Turned on."

"Good."

"Like a piece of meat."

Alastair laughed. "Fantastic."

I blinked, then looked back at the frightening structure. "Do people really use this?"

"Oh yes."

"Have you?"

"Yes. I like it a lot. It keeps my submissive humble and obedient, and I have access to do just about anything."

I glanced at him, then looked back at the cross. "Most of this stuff works the same way...holds someone the way you want them."

He pushed off the wall and stalked toward me. A shiver slithered down my spine and right to my balls, as my dick plumped all the fucking way.

"Yes. But there's something about the pillory. It's more...undignified. More debasing, you know?" Alastair explained. "The cross, the spanking bench? They keep a submissive in a convenient position. This"—he reached past me and stroked the polished top of the cruel-looking device—"this can put a sub into a very humiliating and powerless headspace."

"No kidding."

"But it can be hard on the back, and I don't think we're going to start with it."

"Fine by me." I already felt overwhelmed, and my body thrummed with anticipation.

He moved closer and took my chin in his hands, examining my face. "What do you say, Toby? The cross or the bench?"

"To start?" I breathed.

"To start," he said. "We have lots of time to explore the room."

"Okay." I let my gaze wander over everything again. Then I pointed to the St. Andrew's cross. "That."

"Yay," he said, and it sounded hilarious coming from him. I must have looked shocked, because he shrugged and minced like a little girl. Then I saw him go into Dom mode as his expression changed, and he dropped his hand from my chin. "Strip."

I got to work, pulling my T-shirt over my head then pushing my yoga pants down and off. I piled them beside me on the floor.

"Oh, goddamn it…" Alastair said, hissing a breath.

I stared at him from under the fall of my mussed-up hair. "Do you like them, Sir?"

I'd worn a pair of neon blue lace hipsters that tucked my bottom up nicely and showed off my package.

"You can leave those on."

"Oh." I smiled. "Yes, Sir."

"And the dog collar stays on," he said as he gathered my clothes and threw them onto the spanking bench.

"Yes, Sir," I said, feeling small, obedient and so, so sexy.

"Come here," Alastair said, motioning me to follow him to the St. Andrew's cross.

I padded over there in my nakedness, looking up at it with awe and excitement.

"Now, should I face you to the wall or toward the room? I'm not asking, just thinking out loud."

"Yes, Sir."

"We'll start with you facing out, I think. But I might turn you later."

"Yes, Sir."

"I'm going to blindfold you, unless you have any objection."

"I don't, Sir."

He took a cloth from his back pocket and placed it over my eyes, tying it snug at the back of my head. And I was in darkness. My other senses took over and I became very aware of the smells and sounds around me.

"Remember your safeword?"

"Yes, Sir."

"What is it?"

"Bloomers."

Alastair's voice was a ballast, and I clung to it. I realized in that moment how rich and nuanced it was, even when he was commanding and measured.

"Turn around and step back. That's right. Now, raise your arms."

He fastened my left wrist to the metal hook in the wood, then did my right one.

"Good. Now try to get loose."

I rattled the cuffs against their hooks and felt deliciously secure. I wouldn't get loose unless Alastair undid them.

"Spread your legs."

Soon I was fastened to the cross by my ankles and wrists, with my lower back positioned where the perpendicular planks met. I couldn't see anything through the black cloth. I'd never even played with a blindfold during sex before, so this was all new. I already loved it.

I sensed movement and got a whiff of his scent as he whispered in my ear: "You okay, Toby?" The fingers of one hand hooked under the waistband of my lacy boy shorts and he drew it down past my erection and tucked it under my balls with a quick competency that impressed me.

"Yes. Yes, Sir." I breathed, my heart doing a dance in my chest, my cock reaching for the sky.

"Good," Alastair said. "I'll check in often."

"Thank you, Sir."

"You're welcome," Alastair said, then his lips were on mine. He kissed me like he had that very first day, and the current that attached us arced like an electrical wire.

"Goddammit," he muttered when he forced himself away, our panting breaths loud in the space.

"I bet you did really kinky things with Nigel," I said. *Oh fuck*. The blindfold had taken away my brain-to-mouth filter.

Alastair was silent, and I wondered if I'd fucked up the whole thing. But then he kissed me again, softer this time, and pulled back, placing a hand on my chin.

"You shouldn't be thinking about Nigel," Alastair said. "I wasn't. Now I am."

"Fuck," I muttered, pulling against my bonds with frustration. "Don't. Don't think about him."

"All right. Let's promise to keep our focus on each other. All right?"

"Yes, Sir."

"Let's focus on the magnitude of our connection, all right? It's still there, even when we're here doing kinky things, right?"

"Right, Sir."

"Then, I'm not imagining it?"

"No, Sir."

He leaned in close, and I scented him again. He kissed me very softly on the corner of my mouth, in a way that made me melt and want to do whatever he asked of me.

"We have a bond, Toby. In this room, getting kinky with you, it's like nothing I've experienced before," Alastair said, with feeling. "With anyone…ever."

"Oh." It was a small word, imbued with a million things.

"Kink is a good time, yeah. And playing with an attractive man you've just met can be intoxicating. But it's nowhere near as erotic as playing with a person you have an intimate connection with." He inhaled a long breath. "Toby, that first time, in the room at the Chateau Laurier? That was more intense, more rousing, and…scarier…than any of the kinky things I've done."

"Scarier, Sir?"

"Terrifying. Because I felt more than a physical attraction to you from the start. I didn't admit it to myself. I told myself it was my mind playing tricks on me, and that you were a hot little piece that I wanted to enjoy for one night. And since you obviously weren't experienced with kink, I didn't want to frighten you by bringing it up." He laughed softly. "I didn't realize how much your…youth and inexperience…would affect me. *Everything* that we do, no matter how *soft* or how *kinky* it is, is better than anything I've ever done, with anyone, before."

His words made my heart sing and my dick weep.

He put his mouth to my ear and spoke in a whisper. "So you don't have to worry about Nigel—or the fuckboy that left the other night or any of the other good-looking men in the city."

"Okay," I said, letting out a long, cleansing breath.

"Better?"

"Yeah."

He waited in silence. The wood creaked when I shifted my weight. Then I remembered where we were.

"Yes, *Sir*."

"There's my *good* boy."

A shudder went through me. The low tones of his voice, the erotic hit of his words and the desire I felt for this man were beyond anything and everything I'd ever known.

My body became suffused with warmth under his gaze, my cock twitched and bubbled over with want. While I waited, tense and excited, licking my lips with the anticipation of it all, Alastair wrapped his hand around my cock.

"Fuck," I stuttered, a jolt of electric need slicing into me.

I struggled against the padding of the cross, gasping for breath, as he stroked me with rough pulls of his slick fingers. I was a toy—a doll—for Alastair to play with however he might like to. My sense of self dissolved into an ocean of pleasure that wasn't gained through deliberate means, or even sought out, but became a mere by-product of Alastair's will. When I got close to coming, I opened my mouth to say something, but all that came out was a broken moan. And Alastair was reading my body and my reactions, because his hand disappeared, and my cock waved in the air.

"Fuck. *Fuck*," I said, desperate and hanging in the purgatory of frustrated desire.

Alastair clicked his tongue. "Silly Toby. Did you think I'd get you off in the first ten minutes?"

I whimpered. "No, Sir."

"That's good. Because this is going to be an exercise in endurance."

Oh fuck.

"Yes, Sir."

And his hand was on me again, smoothly stroking and teasing, until I got close once more. His touch disappeared.

I made a frustrated, angry sound.

"Quiet. This is nothing. And you need to learn control."

I didn't reply. I didn't think it was a question.

He worked me to the point of orgasm too many times, leaving me in a state of paralyzed agony.

"Please, please, Sir! Please...I need to come," I whispered, thrusting into the air and rattling my bonds.

"No, I don't think so."

I made a noise of desperation, and Alastair laughed. He *laughed*!

"I'm going to turn you around."

All the nerves under my skin crackled as he pressed himself against me and unbuckled my wrist restraints. He backed up and brought my arms down.

"Don't touch yourself," Alastair commanded, as he bent to my ankle restraints. "Let's get these off," he said, pulling my sexy boy shorts down as I stepped out of them. He turned me so that I faced the cross then refastened the cuffs, the length of him pressing against me, the jut of his erection a teasing reminder that he got off on my struggle.

When he finished, he kissed my cheek and stepped back.

"Oh, hell," he sighed.

"Yes, Sir," I said, my voice tentative and unsure. I felt more vulnerable with my back to the room, to him. What was he going to do? When would he let me come? There were so many questions that I didn't dare ask.

"You look fucking profane and *so* goddamned beautiful."

I gripped the chains and thrust my hips forward to brush my cock against the leather padding.

"Uh-uh. No frotting the cross. Keep still."

Oh my God. How was I not going to shove my aching, dripping cock against the cross when it was *right there.*

I tried to keep still. I wanted to please him.

His hand came down on my right buttock, hard, and I grunted. I hadn't expected it, but it seemed obvious he'd start with that. Then he spanked the other side, and I moaned. I was getting used to the pain of a hand spanking now, and it was everything I'd ever hoped for. Here, though, where I was blindfolded and attached by each limb to this inanimate object, it was so much more. Pain and pleasure, discipline and care, correction and guidance—a decadent debasement at the hands of my talented Dom.

Who knew that Hell was actually a gateway to Heaven?

The clomp of Alastair's boots echoed in my ears as he walked away. I heard him whistling an unfamiliar tune as he rifled through the implements that hung to my left. My heart pounded in my chest and my cock surged, wondering what was coming.

He came back and stopped behind me. A rectangular object pressed against my bottom.

"*Ungh,*" I moaned.

"Guess what this is."

"A paddle?"

"Hmm. Yes, that's right. How does it feel?" he asked as he smoothed the surface of it over my bottom.

"It's cold—and flat, and hard." I shuddered, squirming away from it.

"Stay still," he said, pressing a hand to the small of my back. The paddle cracked against my ass, and I gasped at the sudden impact.

"Oh, fuck. Fuck."

"Did it hurt?"

"Yes."

"Did you like it?"

I hesitated. If I told him I'd liked it, he was going to do that again. And I didn't know how many times it would take for me to stop liking it — or if I ever would.

"Tell me."

"*Yes,*" I said. "But, Alastair — I mean, Sir — I...I'm scared..."

He was suddenly there, right next to me, stroking my hair. "What are you scared of?"

I swallowed thickly. "Of what I'm feeling. I'm scared that I'll want to give you everything and anything. And I don't know if I can control it."

"Your submission, you mean? You're worried that you'll submit to whatever I want to do to you?"

Was I? Would I? I swallowed. "Yeah."

He kissed my cheek and smiled against my face. "I won't let you, my lovely boy. I'm here to protect you as well as to control you. Promise me you'll tell me if it's too much, and I'll take it from there."

I breathed a sigh of relief. "Yes, Sir. I promise."

"And I'll be watching. I know you find the fact that I'm so experienced in this world a bit intimidating, but the benefit of that is that I can read a submissive very well. And trust me, I'm going to be paying very close attention to everything you do, everything you say and everything you are."

I sobbed a breath. His reassurance that he had my back and wouldn't take me farther than he figured I could handle, no matter what I said or didn't say, sent a wave of relief through me.

"Yes, Sir."

"Good." He kissed my cheek again, then he was gone from my side. "I'm going to warm you up. Use your safeword if it gets to be too much, you decide you don't like it or for any reason at all."

"Yes, Sir."

"What's your safeword, Toby?"

My mind was a blur of sensation and the image of Alastair standing behind me with the paddle and what that must look like…and what it *meant*.

It took me a second to remember. "Bloomers."

"Good."

I'd turned my head to the side and pressed my cheek against the headrest—seriously, this was the Cadillac of crosses—so I could hear him better and show that I was paying attention. I wanted to be good for Alastair. The need came from somewhere deep inside me, where perhaps I'd lacked a male authority figure to impress. I craved Alastair's approval with a physical hunger.

The next slap of the paddle wasn't as bad as the first. I knew what to expect. The second and third slaps were okay, too. I kind of liked the feel of it and the thud of pain it gave me that was different from the sting of hand spanking.

"So far so good?" Alastair asked, leaning in close again and kissing my cheek.

"Yes, Sir."

"All right. I'm gonna go a bit harder."

"Yes, Sir."

He continued with a little more force and a quicker rhythm. My ass started to burn and protest, but then the spread of heat morphed into a whole-body pleasure as the endorphins helped to dull the pain. It hypnotized me. I clutched the chains of my bindings as I went into an instinctual pattern of tension and relaxation.

"Breathe, Toby. Don't stiffen up so much."

Easy for him to say.

"Try to relax into the rhythm of it. Accept it. You're not getting away from it. You might as well enjoy it."

I did my best to keep my muscles as relaxed as possible while still bearing my own weight and counterbalancing the forward momentum from each hit. Because every time the paddle made contact, my hips jolted forward and my cock bumped the padding. *Excruciating torment at both ends.*

Finally, he stopped. I was breathing as hard as if I'd just finished a run, and a warm glow enveloped me. My skin hummed with heat and energy, and it wasn't a terrible feeling at all.

"Okay. I'm going to try a different instrument," Alastair said.

I floated on the ache and the burn while Alastair was gone. But he was back after a moment, and he pressed something larger against my tender flesh.

I whimpered, because my ass was already smarting from the other paddle, and this inflamed all my nerves at once.

Alastair chuckled. "You doing okay?"

"Yep. Sure."

Fine. Just dandy. Naked and strung up, at the whim of a cheerful Dom with multiple instruments at his disposal. Never better.

"I beg your pardon?"

"Oh shit. Yes, Sir. That's…that's what I meant to say. Sir."

"Uh-huh," Alastair said with a hint of amusement. "This one is polished wood, but it's wide and flat. It's going to be a bit more thuddy. I want to see how you like it—or if you like it at all. Ready?"

I grabbed the chains harder and took a deep breath.

"Yes, Sir. Paddle me. I've been a very naughty boy."

Might as well lean into it.

He didn't laugh. "Yes. Very, very naughty."

When the wide flat of the wooden paddle slammed against my ass, it took my breath away. I made a choking noise.

"Fuck!"

"Again?"

I thought of saying no.

"Yes, Sir."

He brought it down again.

"Oooh, God. *Fuck.*"

"Again?"

"No. No, stop. I don't—"

The paddle landed again, and I inhaled with a cry, soaring on pain and pleasure and shock.

"Toby, if you want me to stop, use your safeword."

Do I want him to stop?

"Do you really want me to stop?"

He thwacked me again, and I felt deliciously chastened.

"No. Don't stop." I trembled.

The head of my cock slipped against the padding of the cross, wet with my excitement. Suddenly Alastair's fingers were there, playing with my dick and rubbing the moisture over the sensitive head.

"Oh. No, no," I protested, squirming against his touch. It was too much, and it was not enough.

"You really are a spanking slut. You don't know how happy that makes me."

Then his fingers were gone, and he paddled me again, faster now, and it became a strange sort of workout. Sweat beaded on my skin, and my legs started to shake. But I was fucking flying. Part of me wanted it to stop right now. Another part wanted it to go on forever.

Eventually, when I started to think about actually using my safeword, if only because I didn't know how far up I was going to float and I didn't want to get so high that coming back down would kill me, it did stop. The paddle clattered to the floor, and Alastair pressed against me. I hissed as his zipper scraped my tender skin. Then he slipped lubed fingers between my cheeks and into my body, breaching me with pragmatic ease. He fucked me with one finger pushed deep, then two, as he moved them this way and that, teasing me and stoking my passion. His breathing was as labored as mine, but I was the one making embarrassing, vulnerable sounds.

It was exactly what I needed. I came back into my body, and it welcomed me, letting me feel everything Alastair was doing to me, and giving me so much fucking pleasure.

He slid his fingers out and pushed his cock in, wider and thicker and everything I wanted. I cried out as he went deep, shoving his pelvis against my sore ass, his cock touching me everywhere.

"Jesus. Jesus," Alastair gasped, his movements getting faster and rougher.

I gasped and tried to breathe as Alastair railed me against the padded cross. The sounds I made were unreal, the cries of a strung-out sex junkie. Sooner than

I expected, Alastair cried out, clutching my hips with a grip that added more pain to my euphoria. Then all thought left me as I yelled and came hard, convulsing around him, emptying onto the leather padding, and sobbing with pleasure, pain and ecstatic release.

Chapter Twenty-Three

Repercussions

We stayed like that for long moments, our breaths the only sound in the space. I whimpered, and Alastair nuzzled my neck and sighed.

"You okay?" His voice trembled in a way that soothed my heart. He was vulnerable, too.

"Yeah. Better than. That was…"

"Yeah. It was."

Alastair took the blindfold off me, then helped me down and cleaned me off. I leaned against him, my knees wobbly.

"Amazing. You're amazing," he said.

"Can you, like just hold me…or something?" I said, because I was starting to shake, and it felt like I was coming down from subspace, hard and fast.

"Yes. God, of course."

He got rid of the condom and tucked himself away, then led me over to the settee. He grabbed a soft blanket from a basket and wrapped me up in it, using a corner to wipe the damp hair off my forehead.

"Do you want to lie down?"

"In a minute," I said, my teeth rattling as a panicky feeling starting to rise, replacing all the sexual tension and positive energy that had vanished in a heady rush and left me feeling bereft.

"Come here," Alastair said, fisting the blanket and pulling me into his arms, which he wrapped tightly around me. "I've got you. Take deep breaths and let them out slowly."

I tucked myself into him, feeling his warmth seep into my bones, stilling the panic and the shakes after about ten minutes. Alastair kissed my cheek and my ear and my forehead and whispered lovely things to me about how brave and strong I was and how beautiful, and how good it had been to be inside me.

"Better?" he asked finally.

"Yeah. Just really tired. I want to lie down."

"Sure," he said, helping me lie down and arranging the blanket over me.

"My ass hurts."

Alastair laughed. "I expect it does. You liked that big paddle."

"I liked both. That was — so weird, but so much fun. I don't know why it was so good."

Alastair spoke to me about the nature of kink and what the psychologists thought it did for people while he tidied up from our scene, and I watched through heavy-lidded eyes.

* * * *

"Hey, Princess. Wake up."

I opened my eyes. Alastair's face was right there, and he was smiling — and he'd never looked better.

"There you are," he said.

"Hey," I mumbled, then frowned. "Why is my ass on fire?"

Alastair gave me a strange look.

"I'm joking. I know why. It's *your* fault."

He had the grace to look chagrined.

"Ah. I was very thorough."

"Very."

"If you can see your way to getting dressed, we can get out of here. I'll draw you a bath at home, like last time."

"Yes, please. I feel like you owe me."

"I owe you *at least* that."

He helped me up and into my clothes.

"Wait, where are my boy shorts?" I turned to Alastair.

He smiled with a smugness I couldn't ignore. "I've got them."

"Oh, really. Well, I'd like them back at some point."

"We'll see."

I couldn't help the laugh that escaped me. God, he was such a fucking pervert.

I was glad I'd worn yoga pants and not jeans, and I wouldn't have wanted to wear the boy shorts over my smarting bottom. Still, my ass did not appreciate the rub of the light cotton.

Alastair opened the door, and I followed him from the room. It seemed strange to be in the club, as if the Bordello was its own dimension, and I was a different person there.

I felt delicate, soft and ached just about everywhere. But like after a great workout, I was relaxed and loose and happy. Alastair took the key back to Sebastian as I grabbed my coat.

"Let's go," he said, when he returned and put on his jacket. He pulled me in for a quick cuddle before pushing the door open and stepping out into the night.

We were at the bottom of the steps before I noticed them. And by the time Alastair had clued in to who they were, my mom was yelling.

"Tobias! You need to get yourself home, pronto. I don't know what you think you're doing prancing around town with that Indian girl and this pervert, but you should be home with me where you're safe."

She reached for me, as her friend or boyfriend or drug dealer stood there with a creepy smile and his hand in his pocket.

I was still dazed from the scene and would have been lost if Alastair hadn't stepped in front of me.

"Get away from him."

The steel in his voice woke me up in an instant.

"What the fuck? Go away," I muttered to them both.

My mom was wearing a fake fur coat, and all I could see were the pantyhose with runs in them and her stupid dirty sneakers.

"Tobias, I'm your mother. You belong at home."

She tried to come for me again, and this time Alastair ·
put his arms out to block her.

"Call the police, Toby."

"Don't you fucking *dare*!" my mom said, spitting at him. "You think you can prey on my son, you dirty fucking *bastard*?"

I dug my phone out of my coat pocket, my hands shaking, my brain sending out alarm bells. What if the guy had a gun?

"Let's just go," I said to Alastair, pulling at his coat sleeve.

But my mom was cursing him, and her friend was getting into it now.

"Be a good kid and go home. Your mom needs you."

I glared at the man. "You know I'm twenty, right? I don't need to go anywhere."

I heard the familiar sound of the door to Maverick Molly's opening, and several things happened at once.

"What do you think you're doing, assaulting people in front of my business?"

It was Jacob.

"I'm calling the cops," Sebastian stated.

"Thank you," Alastair said.

He had placed himself in front of me, and I was happy to have that shield. For the third time this month, it felt like people were actually standing up for me, and I knew if Esther were here, she'd be hooking arms with Alastair to protect me. The thought made me emotional.

My mom stared daggers at me.

"You're a fucking loser, Tobias. You know that, don't you? I don't know why I ever thought having a kid was a good idea. I should have gotten rid of it when I had the chance. You've ruined my fucking life, Tobias."

That hit me like a knife to the chest, but I recovered fast.

"Fuck you," I whispered.

Sebastian was talking to the police on the phone, and my mom and her dealer/boyfriend decided they didn't want to be arrested and left, my mom cursing as she walked, the sketchy guy trying to comfort her with an arm across her back.

I just wanted to go home.

"Can we leave?" I asked, as Alastair watched them go, and Sebastian ended his call.

"They're sending a police unit, so you'd better stay." Sebastian's voice was grave. "I'm sorry."

Alastair turned back to me. "It's all right. We'll go inside and have a drink. You need some water and a Coke."

"Whatever," I said. I was so done with everything.

"The police are coming, Toby," Alastair said, walking me inside. "And you're going to tell them everything."

* * * *

I did tell them everything — about all the times she'd hit me and the *one* time I'd hit her, about her emotional and psychological manipulations, about her multiple boyfriends who had treated me badly, about not having enough to eat and about cleaning the entire house myself.

I told them all of it.

Jacob and Sebastian plied me with cold drinks and tea, the other servers left me alone, and Alastair sat with me and heard it, too. But I didn't care.

That part of my life was officially over.

Eventually, we Ubered home, Alastair cuddling me close the whole way.

By the time we got there, I didn't even want the bath that Alastair had promised. He gave me one of his oversized shirts to wear and insisted on seeing to my ass with the Arnica gel.

"Toby, I had no idea she was so fucked up, even after the driveway incident."

"Can we stop talking about her, please?"

"Yes. Absolutely, except for one thing. I want you to know that you are not to blame for her problems.'

"Duh," I said.

"Okay. And Jesus Christ, if you'd never been born, I'd —" He choked on a breath.

"Oh my God. Do *not* cry — over *me*," I ordered, as my own voice broke.

He nodded, trying to smile.

"I'm sorry. I'm just — I'm rattled by what happened." Alastair swallowed with difficulty, as if he had something in his throat. He blinked at me. "I love you, Toby, and I'll always protect you from anything or anyone that threatens you."

I stared at him, not breathing.

"Pardon?" I whispered.

"Yeah, you heard that right. *I love you.*"

"That's what I thought you said. But…but you can't love me…"

Alastair looked genuinely confused. "Why the fuck can't I? And if you say it's because you don't love me, well, I'll deal with that. I can still love you, even then."

My heart literally spasmed. "Of course, I fucking love you, Alastair. How could I not? But…but…" I looked around the room for some kind of explanation as to why this seemed so unbelievable. "How is this my life?"

I started to laugh, because if I didn't, I might end up crying — then *he* would cry, and everything would be ridiculous. I'd *never* get any sleep.

"I'm sorry. I'm not laughing at you," I said, trying to control myself. "Just the situation. We were literally leaving a kink club where you paddled my ass and told me I was a naughty boy, then my *actual mother* starts hurling insults and threatening me…" I gasped a breath. "It's all kinds of absurd, you know?"

He made a sound of agreement, the feel of his soft hands rubbing the soothing gel into the muscles of my ass a comforting and calming accompaniment.

"And now you say you love me."

"I did say that. I mean it."

I stared at the blue walls of his — *our* bedroom, a happy smile on my face.

"I love you, too. You know, you've got a really sappy heart. And I'm going to take care of it," I said. "Now, please, can you," I asked, yawning, "get under the covers with me, or I'm gonna go to sleep on top of the comforter."

"Sure."

We cuddled together under the blankets, our skin and emotions bare.

"Will you make me pancakes for breakfast, Sir?" I mumbled, somewhere on the verge of sleep.

"Always."

* * * *

Jacob had insisted on giving me a few days off, so when I woke up on Saturday morning cuddled up with a snoring Alastair and the memories of what had happened rushed back to me, I was able to temper my annoyance and anger with thoughts of a three-day weekend.

Alastair Kenney loved me. Alastair Kenney, the man who had turned my world upside down in so many ways, fucking loved me. Me. Toby Dunn, the femme boy, whose mother said was her biggest mistake, the wide-eyed kink newbie who'd only just moved out of that toxic environment and for the first time in maybe ever, felt safe, and, yes, loved, and cared for. It seemed like a dream that I might wake up from, but hoped I didn't…ever.

My ass wasn't as achy and tender as I'd expected, and I shifted under the covers to rub some of the pain to life.

Ah, there it is.

I didn't understand why getting spanked or paddled was such a turn-on, but the way Alastair looked after me in the Bordello and here at home was something I'd never experienced before. It did feel like I had missed some sense of competent male energy in my life. Maybe that's what I saw in Alastair, and what made his taking me in hand so appealing — or maybe I simply liked being spanked.

I lay in bed enjoying the warmth and security and Alastair's gentle snores, until I couldn't ignore my bladder anymore. As I slid out from under the covers, Alastair closed his fingers around my wrist.

"Don't go…" he mumbled.

I sank back and kissed his sweet face. "Good morning. Unless you want me to piss this bed, I have to go."

He didn't open his eyes, but he did release me. "As long as you come back."

"I will."

I took care of business and went back into the bedroom. A gap in the curtains gave me enough light to see Alastair lying there, all tousled and sleep-sexy, watching me.

"Turn around and lift your shirt," he said.

I squinted into the dimness.

"Alastair? Is that you or someone else?" I asked, pretending I didn't have a clue who had said it.

"Very funny. Yes, it's me. Who else would be in your bed this early?"

"Good point. Wait! You want to ravage me already? You're not even properly awake."

He sighed and rolled his eyes. "I want to see how your bottom looks."

"Oh." I spun around and lifted my T-shirt, waving my ass at him.

"Hold on," he said, reaching behind him to tug at the curtain. A flood of sunlight illuminated the room. He examined the body part in question.

"How does it feel?"

"It's sore. But that Arnica gel works like magic. I thought it would be pretty bad today, but it's okay. I like it." I crawled under the blankets and snuggled up to Alastair, who laughed softly and tousled my hair.

"How did we ever think you were vanilla?"

We lay in a cozy embrace for a bit, and I almost went back to sleep. Then Alastair said, "Don't forget, Nigel's coming over."

I rolled my eyes. *Sexy fucking Nigel.*

"Yeah, yeah."

"I can call him and postpone, if you're not feeling up to it," Alastair said.

"It's fine. I want to meet him."

"Yeah?"

"Yeah."

The whole thing with my mom had put the Nigel issue into much needed perspective.

* * * *

I phoned Esther and told her what had happened.

"Oh, my fucking God. I'm going to *murder* that woman."

"Then you'll both be in jail."

"I fucking hope they lock her up. What's the likelihood of that?"

"I don't know...probably not high. But she'll be scared enough to stay the fuck away from me. I can't see her risking police involvement again if she manages to evade any consequences this time. She's got too much sketchy stuff going on."

"Yeah," she said. "Are you okay?"

I was sitting in the living room and Alastair had the fan over the stove turned on, so I knew he couldn't hear me.

"Except that I'm craving a cigarette pretty fucking badly, I'm pretty good," I muttered. "God, Esther, you should have seen Alastair. He went all caveman on me. I barely had time to figure out what was going on, and he was standing in front of me, protecting me. He put that beautiful, Dominant body in between me and her, and I think I kind of died right there. It was *amazing*. You're the only other person who's ever dared get between me and her."

She sighed. "I'm glad Alastair has your back."

"He's making me pancakes right now."

She laughed. "Toby, he's a total catch. Don't let him go."

"I won't." I cleared my throat. "I made an official statement to the police."

"You did? How did that feel?"

"Kind of scary...but all kinds of right."

"Awe, babe. I love you so much."

"Thanks. I love you, too."

"I gotta go. But we need to go out for drinks with your man. Text me."

"I will."

A stack of pancakes was exactly what I needed after yesterday. Alastair watched me slather them with butter and syrup.

"What?"

"I should have served them in a bowl," he said.

"Next time," I suggested, and he laughed. I gave him a grin. "Hey, I happen to like messy, sloppy, goopy things in my mouth." I popped a dripping piece of pancake onto my tongue and chewed blissfully.

"You…are disgusting," Alastair said, stabbing another piece of pancake off my plate and plopping it into his own mouth. He made choking sounds and his eyes bugged out. "Holy shit. I'm going to get diabetes."

"Don't be so dramatic." I leaned over to wipe a bit of syrup from his chin.

If we weren't careful, Nigel would arrive in the middle of a full-on fuck-fest.

But we were too tired from the night before to do anything but lounge around until a strange car pulled up and let the stunningly gorgeous Brit out onto the drive.

"He's here," I said, peering out of the window as he strode toward the door.

I'd elected to go full-on Toby Dunn for this rendezvous. That meant silver sparkly leggings with a pair of fuzzy socks and a baby blue cable-knit sweater that exposed one shoulder. I had also put on the dog collar because, fuck it. I'd outlined my eyes in black kohl and gelled my hair into an artful mess. Alastair had gasped his approval when I'd come downstairs and promptly pulled me into his arms for a hungry kiss. It was a good thing I hadn't put on lip color. Although, come to think of it, him opening the door to Nigel with my lipstick all over him would have been a-mazing.

"Nigel Farrow!" Alastair stated with joy as he opened the door to his friend.

Nigel gave him a huge smile and stepped forward into Alastair's embrace.

"Alastair! So good to see you!"

I hung back as they kissed each other on the cheek — *thank God* — and Alastair ushered Nigel into the room.

"It's great to see you!" His gaze traveled over Nigel. "You look — "

I cleared my throat.

Alastair spun around and smiled. He turned back to his friend. "Nigel, this is my boyfriend, Toby Dunn."

"Fantastic! I thought you had a very sexy housekeeper."

The burn of being thought of as the hired help was much assuaged by Nigel calling me sexy. I tried not to simper.

"I'm living the dream," Alastair said, putting an arm around me.

"You certainly are," Nigel said, and, swear to God, he gave me an appreciative once-over.

I rolled my eyes. "Great. You're not only incredibly sexy but charming, too? How will I ever compete?"

"Ha! You're not competing with anyone, by the looks of it," Nigel said. "He's obviously smitten." Nigel gestured to Alastair, who did look very happy and content.

"So, you and Alastair had some fun a long time ago?" I asked.

"We did, absolutely. I will think back on those times with a melancholy fondness now, as I know they have been relegated to the past."

Okay, Nigel was a king.

"Here, come to the living room. You want some tea, or a glass or wine? Coffee?" Alastair asked.

"Oh, darling, tea would be fab."

"Great. I'll put the kettle on while you and Toby chat."

Alastair had become Mrs. Doubtfire. I tried to keep my smile from turning into a laugh.

"So, whereabouts do you live, Toby?" Nigel asked, sitting on the couch and stretching his long legs out in front. He was dressed in some kind of hip business suit, and boy, did it work for him.

"Oh," I said, blinking. "Here. I live here."

Nigel gave me a weird look. "*Here*? With Alastair?"

"I needed a room, and we were already kind of seeing each other. We weren't sure it would work out."

"So, this really is serious! Well, I'm thrilled for both of you."

He sounded sincere. When Alastair came back with a plate of cookies and some mugs, Nigel said, "You didn't tell me you and Toby were living together. I think it's wonderful."

"Oh, yeah. Sorry. I'm just so used to it now."

"I'm happy for you. Although it does throw a wrench into the mix."

"How so?" Alastair asked.

"Well...I was going to ask if I could stay here, just until the end of next week. I have a shoot and another contract to negotiate before I go back to London."

Alastair looked over at me, and I looked back at him. I didn't know what to say.

I wanted to say, 'please don't tell him he can stay here,' but I knew I didn't have that right. And it wouldn't be fair to Nigel, because he'd been a gentleman so far, and why couldn't he stay for a temporary length of time? We were all adults.

"I'd offer you the guest room but Toby's renting it from me and all of his stuff is in there," Alastair said.

"No, no. All I need is a couch."

"Are you sure?" Alastair asked, and I realized that this had become a done deal while I wasn't looking — or, while I *was* looking but standing there gaping like a startled goat probably.

"Yeah, yeah. I'll hardly be here. I have lots going on," Nigel said.

Alastair glanced at me and smiled, obviously not perturbed by the fact that his former friend-with-benefits with the sexy-ass accent and gorgeous bod would be sleeping on our living room couch all next week.

Chapter Twenty-Four

Where It Started

I tried not to let it bother me. I really, really tried. But I'd only recently gotten used to living with Alastair, and now there was a super sexy guy walking around in boxer briefs and slouch socks, and I was going to lose my mind.

And Alastair fucking called me on it.

"You know, I'm starting to think that the problem you have with Nigel—"

"I don't have a problem with Nigel."

"—is that *you* find him so attractive."

I narrowed my eyes at Alastair. How dare he be so fucking perceptive.

He shrugged and sipped his coffee. "I've tapped it. He's old news to me."

"Fine. That might be why—"

"It is! It so is. Maybe *you* need to have sex with Nigel," Alastair stated triumphantly.

I started to consider it.

"That was a joke. Don't fucking touch him."

We gazed at each other, and Alastair reached out and took my hand.

"Hey, look. You've got some time off. Do you want me to see if I can book the Bordello for tonight? Or we could go out to dinner, instead? What do you want to do? I'm yours."

"Really?"

"Yes. Whatever you want."

"Huh. Normally I'd be all over the Bordello idea, but since my ass is still sore, could we go somewhere nice for dinner?"

"Absolutely," Alastair said, picking up his phone. "I need to make a call. Shoo."

My mouth dropped open. "Did you just…tell me to *shoo*? Like a *dog*?"

"Yeah."

"Jesus," I said, shaking my head as I left the room. I had to piss anyway.

When I came back, Alastair was smiling like he had a secret.

"What? You might as well tell me."

"I got us a reservation at Wilfrid's," he said, with pride.

"Okay?" I'd never heard of it.

"Toby, it's the restaurant at the Chateau Laurier. It's very expensive and swanky."

"Oh," I said. "Oh! Wow. Okay."

"*And* I got us a room."

Oh, hallelujah, praise the Lord.

"Seriously?" I said, eyes wide and spirits lifted.

"Seriously."

"I love you," I crooned, making goo-goo eyes at him.

"I love you, too. Now stop obsessing over my friend and figure out what you're going to wear."

* * * *

What *was* I going to wear? In a moment of clarity, I decided I wanted to wear a dress. Dinner and a room at the Chateau Laurier with my incredible and kinky boyfriend called for something special.

I actually had two dresses. One was a casual navy sweater dress that I'd borrowed from Esther and that she'd told me to keep. But I also owned a deep burgundy sheath number that did incredible things for my ass, thighs and arms. I'd worn it to various queer venues in Montreal with Esther and Lev. And I really, *really* wanted to wear it tonight.

I decided I should run the idea by Alastair. Not that I was asking for permission. If I really wanted to wear it, I'd wear it. We'd probably get some looks. I didn't give a fuck, but Alastair might.

I texted Alastair as I stood there looking at the two dresses.

Yeah?

Would you mind if I wore a dress on our date tonight?

There was a pause, then three dots as Alastair typed.

I don't think I mind. What kind of dress?

I took a photo of the burgundy dress on its hanger.

This one.

He sent a shocked emoji…and a tongue hanging out emoji…and three fire emojis. Then…

Please wear that. I'm begging you!

I laughed as I typed back.

Save your begging for later.

* * * *

Nigel had gone to his preliminary photo shoot and apparently had a date later, so might or might not be sleeping on the couch tonight. Alastair had given him his own code for the door, just in case, and told him we were staying at the Chateau overnight.

I stomped down the stairs in my burgundy Doc Martens, opaque black tights and my dress in almost the exact same color as the boots. The dress hugged me in all the best places. It had long sleeves, a boat neck, and a slit up one side. Esther had given me a pearl choker that she'd inherited after her grandmother passed away. I would have worn my dog collar if we'd been going to the bars, but Wilfrid's was a classy joint.

Alastair's chin dropped when he saw me. But I almost didn't notice, because of how good *he* looked.

"Oh, hell yes," I said, checking him out. He was wearing a navy-blue tuxedo ensemble, with a white shirt and light-blue waistcoat embroidered with silver. There was even a bowtie and a light-blue pocket square.

"No, no, no," he said, shaking his head and walking toward me, and for a split second I thought he didn't like the dress. "How can you possibly be this stunning?"

He held out his hand for mine and spun me around, his expression ecstatic.

"You look incredible. You're not tucking, are you?"

"No. But I am wearing panties. They're keeping the goods together."

"Well, you look fucking edible."

"Perfect. Because at some point tonight, I'm going to want you to eat me."

He chuckled and took my chin in his hand, examining my face. "Nice eye shadow."

"Thanks."

I'd lined my eyes with kohl but added sparkly silver shadow and a touch of blush on my cheekbones. I'd done my hair in a pompadour style. I looked smashing, and I was glad Alastair appreciated it.

We ordered an Uber and got to the Chateau by six-thirty.

I was busy taking selfies and texting with Esther while Alastair checked us in. Only when we got off the elevator on the sixth floor and stopped in front of the door did I realize—

"This is the same room," I said.

He simply smiled and swiped his key card, pushing the door open.

I stood there gazing at the familiar space, which now contained a large gift basket wrapped in cellophane.

"Oooh, what's that? Is there chocolate in there?"

"Of course there's chocolate in there, Toby. It's for you."

"It is?"

"Yes," he said, gazing at me warmly. "Happy hookup anniversary."

"Wait! Is it?

"It's been exactly eleven weeks and three days. Almost three whole months."

"Impressive," I said. "I didn't get you anything."

He smiled and pulled me forward. "I'll collect my gift later, if you don't mind."

"Oh, I don't think I mind at all."

* * * *

I'd hate to say I was surprised that nobody at the restaurant put up a fuss about a guy in a sexy dress, but it threw me. I was absolutely ready to counter any ill-informed comments with icy politeness and an explanation as to the un-gendered nature of clothing, but I didn't need to. Sure, Ottawa was conservative compared to Montreal or Toronto, but downtown, in a classy establishment like the restaurant at the Chateau, my dress was a non-issue.

Alastair impressed me by pulling out my chair.

"Thanks, darling," I said. "You're a peach."

He rolled his eyes at my overacting and sat in the chair opposite me, steepling his hands and mouthing "Behave."

I gave him a saucy look and picked up my menu.

"Oh," I said and put it back down. "Were you going to order for me?"

"I wouldn't fucking dare," he said.

I smiled. "Good man."

We both had the salmon, sparkling water to drink and desserts to go, because we were looking forward to shenanigans in the privacy of our room, and a heavy meal would be counterproductive.

Alastair declined the offer of an alcoholic beverage, either in deference to my preferences or because of our other plans.

"So, Mr. Kenney," I said, as we rode the elevator up to the sixth floor. "We have the Bordello again this week. What are your plans for me?"

He grinned. "Oh, I'm not going to tell you that."

I pouted and played with the pearls around my neck. "Oh, come on. You don't have to be so secretive."

"Stop talking. I'm trying to focus."

I blinked. "On what?"

"On trying not to fuck you until we get to the room."

"That's presumptuous of you. Just because you took me to dinner doesn't mean you can fuck me, Mr. Kenney."

"Oh my God," he sighed.

"Just kidding." I flashed him a huge smile. "Of course, I want you to fuck me."

He rolled his eyes as the elevator pinged and the doors opened. He took my hand and started striding down the hall. It was a good thing I was wearing Docs and not heels, or I would have tripped.

By the time Alastair swiped his key card, we were panting and desperate, just like we had been the first time we'd been here. But instead of kissing me, Alastair growled, "Get on the bed."

"Wow. I guess the romance is gone," I said, taking off my shrug and bending to untie my boots, but not before turning so that Alastair got a good view of my ass as I did.

He laughed but it sounded like a gasp. "I just spent two hundred dollars on fucking salmon! And this room isn't cheap, either."

"Don't forget the desserts," I said, pointing to the cardboard containers Alastair had thrown onto the table. I bent to untie my Docs with frantic fingers.

He landed his hands on my hips and pressed his erection against my ass, hissing his desire. "This is the only dessert I want, pretty girl. Pretty boy. Pretty girly-boy. I don't know what to call you."

"Just call me Toby," I said, kicking off my boots and turning to face him.

He held my hands still by my sides as he kissed me hard, stealing my breath and my will in one delightful swipe of his tongue.

"*Fuck me.*" I gasped into the kiss, enunciating the words clearly so there could be no confusion.

He let one of my wrists go and slid his fingers up my leg and under the slit of my dress to find my cock nestled in its lace cradle. Since the tights I had on left my upper thighs and bottom bare, he had easy access to the good stuff.

I groaned and held onto Alastair's arm as he stroked his fingers over my erection. "You fucking tease."

He grinned wickedly. "Just wait."

"I'm tired of waiting. I want you...fucking *now*."

He raised his eyebrows.

"You can't be the Dom all the time."

"Watch me."

"Well, that's just not fair," I said, as he slipped his hand into my panties and my eyes rolled back in my head. "*Fuck...*"

"I want you to get on that bed, and take off your clothes, while I watch. Your safeword is 'bloomers'. Use it if you want."

"Yes...Sir," I sighed, leaning into the pressure of his hand.

Then it was gone.

He spun me around and laid a spank on my ass that sent me lunging for the bed.

"Jesus. Hold your fucking horses," I said, but I grinned and climbed onto the mattress, kneeling up and facing him. I hiked the dress up to my waist, showing off my hard cock behind the pink lace.

"Oh, my fucking God. Toby, you're stunning — and so, so hot."

"I know."

He laughed, but his hand worked at his belt buckle and fly. In a moment, he had his own erection in hand. "This is for you. But you have to work for it."

I nodded. "What do you want me to do?"

"Take off the dress. As gorgeous as you look in it, I want to see what's underneath."

"Fine," I said, reaching around me to unzip it.

I gathered the hem and pulled it slowly up and over my head, then tossed it to the floor.

"Whoops."

Alastair made a sound in his throat and pulled at his cock.

"Now take out your dick, you pretty girl."

I parted my lips as I scooped my dick and balls out of the panties, tucking the lace underneath and giving myself a solid stroke before my hands dropped to my sides.

"Oh, yes. Yes, yes, yes," Alastair moaned, hurrying out of his pants and shirt while I waited.

"Don't use a condom," I said.

Alastair froze, his eyes gone wide. "Are you sure?"

"Yes, I'm fucking sure. I want all of you — your jizz, your undying devotion… Everything."

"Huh, not greedy at all, then."

"I saw your test results. I'm not worried."

"Neither am I."

I burned with need as I watched him bare himself to me. In a minute he was naked — a sex god and natural Dominant who just happened to be my boyfriend. How I'd ended up here was anyone's guess, but I was done questioning it. I didn't know if I deserved him or not, but I was definitely keeping him.

"Turn around. I want you on all fours," he said, drilling me with his Dom stare.

"Yes, Sir," I said, turning lithely and gracefully and giving him my ass to gawk at as I stretched and arched like a cat. I still had the pearls around my neck — warm from my skin and a pleasant weight. "Oh, God, hurry up, Alastair. Do something."

"So fucking demanding," Alastair said. "It's almost like you don't know your place."

He slapped my ass, and I keened with the pain and the excitement of being owned. It was still tender from the other night.

"Again," I said.

He spanked me several times and watched me squirm and cry out, before he grabbed my ass and pulled my hips toward him.

"Now stay still and let me worship you."

I nodded, beyond words as he tugged the panties down, spread my cheeks and buried his nose and mouth between them.

"Oh, fuck, fuck, *f-fuck...*" I stuttered, dying as Alastair licked and sucked at my most secret places. He bathed my balls with his tongue and went at my hole as I wriggled and protested.

I sucked in air and tried to stay still under his assault, but it was impossible. I made the most desperate and embarrassing sounds while he used his fingers, his tongue, his chin and even his nose to undo me.

He wouldn't let me touch my cock. He kept batting my hands away, until I growled out of pure frustration.

"That sweet cock is *mine*, and you're not coming until I say so, Toby Dunn."

"Yes, Sir!" I sobbed, grabbing at the bed clothes and fisting them tight.

And there was slickness on my hole as Alastair primed me for his cock, then left me a whimpering mess as he lined up and pushed in.

I groaned and arched my back, pushing against the welcome invasion. Alastair stuttered and lost his grip on my hips, bottoming out with a cry and a curse. I still had the assless tights on, the lace panties stretched out between my spread thighs and the pearls. It was a delicious debauchment.

He grabbed my hips and started to fuck me, as I hung on his cock like a helpless puppet, groaning and twitching helplessly.

"Fuck, you are so fucking snug and perfect. I love your ass so much."

"Please touch my cock. Please touch my cock. Please, please, *please*."

"No."

"Alastair! Come on," I whined.

He appeased me with a faster rhythm. Then I was too busy to complain, riding his cock and trying not to jerk my own, because boy did I want to.

Finally, finally, he sped up and seemed on the verge of release. I wanted to clinch it, so I moaned and said, "Give me your babies, Sir! Bury your dick and fill me with everything you've got!"

I sounded ridiculous, but it worked.

Alastair's grip on my hips tightened, a cry left his throat and his thrusts lost their even rhythm. He froze deep and groaned, emptying into me like he'd gone without an orgasm for weeks.

Pretty fucking melodramatic but super satisfying for both of us.

"Now? Now?" I panted. "Please, please, *please*! Sir!"

He wrapped his hand around my cock and jerked me, his still hard and buried in me. I spurted all over the fancy comforter in our room on the sixth floor of the Chateau Laurier, as Alastair purred words of praise in my ear and finished riding the waves of his own climax.

I collapsed into my own fucking mess with Alastair atop me as I grabbed for his hand. He entwined our fingers as we came down from it.

"I love you, you slutty boy," he whispered.

"You're my favorite fucking pervert in the whole world," I said, bringing his knuckles to my mouth and licking them.

"Right. You get ten minutes to rest then we're doing that again," he said. "I'm determined to get my money's worth."

I gasped in dismay.

"For the *room*, I mean. For the room!"

He laughed, and I smiled, and we lay there in a tangled heap on the expensive bedding.

Want to see more from this author? Here's a taster for you to enjoy!

Parlor Games: Forfeits
AE Lister

Excerpt

There were times in my life when I'd had to put my foot down.

"No, Lucy. We are *not* getting a baby goat."

"But, Dad! Come on! I heard they can live indoors, and you can train them to—"

"I said no. Not up for discussion."

"But, *Dad!*" Lucy tossed her strawberry-blonde, shoulder-length hair and huffed a long-suffering sigh. Her blue eyes, *his* eyes, sent me an accusatory glare.

"Are you ready to go? The bus will be here in a minute, and I've got to get to work."

Lucy side-eyed me as she grabbed her jacket and picked up her backpack. "You work from home."

I shook my head. "Not today. I'm going into the office."

"Fine. I'm leaving."

"Patrick will be here when you get off the bus," I said, ever grateful that my nephew didn't mind spending a couple of hours with his younger cousin a couple of times a week.

"Cool. Hey, Dad, think about the goat idea," she said as she opened the door and slipped out, shutting it behind her.

"Fuck," I said. "No fucking goats. Jesus."

I turned to look down at the dogs, who gazed at me with expectation in their eyes. "The two of you are enough."

I slipped on my fall boots and leather jacket, then hitched the dogs to their leashes and we left. I took a direction opposite to where Lucy would be waiting for the school bus, since she'd probably start talking to me about goats again. It was a good thing that she was so tenacious. It would serve her well in the future. But right now, with only me to win over, it was annoying and exhausting. For about the hundredth time, I wished that Daniel were still here helping me to raise this spitfire of a girl that had many of his physical characteristics and his outgoing personality.

I didn't regret being a dad. Lucy was my reason for getting up in the morning and for fighting against the grief that had threatened to pull me under those first couple of years. I loved her so much, and it would have been nice to have had someone to help me raise her.

But, yeah, sometimes the best laid plans go to shit. I pushed memories of Daniel and our life together out of my head and took the dogs over to the neighborhood park so they could do their business. This was my morning ritual, and it wasn't a bad one. I had Lucy and I had the dogs—Cocoa, an overweight chocolate Lab just shy of being a senior, and Eddy, a younger, more energetic corgi cross. I had a job I enjoyed and only had to go into the office two days a week—and my twenty-one-year-old nephew, Patrick, who looked after Lucy for me when he could.

It wasn't a terrible life.

I was an editor and copywriter at a Toronto-based publisher, and the Ottawa offices were located smack downtown in a sun-filled building on Slater Street. It wasn't a hardship to be there, but the fact that I could spend most of my week working from home was a godsend, especially as a single parent. Even the two-day-in-person per week requirement could be adjusted if there were events at home that required attention. It did me good to get out of the house. Most of my life revolved around Lucy and the animals, so to be in an adult environment with no distractions was a good break from it all.

My day went predictably well. I was working on a couple of different projects so could switch things up if I got bored. The deadlines were still a couple of weeks away, and I was making good progress, so I wasn't stressed about getting them done.

When I got back home at five-thirty, Patrick and Lucy were in the middle of a game of Monopoly.

"Who's winning?" I asked.

"Me!" Lucy stated.

I laughed and met Patrick's gaze. "You've got to stop letting her win."

"Hey!" my daughter said with indignation.

"I'm not. She's got good instincts and a way with money. You'd better watch out." Patrick stood. "Sorry, cuz, I've got to go," he said to Lucy. He looked at his watch.

"But we're in the middle of a game," Lucy whined, "that *I'm* winning!"

"Just leave it, and we'll continue it Thursday when I'm here again."

"Fine."

"I have to drive Patrick to work. See you in about thirty minutes?"

I was only beginning to feel comfortable leaving Lucy on her own for a half hour every now and then. It was possible that, if Daniel hadn't died, Lucy and I would be further along on our journey toward her independence, but his unexpected passing had affected every part of our lives.

"Yep."

"Don't answer the door to anyone, okay? You know the drill."

"I know the drill."

Come to think of it, Lucy didn't answer the door when I was here. She waited for me to do it.

"So how is Maverick Molly's these days?" I asked Patrick.

He was a server at a relatively new entertainment venue that had set up in a quieter part of Centertown about a year ago. It was called Maverick Molly's and heralded itself as a kink club and gaming parlor. I'd never been inside but Patrick raved about the place.

"It's fun. I get great tips," Patrick said, grinning.

Patrick had told me that the owners, Jacob and Sebastian Moriarty, had the young male servers dress in vintage Victorian undergarments. It sounded bizarre, and I couldn't imagine it. I didn't acquaint myself much with historical dress, so I didn't even know what that meant.

There had been a day when the appearance of a new kink club in town would have been of interest to me, but those times were gone—buried with Daniel and better off laid to rest.

As I drove out of the driveway and down the street, I realized that I should have used the bathroom before we'd left. I needed to piss, but Patrick's workplace was only a ten-minute drive away. I could hold it until I got back home.

Or could I?

By the time we pulled up to Maverick Molly's I realized the situation was more urgent than I'd thought.

"Um, Patrick?"

"Yeah?" he asked, his hand on the door handle.

"Do you think I could come in and use the washroom? I should have gone before we left my place…"

"Sure. Of course. There's one in the staff changing room."

"Oh, thank God," I muttered, embarrassed.

I parked in the spot right behind where we'd stopped and followed Patrick up the steps and through the front doors. The sounds of conversation, laughter and light jazz piano, trickled out of a nearby room and into the carpeted hallway. A rack of hangers with jackets and coats on them sat to the left, and I could see doors to another room at the end of the hall.

A tall man with blond hair in a ponytail, holding a bar cloth and wearing fancy clothes from another time that made him look like a Victorian gentleman, came toward us.

"Patrick, hey." He smiled. The lines on his face spoke of a good disposition and graceful aging.

"Hey, Sebastian! This is my Uncle Fletcher," Patrick said, gesturing to me.

"Lovely to meet you. Welcome to Maverick Molly's. Sebastian Moriarty."

He held out his graceful hand. I shook it and looked around.

"This is…a cool spot."

Even the entry hall gave off Victorian vibes. The interior design had been expertly done. There were crown moldings on the high plastered ceiling, what looked like hardwood underfoot and pieces of antique furniture against the walls. Replica oil lamps hung on the walls to give the place the soft glow of a decades-old salon.

"Thank you so much," Sebastian said. "Are you here for a drink or—?"

"He needs the washroom," Patrick said.

"I'm so sorry. I should have gone at home," I said.

"I'll just take him into the changing room."

"Of course. All the servers are on the floor." Sebastian nodded to me, then said to Patrick. "I'll see you in a few minutes."

"Yep."

"Thanks so much," I said.

"No worries at all." Sebastian smiled and went into the other room, above which a sign said 'Gaming Parlor'.

I followed Patrick through a door marked 'Staff Only' into a large, sparsely decorated space with a couple of chairs and a beat-up settee.

"Washroom's just there," Patrick said, pointing to a door at the back.

"Thanks." I hastened into a room with two stalls and a urinal, did my business quickly and washed my hands.

When I came out, I was greeted to the sight of Patrick sitting on the settee in a pair of lacy panties and a garter belt, pulling a black stocking up his calf.

"Better?" he asked, as I stood there, staring.

"Oh my God, yes. Thank you." I stood there, gobsmacked. "They really get you to dress authentically, don't they?"

Patrick smiled and attached the top of his stocking to the belt.

"Uh-huh. It takes some getting used to."

The door to the changing area swung open. A young man wearing white bloomers and a corset over a white linen blouse came into the room. He had makeup on, black nail polish and spiky, shortish hair.

He stopped when he caught sight of me.

"Oh shit. I didn't know we could have guests in here." He looked back and forth between the two of us.

"Hi, Toby. This is my Uncle Fletcher."

"Oh, okay," Toby said. "That explains everything."

"He needed to use the washroom."

Toby put a hand on his hip. "A likely story. Or did he only want to see me in my bloomers?"

"So sorry, I'll get out of your way," I said, moving toward the exit.

"Not so fast Mr...." Toby crossed his arms over his corset and looked at Patrick with raised eyebrows.

"Marin. Fletcher Marin," Patrick said with an amused look at his saucy coworker.

"Mr. Marin. I need to memorize the way you look standing in the midst of a pile of Victorian undergarments in your" — he looked me over and sighed — "fancy business suit."

"Toby," Patrick warned, standing up and pulling on a pair of white bloomers that he buttoned at his waist.

"What?" Toby said, keeping his gaze on me.

I was starting to feel uncomfortable. Ironic that I was the one on display when the two of them were wearing vintage underclothes.

"I'm enjoying the aesthetic," Toby murmured, his eyes still on me.

"Did you need something?" Patrick asked.

"Oh shit. Yeah. I forgot my choker."

Why was I still standing there?

"Oh," I laughed awkwardly. "I'd better get home to Lucy."

Toby gave me a piercing look. "Your wife?"

"Oh no," I laughed in earnest this time. "Lucy's my daughter."

Toby whistled. "I knew there were daddy vibes." He looked me over wistfully.

If these were the kind of theatrics that went on at Maverick Molly's every day, no wonder it was doing so well.

Now Patrick was laughing. "Oh my God, Toby, stop. I don't want to think about my uncle that way."

I started for the door.

"Wait," Toby called.

I turned to see him standing by a row of cubbies, holding something black in his fingers.

"Would you help me with my necklace, Mr. Marin?" He batted his eyelashes at me with a saucy grin.

Patrick rolled his eyes. "How does Alastair even put up with you? I'm gonna tell him you asked a strange man in a suit to dress you."

Toby collapsed into irreverent laughter and put on the choker, attaching the clasp in the back and meeting my gaze with dancing eyes. "Ah, he's not that strange. Sorry. I'm a fucking brat. Can't seem to stop."

"Cute," I said. He was *very* cute. "I'd better go. Thanks, Patrick."

"You're welcome. See you."

I took one more look at saucy Toby and got the hell out of there. Those outfits were incredibly titillating — not so much on my nephew, although he did look adorable.

But on Toby? I didn't know who this Alastair guy was, but if Toby was his partner, he was a very lucky man.

When I got back home, Lucy was doing homework at the table and feeding Eddie bits of cheese off her plate.

"Lucy," I said, "you know I don't like you feeding him from the table."

"But he's hungry. And he loves cheese so much."

Pick your battles. Pick your battles.

I went upstairs to change out of my suit, thinking about Maverick Molly's and the pleasant atmosphere and good-humored employees. But there was no point, because I didn't have anyone to take there, and I'd be damned if I'd go by myself. And anyway, I didn't have time, with Lucy and the dogs and work.

I sat down on the bed in my boxer briefs and picked up the photo of Daniel that I kept on my bedside table.

"You would love that place," I said, talking as if he were in front of me and not six feet underground in the Capital Gardens Cemetery. "I wish it had been there before you…"

I blinked, thinking I had more tears to shed over the loss of my husband and partner and co-parent. But there was nothing. Only a memory that came to me of holding Lucy for the first time. Lucy, our daughter, who was now my number-one priority, and meant I didn't have time to go gallivanting around to kink clubs or even to find someone to share a pleasant meal with.

The loneliness of my current existence hit me all of a sudden, but I pushed it away and thought back to that incredible moment twelve years earlier.

"My God," I said, as Daniel placed our baby in my arms. "She's so beautiful!"

I blinked back tears as I stared at our daughter's — our *daughter's! — perfect face.*

"She does have my genes," Daniel said, touching his fingertip to her cheek. "Of course she's beautiful."

I nodded, at a loss for words. She was so tiny and miraculous! I thanked the universe for Daniel, for our surrogate, Tamara, and for a world that allowed us to experience parenthood the way we wanted. It hadn't been easy, but Daniel had wanted a child so badly and I loved him so much, and even though I was scared of the responsibility of guarding and guiding a new life, I'd been a hundred percent on board.

"So...what do you think? Do you still want to go with 'Riley'?"

"I don't know. She looks more like a 'Lucy'."

Daniel rolled his eyes. "So traditional."

"But everyone's naming their kids 'Riley' these days. 'Lucy' may be kind of traditional but it's not common."

"Lucy, huh," Daniel said, moving the cloth of the hospital blanket so he could see our daughter's face. "All right, then."

As it always did, my gut clenched at these heartwarming memories, and now the tears threatened. I sighed and stood, blinking them back, and got dressed.

About the Author

Alison Lister is a Canadian non-binary author.

They write graphic erotic romance (contemporary/historical/paranormal) as AE Lister, and sweet Young Adult LGBTQ+ romance as Alison Lister.

She/he/they

Alison loves to hear from readers. You can find their contact information, website details and author profile page at https://www.firstforromance.com/

PUBLISHING

Sign up for our newsletter and find out about all our romance book releases, eBook sales and promotions, sneak peeks and FREE romance books!